A

Season

For

Shariton

Park

Edited by Lynne Riffenburgh, Alexa Martineau, and Lauri Schoenfeld.
Book cover design by: Sapphire Midnight Designs

A Season for

Shariton

Park

Christine M. Walter

Dedicated to Audrey

Don't give up on your writing dream

To everyone else, thank you for picking up this book! Hopefully you've already read the first book in this two book series. If not, please read *A Time for Shariton Park*. You'll be confused if you don't.

I've decided to rate my book using Michelle Penninton's rating system found at https://thewritinggals.com/michelles-clean-and-wholesome-category-content-diagram/

This book is rated at level one. :)

Soundtrack for this book:
*The Carnival of the Animals: XIII, The Swan- Saint-Saens
*Orchestral Suite No. 3 in D Major- Bach
*Yesterday- Beatles
*Stairway to Heaven- Led Zepplin
*The Duke of Kent's Waltz
*This Old Guitar- John Denver
*Corn Dogs- Ryan Shupe and the RubberBand
*Leaving on a Jet Plane- John Denver
*Serenade for Strings in E Minor- Elgar
*Blackbird- Beatles
*Young Widow/Fourpence Ha'penny Farthing/Grimstock
*Begin Again- Taylor Swift
*Like I'm Gonna Lose You- Meghan Trainor feat. John Legend
*Piano Man- Billy Joel
*Let her go- Passenger

Chapter One

1812 England, Ruth

My decision to skip a meal before the night's event had not been wise of me. Nervous anticipation of the ball had prevented me from taking even a bite of our cook's delicious pastries. Now, the odors of London caused my stomach to boil like a simmering stew. Thedrizzle had stopped only a short time after it began, which meant it had not rained enough to rid the London streets of its daily grime and stench. Given the number of horses passing through, stepping from the carriage to the Bowers' walkway proved challenging, but I traversed it well enough.

I pressed a hand to my stomach. *Please, let my dreams come true tonight.*

I held my gloved hand over my nose and hurried inside the open door after my brother, Charles, and his wife, Celeste. Our smiling hosts stood in the foyer next to the ballroom's entry with its high ceilings, crown moldings, and arched windows lit by chandeliers and collections of wall sconces.

"Miss Elsegood!" I heard my name and turned to answer. Mrs. Bower smiled, her plump face as rosy as ever and bulbous eyes made larger by the blue of her gown.

"Mrs. Bower, I cannot tell you how delighted I am to be here," I half lied, smiling. "What a grand party it is." I took her hand in mine, and we both curtsied.

"It is always a pleasure to have you, Miss Elsegood. And you will be even more delighted, I am sure when you learn that a certain someone is here tonight," she laughed, her large chest jiggling up and down.

"I am sure I do not know of whom you speak." I forced myself not to search the room but kept my eyes steadily upon her.

"Come now, Miss Elsegood. Do not toy with me. I know where your heart lies. He has paid you a great attention over the last few weeks. I am quite certain I will be hearing wedding bells soon." She did not give me a chance to reply before she turned to greet the guest in line behind me.

I greeted her husband, then followed Charles and Celeste into the sparsely decorated ballroom. The doors at the far side stood open, letting in the cool night air, which drifted up from the London streets and over the hundred or so guests who mingled within. However, little improvement was made, as London streets were not known for their fresh, clean air, after all.

Celeste laid her fingertips on my upper arm and whispered, "Ruth, keep clear of Mrs. Reid. It looks as though she has had too much already."

I followed her line of sight and spotted Mrs. Reid's red face. I nodded, trailing behind Celeste and Charles to an open alcove. Celeste rested her cheek against Charles's shoulder for the briefest of moments in a gesture of affection. Four years previous, I had joyfully watched my only brother wed my dearest friend, who had mysteriously entered our lives from the twenty-first century. I had rejoiced in their union every day since, not only for her welcome companionship, admirable intelligence, and wild stories of a time we could hardly comprehend, but also due to her genuine sisterhood. Seeing the two of them even more in love today warmed my heart … and filled me with envy.

I found Captain John Hughes among the crowd, the "certain someone" Mrs. Bower had mentioned. He stood straight and tall, speaking with another gentleman, most likely about politics—his favorite topic next to horse racing. I smiled when he noticed me. He winked behind his comrade's back and made his way through the throng to join me.

I had thought of Captain John Hughes every day since our first meeting soon after I arrived in London, although he did not begin to call on me until later in the season.

Celeste gave me a pointed look, then nodded toward Charles when she noticed the Captain's trajectory. I glanced at Charles' stiff posture. My brother showed less enthusiasm than Celeste on the subject of my affection. I cannot say I blamed him. On more than one occasion, he had remarked that a young lady such as myself should seek a gentleman of good fortune who stood to inherit a title. Captain Hughes would inherit the title of Earl only if something should happen to his elder brother. Thus, his pursuit of a military career to make his way in the world.

His attention toward me came as a relief. People had begun to talk. I knew they whispered that my youth was fading and I was well on my way to spinsterhood. I nearly believed their cruel gossip. Celeste was my saving grace. I could always count on her to set them straight. After all, I was only four and twenty, though at times I felt older.

"Good evening, Ruth. You look enchanting." John bowed over my hand, keeping his eyes locked with mine.

My heart leaped at the sound of my name on his lips. I had not permitted him to use my given name, but I did not mind in the least.

Does this mean he has decided? Am I to be wed? "I am glad you think so. It took me hours to become this enchanting."

"Now, Ruth, lying does not suit you. You are a natural beauty— anyone can see that." He glanced down, brushed his fingertips against my arm, and locked eyes with me again. "Your beauty is the envy of all the *ton*."

Can he possibly love me? Does he see beyond my freckled face and full cheeks?

My face warmed at his compliment. "How would you know what the *ton* think of beauty?" My voice cracked, and the pain in my throat filled my eyes with tears. I blinked hard and resisted the urge to rub my neck.

"Are you feeling quite well, sweet Ruth?" he asked distractedly, his eyes following something across the room. "You sound a little hoarse."

I hesitated, wishing he had not noticed. It took great effort to maintain my serene expression with the mysterious and persistent pain as of late. It frightened me. Voicing my weakness and discomfort would only make it more real. Before I could reply, an acquaintance approached, wishing to speak to him.

He paused before whispering in my ear, "You will save the supper dance for me?"

"Of course." My heart fluttered in a joyful flurry, hoping it would not be our only dance of the evening.

The ensuing hours crept slowly by. Several gentlemen asked me to dance, and I obliged reluctantly, wishing to save what little energy I had for Captain Hughes. My gaze moved through the room in search of him. With a wistful heart, I watched the supper dance come and go without a sign of him. Had he left the ball on some urgent business? Had some tragedy befallen him? In my mind, I continued to make excuses for him when I overheard a lady mention some "juicy bit of news" to Charles and Celeste, standing beside me at the edge of the room.

"There must be some mistake," Celeste protested.

"No, indeed. He was found in the library with her, wrapped in an embrace. Such shocking behavior requires that a match be made." She sounded like a clucking hen gloating over a choice worm. "*Scandalous*, to be sure!"

"But are you sure the gentleman was Captain Hughes?" Charles asked, looking as if he'd love to run the man through.

My chest constricted, gripping my lungs to the point they may never fill again. *No. Not my Captain.* Celeste's hand clamped down on my arm.

"Of that, there is no doubt," the lady replied with satisfaction.

Another clucking hen, in the form of Mrs. Reid, hurried to our side and hiccupped, "Have you heard? Everyone is in an uproar. Captain Hughes is engaged to Miss Webb!"

Celeste glanced surreptitiously at me. I avoided her gaze and swallowed hard, raising my fan to my face. My eyes fell upon a young couple by the windows, speaking to one another with their heads bowed together. The lady's eyes were downcast, and her cheeks were pink with pleasure. Pain shot through my heart like a bullet hitting its mark, and I could not draw proper breath. *I hate them.*

The first clucking hen placed her hand upon my arm, bringing me back to the conversation. "I must say I am surprised, for I thought his affections were more drawn to *you*, my dear. I expected to hear of your engagement these two weeks!"

"Perhaps he thought Miss Webb's forty thousand pounds prefera-ble," I replied, my words sharp. "If you will excuse me." I nodded curtly and hurried quickly away, needing room to breathe.

I hated this. Not just tonight. All of it. Over the last few years, I had increasingly felt as though I had a price written on my person, advertising my worth. The buyer would stop, assess the merchandise, and move on when a more valuable object stepped into view. I was tired

5

of feeling like a banknote. I wanted someone to *love* me.

How could I have been so mistaken? He seemed genuine in his affections and was attentive and kind. He had made me blush on more than one occasion and caused my heart to flutter. Now I felt as if my heart were tied to my ankles, and I was dragging it through the room for all to see and step on.

"Would you like to return home, Ruth?" Celeste hurried to my side as I made my way out into the crowded hall.

I answered without looking at her. "I want to go home ... to Shariton Park. I have had enough of London." Someone bumped my shoulder, and a sharp pain pierced my neck. I winced and gingerly put my hand on the spot.

Celeste gave the signal to Charles, and we quickly said farewell to our hosts. I carefully hid the turbulence in my heart during the short ride to our London home. When we arrived, I changed into my nightgown and lay safely in bed before I let myself feel the pain. My body racked with sobs, further irritating my aching neck. The unfairness made me want to break something, just as my heart shattered. I clenched the pillows, wishing I could tear them apart, but my strength was spent. I could only lie there and weep.

* * *

Present Day Denver, Colorado, Abbie

I was ready. *So* ready to get out of dodge. Rocking back and forth on the balls of my feet, I waited for the line in front of me to grow shorter. The cheers grew louder as my peers stepped onto the stage to receive their diplomas. I'd waited for this day for ages. The only other day I'd looked forward to with as much anticipation was my eighteenth birthday, which I had celebrated more than two months ago, on April

6

1st. With that and graduation all but behind me, I was finally free.

"Abbie Lambert."

I stepped forward into the spotlight from backstage. There was some applause, but no cheers. I shook hands with the principal and a few other people I didn't recognize, and was handed my diploma by the last person in line. I smiled at the camera and returned to my seat.

I didn't try to search for anyone I knew—no one would be there. My father's permanent residence was in prison, an obvious no-show—not that it mattered. I'd never met him and only thought about him when my friends' dads were around. My mother flitted in and out of my life so often that her coming and going gave me whiplash. My grandmother, who took me in each time my mother decided to split, passed away more than a year ago. At last, for the past nine months, my luck had taken a turn for the better when my friend's family opened their home to me. I owed them everything.

Kacie's name sounded over the chaos. She was one of the last to receive her diploma. I watched her wave to her cheering family, and I called out, clapping along with them. The crowd settled down the moment someone began to speak again.

Oh, come on! Not another speech!

I leaned forward with my elbows on my knees. My palms pushed my cheeks into my eyes, forcing them into a squint. *It would be much more interesting if the speaker had a guitar.* Too much energy for the anticipation of the future kept me at the edge of my seat, ready to bolt for the door. It felt like an eternity before we could finally participate in the traditional throwing of the cap. The moment it ended, I raced outside. Kacie's parents cried and kissed us both. I returned each hug and kiss, thanking them repeatedly for all they'd done for me over the years. They were wonderful to take me into their home and treat me as one of their own.

"Abbie!" Someone called from behind me. I turned and my eyes

7

landed on the source of my greatest excitement the past few weeks. "Grace!" I threw my arms around her.

"Green?" She took a lock of my long hair in her hands and examined it closely.

I laughed and batted her hand away. "Yeah. I tried to dye it with blue Kool-Aid last night, but with my blond hair, it turned green. Figures, right? I would've used real hair color if I hadn't been saving up for our big adventure and how long my hair is. But, whatever. It's fine."

"Speaking of, our flight leaves in four hours, so we should get going. Traffic's only going to get worse."

I held up my hand. "Let me say goodbye to my friends first."

She nodded and waited amid the noisy crowd.

I wended through the crowd, deftly dodging a large family group, all gesturing adamantly with their arms, on my way back to Kacie. "Hey, I need to get going. My flight leaves soon."

"I'm gonna miss you." Her spiky hair poked my ear when we hugged.

"I'll miss you, too."

"When you get to France, don't forget to kiss a French man for me. Maybe a Scottish one, too," she said, wiggling her eyebrows.

I gave a snarky laugh. "Yeah, like I'm going to walk up to some French guy and kiss him."

"If he was cute, I totally would."

"If I were to kiss any foreign man, it would be an Irish man. They have the best accents." I placed my hand over my heart, sighed, and fluttered my lashes.

"Seriously, though, be careful and keep your distance from Ray. You have plans to go to college, after all."

I scrunched my nose. "Why would I hook up with Ray? He's Grace's cousin, and he's *old*."

"He's only five years older than you."

8

My stomach twisted, as it did every time I spoke with Kacie or her mom about my trip—and my tour guide. They were right. The group wasn't ideal, but it was my only opportunity to travel before real life began. "Don't flip out. I'll keep my distance." I took hold of the bottom of my graduation gown and pulled it over my head to reveal jean shorts and a T-shirt. I pushed my many bracelets back down my arm and handed over my cap and gown. "Could you turn these back in for me?"

"Sure thing. Have fun."

After saying my goodbyes, I followed Grace to her cousin's car. Ray parked in a "No Parking" zone, kept the engine running, and slumped behind the wheel beside another guy riding shotgun. My insides felt as though they'd all switched places. I hadn't mentioned to the Zimmermans that Ray's friend was also traveling with us. If I had, they really would've put their foot down. Not that they had any say in the matter, but I liked giving them the impression that they did. Mason's numerous tattoos and piercings would've done little to ease Kacie's parents toward acceptance. Fortunately, his bad-boy reputation and rumors of the girls he'd dated remained secret. Even Kacie hadn't heard the whispers.

Well, the gossip didn't matter much. If Ray wanted a friend who'd taken French class and might help with the language barrier, it was fine and dandy with me. Coincidentally, French class had a lot to do with the rumors, and they were not about french bread or french fries. What did I care if he practiced more than the language with the girls in class? He was a good guy … just misunderstood.

My conclusion did little to ease my nerves as my insides still protested.

"I know you're thinking it, and yes, your backpack *is* in the trunk. I didn't forget it." Grace opened the back passenger door and climbed in. I followed.

"You got my guitar, too, right?" I asked.

"Yep."

I settled into the seat and buckled up. "Hey, Mason. Hey, Ray."

"Hey, Abbie," they said together.

"Are you ready? By tomorrow you'll be eating corned beef and cabbage," Mason said in his best Irish accent, which sucked.

I laughed. "Can't wait." The four of us had spent a month planning this trip, which would last the entire summer. It was going to be unforgettable.

Chapter Two

1812 England, Celeste

"There you are." I moved into the sitting room. Ruth looked up from her needlework. I pretended not to notice her rubbing her neck again. She hated it when I mentioned her aches. "I wondered if you would like to go for a ride with me. Charles is busy in the fields, and you know how he doesn't like me to go alone."

Ruth frowned. "My apologies, Celeste. I do not feel much like riding today." She bent her head over her work. I pursed my lips.

"It has been a month now since we returned to Shariton. You need to get back into your regular routine. You would feel much better doing so, and I daresay you will get over the Captain that much sooner."

"Believe me, Celeste, I have moved beyond my infatuation for him. I have not thought of him in weeks," she insisted, her fingers working the needle deftly through the delicate fabric.

11

I moved to sit beside her. "Then what keeps you in such melancholy spirits all the time?"

"Nothing, really," she shrugged.

"Please tell me."

"I am at a loss as to what it might be. I do not have the energy I used to. Perhaps I have lost my zeal for life." She gave me a small smile that faded slowly from her lips.

"Are you unwell?"

"I am well enough."

"You sound a bit like you have a cold. Are you coughing still?"

As if on cue, she began a coughing fit. "It helps me fight it off if it is not mentioned."

I studied her momentarily, then leaned back into the sofa and sighed. "You know, our situation isn't that different."

Her brows pulled together. "How so?"

"We both want something so much it hurts at times, but we can't have it—and because we can't have it, we've lost our passion for the usual daily life. We just want to sulk away and wallow in our own misery." I smiled, though I knew there was sadness in my eyes. My empty, childless arms ached with each mention of it. "But that will not do, will it?"

Ruth shook her head.

We sat there for a few thoughtful moments until she broke the silence.

"How are you doing, Celeste? You do not speak of it often, and sometimes I wonder how you can hold your head up."

I shrugged. "I'm still clinging onto hope. The Elsegood name must continue, right? I guess I'm being too impatient. Perhaps I need to relax."

Ruth lowered her voice. "What do they do for women in the twenty-first century? With all the medical miracles you have described,

12

surely there is something they can do for you."

I blinked hard to keep from tearing up. "You know that Charles won't agree to letting me go back. It scares him."

"Can you not persuade him?"

"Honestly, I've never tried very hard to convince him. I'm still hoping that my miracle will happen on its own."

"I see no reason why the two of us should not go. We could leave in the morning. You could see the doctor, and we would be home before supper."

I chuckled. "I wish it were that easy."

* * *

1812 England, Celeste

A week had passed since Ruth casually proposed that we visit the future to see a doctor. Since then, she had brought it up on several more occasions. It seemed as though it were her new ambition to get me there. I brushed the thought away and did not mention it to Charles.

It was not until one rainy day in late June that I felt a greater need to go, though not for myself. I noticed her energy suddenly decreasing at an alarming rate, coinciding with more intense neck pain. On this rainy day as we sat talking on the window seat when Ruth suddenly reached for her neck. Her sharp gasp and abrupt movement caught my attention, and I turned to her in alarm.

"Ruth! What is it?"

Charles sat on the sofa, reading the paper. He set it aside and came to his sister.

"Oh, it's nothing. It will go away shortly," she replied, massaging her neck and grimacing.

"Does this happen often?" I asked.

She nodded slowly. When she removed the scarf from her neck, I caught sight of a large lump at one side, right above her collarbone.

I stood, walked to the door, closed it, and returned to Ruth's side. I cleared my throat and stared directly at Charles. "Charles dear, I know how you feel about my going back through the tree root and into the future." At the look on his face, I quickly held up a hand, "Let me finish. Up to this point, I've agreed with you. Now, I must tell you that I'll be going back at the earliest opportunity, and I'll taking Ruth with me."

"What?" they both cried out in unison, though Ruth's tone sounded more hopeful than Charles'.

"You cannot be serious." Charles nearly choked on his words.

"There's obviously something wrong with Ruth's health, and I'd like to find out what it is before it becomes too serious."

"You believe a simple neck pain could be something serious?" Ruth asked, suddenly alarmed.

"A moment, please. Can we not have her looked at here? Surely, it is easily remedied," Charles interrupted.

"No. I will not take that chance. I know you're afraid of what might happen if I go back, but I've been pondering it for weeks now. I feel deep in my heart that it's right. We must take her there. It may save her life."

"And while we are there, you can be seen by a doctor as well. Besides, having you with me would make me less anxious," Ruth chimed in with excitement.

Well, at least I do not have to convince her to be seen by a modern doctor.

"No," Charles said so quietly that I would have missed it if I had not been watching him.

"Charles—"

"No," he said a little louder.

I narrowed my eyes. "You do remember why I survived the gunshot wound that day four years ago, do you not?"

He stiffened.

"We *will* be going." I lifted my chin. "I would like it if you would accompany us, but if you refuse, don't be surprised to find us missing one day soon."

He narrowed his eyes, turned on his heel, and left the room without a word.

"Do you think he will consent?" Ruth asked anxiously.

"I hope so. I would hate to go back without him, and without his consent," I sighed.

* * *

1812 England, Ruth

A nearby bird stopped twittering when my foot snapped a twig. "How did he consent so quickly?" I whispered to Celeste while we made our way on foot through the forest. I was more than a little surprised that we were already on our way the following morning.

"I suppose he realized we were going regardless of whether he came or not. He didn't want us going alone," she whispered back.

"And I would not like to miss another ride in a *motorcar*," Charles said sarcastically.

"I should have known better than to whisper behind your back. You have excellent hearing, dear brother," I said. I was not watching where I stepped, and my foot slipped on a rock, startling me into a scream.

"Are you alright?" Charles asked anxiously, stopping to assist me.

"Why could we not ride there?" I complained, clearing my throat painfully.

"We could hardly leave the horses alone in the middle of the woods, nor could we involve all of our staff. It is imperative they believe us to

15

be taking the carriage to London. Only John knows *some* truth to our plight." Charles spoke of our stable hand. John grew up working alongside his father in the stables, so Charles and John grew up as friends. We knew him to be trustworthy, but with this secret, I had my doubts.

"You think it wise to involve him?" I asked.

"I trust John with my life," Charles replied.

I paused to rest yet again. We had passed through the mysterious archway some time ago, and Celeste assured me we had not far to go. I sat on a boulder and let my breathing slow. When it did, I could make out a noise like a distant waterfall, but not continuous.

"Do you hear that?" I asked.

They nodded.

"That's the dreaded motorcar," Celeste laughed. "We are nearly there."

I stood, and we continued. I felt sorry for Charles as I watched him tow a small trunk. It was not large or particularly heavy, but it could not be comfortable to carry the cumbersome thing such a distance, regardless.

The noise grew louder as we walked on, and I could see the forest's edge ahead.

"Now, prepare yourself, Ruth. It will be quite a shock. Remember what I told you and what we practiced with speech. It's different now. Oh, and I should tell you, the words 'making love' don't mean the same here as they do in our time." She grinned and winked.

I nodded, feeling my face heat. "You have told me that before." Celeste had warned me about many things in the future. I tried to imagine the wonders she spoke of so that seeing them would not be such a shock. When I stepped out of the trees and saw what I supposed to be a motorcar speeding swiftly past on the smooth gray road, my jaw dropped. The shape of the thing and the way it moved was so strange and frightening I could not help but feel overwhelmed.

"Close your mouth, Ruth. Don't look so surprised. You'll stick out like a sore thumb if you react that way to everything," Celeste said.

She waved her hands wildly above her head before an oncoming motorcar and it came to a stop along the side of the road just beyond us. Celeste hurried to it and spoke with someone sitting inside. A moment later, the door was thrown open, and Celeste waved for me to enter.

My heart quickened as I climbed inside. "Incredible. It is so soft to sit upon," I said and laughed, until I noticed a man in front of me. "Oh, good morning—er, afternoon," I greeted him.

He stared at me in confusion, giving me a wane smile. "Good afternoon."

Celeste slid in beside me, then Charles beside her, with the trunk on his lap. Once the door shut, the motorcar began to move, and my arms flew out, one clinging to the door and the other holding Celeste's arm. I watched the trees pass by faster than I believed possible and other motorcars moving equally fast in the opposite direction. Each time one passed, I jumped, and a small squeaking sound escaped my white lips.

"Where would you like to be dropped off?" the older man asked over his shoulder.

"The bank, please," Celeste smiled.

"Is she all right?" he gestured toward me. "She looks a little ill."

"She gets carsick," Celeste replied briskly.

"Good thing for the both of us that we're almost there," he chuckled, still casting uneasy glances my way.

A moment later, the great metal beast came to a halt outside an imposing building. We thanked the nice man and watched him drive away.

"How did you like your first ride in a car?" Celeste asked.

"I will let you know when my sickness passes," I replied.

"Left your stomach behind, did you?" she winked. At least one of us was enjoying this. I glanced at Charles. He met my gaze and shook his head helplessly.

Celeste led us to the entrance. I could not help but stare at the bewildering sights all around me, amazed by the glowing red and green lights that seemed to go on and off of their own accord, the strangely dressed, oddly coiffed—positively shocking—people walking about, and the cacophony of unfamiliar sounds. It was all I could do as I followed Charles and Celeste up the stairs and into the bank.

The coolness of the room caught me off guard. My attention darted from one shining surface to another, and I noticed Charles also studying the room with interest. Celeste spoke to a polished-looking gentleman with slick black hair sitting behind a large desk, then made her way back toward us.

"Well, that was easier than last time! I'm happy my identification has not expired yet. Things will be a little easier now." She slid a sheaf of papers into her cloth bag and cinched it up. "Our next stop will be to purchase some modern clothing. We need to blend in. Then we'll find a place to stay for the night."

"I should be taking care of this, not you," Charles grumbled. "I feel completely useless."

Celeste touched his cheek and smiled at him. "I know, love. Soon, you'll know enough to be the one to handle all of our affairs."

"What is that man doing over there? Everyone seems to be doing the same thing." I gestured toward a man holding a rectangular object against his cheek as he spoke.

"He's using a mobile phone. You talk into it and someone talks back. You can speak to anyone anywhere in the world on one of those," Celeste responded. "Amazing, isn't it?"

"Yes. I believe you have mentioned those contraptions before." It seemed impossible that it could be true. What had she meant by talking to anyone in the world? I struggled to grasp the meaning of her words.

Over the next few hours, we went shopping. The sheer volume of clothing in the stores was extraordinary. The colors, fabrics, styles, sizes, the shoppers and salespeople, and the noise were almost too much to bear. I rubbed my neck and closed my eyes, trying to steady my breathing. At Celeste's request, I tried on several different types of clothing. Most left me feeling scandalized and self-conscious. In the end I settled on two long summer dresses with pretty puffed sleeves, a pair of *leggings*, and a pair of *sandals*. Celeste did not buy more than that for herself and Charles. She hoped we would be heading home in a few days.

It was growing dark when we arrived at our bed and breakfast, having picked up *takeout* for supper. I carried the food and parcels into the small, dimly lit room. It was furnished with a sofa, a short table, and a cupboard upon which stood a black box. I could see a neat looking bed through a door that opened into another room containing many objects I could not even begin to describe.

I unloaded my arms on the short table and glanced around once more. "Are there no other rooms? Surely this is not all. Where are we all to sleep? And where are we to dine?"

"It may be small and plain, but we'll only be here briefly." Celeste crossed the room to a table that appeared built into the wall. "Take a look at this." She smiled and lifted a metal lever. Instantly, water poured out and flowed down a hole in a bowl.

I laughed, "Is that the running water you spoke of?"

"This is called a sink. The faucet is where the water comes out." She gestured at the black box on the cupboard. This is a microwave—it warms food." Then she pointed to a taller black box standing upright on the floor. "And this refrigerator keeps food chilled." She moved around the room, showing me how lights could be turned on with the flip of a switch, how music could be heard from the digital clock radio, and how the room temperature could be adjusted using the thermostat. Then she took my hand and led me into the room with the bed. To our left was another, smaller room.

19

She stepped inside, and I followed. "This is a shower. Take a look." She lifted the lever, and out came a waterfall. It showered down as if it were raining.

"Incredible." I reached in and let the water fall on my fingertips. I laughed, "It is warm!"

The rest of the evening was mostly spent in awe over all that surrounded me—some of it was unnerving, and some parts left me wanting more. I asked Celeste what the large black glass was that hung on the wall. She told me it was a telly—or television. She would not tell me what it was used for and said I was better off not knowing. I found myself glancing at it throughout the evening and wondering what it could be, curiosity burning inside me with every glance.

Chapter Three

Present Day England, Celeste

The next day, it became quite clear that obtaining medical help without some sort of identification for Ruth would be difficult. Four years ago, when I'd stayed at the hospital due to a gunshot wound, I didn't have identification, but being treated for an injury was a far cry from trying to get blood tests and the like for Ruth. They needed all kinds of information.

When it came down to it, I had to choose between Ruth getting medical attention or being seen myself. Ruth needed answers more than I did, so I chose to pretend Ruth was me. We filled out the questionnaires and medical history as if Ruth's name were Celeste Marie Roberts. We even went so far as to dye Ruth's strawberry blond hair brown, hoping to match her appearance to my old identification card.

In time, when Ruth was fully recovered, maybe I could see the doctor.

More than a week went by, and in between doctor visits, we tried to lay low. People from the past wandering about the city could be a bad idea. It worried me a little how much they would learn of the future, and I didn't want to shift events or alter time.

"Welcome back." Dr. Delauney shook Ruth's, Charles', and then my hand before sitting behind his desk. This was Ruth's second doctor and our third visit with him. Following her first visit with Dr. Delauney, she was sent to a different facility for various tests and an MRI. At her second appointment just two days ago, she had a lump removed, and it was sent out for a biopsy. Today, we sat on the edge of our seats, awaiting the results.

From the corner of my eye, Ruth fidgeted, most likely having difficulty getting comfortable with her new clothing. I took her hand on one side and Charles' on the other.

The doctor cleared his throat and opened his laptop. Something in his eyes filled me with misgiving. "I'm afraid we don't have good news for you, Celeste," he said, looking at Ruth. I strove to stop myself from answering each time he used my name. "Your blood work came back with no sign of infection, so we know you're clear on that front." He turned the computer screen toward us and cleared his throat again, pointing at several places on the x-ray. "If you can see this here … I've zoomed in on your neck. The lump we removed was taken from the lateral region, here." He pointed with the tip of his pen. "That lump doesn't belong here, so I was concerned about that. The biopsy confirmed my suspicions, coming back positive for cancer. You have Non-Hodgkin lymphoma." He sighed heavily and looked at Ruth pityingly. "I'm sorry. Though, all is not lost. You're young and have an excellent chance to beat it."

My jaw fell slack. How could this be? I glanced at Ruth. She stared at the black-and-white image. Her expression showed confusion and

22

awe. I wondered if she understood what the doctor had said. I gazed at Charles, and he, too, appeared bewildered.

"The next step is to refer you to a medical oncologist at the nearest hospital."

The trepidation that had begun to build inside of me bubbled over. I couldn't let Ruth receive anything less than the very best care available. "I have money," I blurted out. "I will pay whatever is needed—whatever it takes to get her better." Charles' hand tightened around my own. I could see the determination in his eyes now, and I knew he understood the severity of the situation if not the precise terms.

Dr. Delauney nodded slowly. "In that case …" He opened a drawer, pulled out a card and placed it before us. "This is Doctor Begum. He'll be the one to do the treatment." He hesitated again before handing me another card. "There's an excellent place nearby for treatment and recovery, if needed. Dr. Begum works there half the week. You may be familiar with it—it's called Shariton Park. It's a historic estate which has been partially renovated into a cancer treatment and recovery center."

I stared at him blankly for several long moments, then peered down at the card in my hand. The words Shariton Park were printed in black script across the top. "What?" I croaked, clearing my throat. "When—when was it renovated?"

"It opened up not even a year ago. It's the best facility in the region, a little pricey, but I would send her there if you can afford it." He smiled at Ruth, who only looked at him in silent confusion.

Dr. Delauney went on to explain what we could expect in regard to cancer, treatment options, timelines, and side effects. "You have a long road ahead of you," he said sympathetically. He paused to study Ruth. "Celeste, you're quite young." His statement sounded like a question. She hesitated, then nodded.

"And you may wish to have a family someday?" he continued.

Ruth swallowed and nodded.

"I'll put you in touch with another colleague of mine. You can consult with him about your options, and he can help with egg freezing if you choose to go that route."

Ruth's eyes widened, and she glanced at me, her eyebrows knit together.

Dr. Delauney must have noticed her confusion. "I don't mean to overstep, but this is another side effect we must consider. The chemotherapy you'll receive is likely to damage any chance of natural conception. For young women who are diagnosed, we try to do what we can to preserve the opportunity for motherhood. It's not always successful, but you'll have a better chance than if you were to do nothing. Are you interested?"

Ruth's cheeks could not have been more red. She nodded, her eyes fixed on the floor.

Dr. Delauney leaned forward, catching her eyes with his own earnest gaze. "I see no reason why you should not overcome this and go on to live a long and prosperous life. You're young and healthy. If I could give you any advice, it would be this: Keep your head up and think positively. No wallowing. Understood?"

I hoped Ruth would take his advice to heart because I'd be doing enough worrying for the both of us.

* * *

Present Day England, Celeste

I pushed aside thoughts of my own childbearing plight. How could I think of anything but Ruth's health?

When we left the doctor's office, Ruth and Charles began peppering me with questions. I told them to wait, for I didn't want to turn into a puddle before we returned to the bed and breakfast. I hated crying in public.

"So, what do we do now?" Charles' voice was weak and quiet, his eyes swollen and red. It was hard to see him like this.

"She will have to start treatments. Chemotherapy."

"I have not the slightest understanding of that word!" Ruth cried.

"I'm afraid I don't know everything there is to know about it, either," I said, taking her into my arms. I was careful not to touch her neck with my shoulder.

"This is terribly irregular. Only a few days ago, I had not heard of Non-Hodgkin ..." Ruth pulled abruptly away and sat down hard on the sofa bed. "Though I have heard of cancer."

I sat beside her. "Many different types of cancer have been around for ages, although most people in your time do not know what it is they are dying from," I replied.

"So this treatment—or procedure—will cure her?" Charles asked.

I shook my head. "There's not a cure, per se. These treatments may kill the cancer, but there's always a chance it could return. Some people do go on to live long and healthy lives with no recurring cancer. Ruth has an excellent chance." I tried to sound optimistic, but feared I fell short.

Charles stood and began to pace the room. I watched him for a few minutes, then realized he was making Ruth nervous. "Sit down, my love, before you wear a path in the rug."

"If you do not mind, I would like to rest now, but we are sitting on my bed," Ruth said to me.

I stood and hugged her. "Are you doing all right with this news, Ruth?"

She nodded, then rose and moved toward the water closet without a word, closing the door behind her. Charles and I made up the sofa bed for her before retiring to our own room.

25

"Are we destined to live out our lives here, dependent upon modern medicine to keep Ruth alive?" Charles asked. "What is to become of us? I do not know how to live here—and what is to become of Shariton Park and all our staff?"

"I don't know, but shouldn't our main concern be for Ruth? We can't leave until she has overcome all of this and is safe."

He paced again.

"This will be exactly as if we were away in London," I said in my best soothing tone. "Your staff will take care of the estate until we return. It will work out. Ruth will live through this, and we'll all go home soon."

"We should get her a room at Shariton Park, where she will be more comfortable," Charles said, sighing.

"I'm sorry. This is the best place I could arrange here on short notice. If we were in London, we would've had better options." The stress of our situation heightened, growing like an inflating balloon of lead in my stomach. Tears spilled over my lashes.

Charles lay beside me and pulled me into his arms. "All will be well, my dear. All will be well."

Chapter Four

Present Day England, Ruth

I blinked slowly against the summer sun peeking from behind a low cloud. The taxi we rode in hit the uneven ground, and my head bumped the window. I rubbed it, then ran my fingers through my hair. It was strange to wear it down. Celeste said it was not common for people to wear their hair up and curly unless they were going to a wedding or a fancy party. Truth be told, I rather enjoyed it long and loose.

I blinked slowly again. Drowsiness still had a hold of me due to the pain medication. Dr. Delauney had warned me that it would feel worse before it got better. Not that I expected life to get better from here, for who would marry me now?

Don't dwell on that, you goose. Think positive, like the doctor said.

Dr. Begum has been great to work with thus far. He was able to help us arrange for me to stay at Shariton. I looked forward to my stay.

It would be far better than remaining in that tiny inn room.

Why did this all have to happen? I should be planning ... planning what? I had no prospects.

I wanted to curl into a ball and cry, but knowing how hard it would be for Celeste and Charles to see me react like that, I kept a straight face and held my devastation to myself.

When the car drove around a bend, Shariton Park came into view. My eyes grew wide as I took in my surroundings. It looked so different from the home I knew. The south side appeared newer, fresher, less familiar, and I recalled with chagrin what Celeste had once said about the building being partially destroyed. Newer tiles on the roof stood out as well. The grounds had undergone an even greater change with the forest cut back. Flowering shrubs and ornamental trees grew in intricate patterns surrounding the house and a wide circular driveway in front. Despite these changes, or perhaps because of them, the estate appeared majestic and awe-inspiring.

Tears pricked at my eyes.

I glanced at Charles. His expression was somber, and I could tell he was conflicted by what he saw. Charles loved the forests he had once played in as a boy. To see them cut down must have been hard on him.

As we neared the gate, a large stone wall with *Shariton Park* carved upon it came into view. More vegetation was beautifully arranged around the wall. The taxi driver stopped at the closed iron gate and spoke into a glowing box where a voice answered back, and the gate swung open of its own accord. As we drove through, I noticed this gate was not the one I remembered. I wondered how much of what I saw would be new. Would the furniture be gone? Would the paintings of my ancestors still be hanging on the walls?

I rested my forehead against the window and watched as we drove toward the large front entrance. My brows rose when the driver did not stop but continued toward the side of the building.

28

"Where are you taking us?" Charles demanded.

"They don't use the front entrance for everyday use. Only for large social events," the driver replied. "Last time I drove someone here, I learned that the hard way. I received an earful from the woman in charge. They should have some kind of sign out front." He stopped before a short stone wall bordering a doorway into the building.

I waited while Charles helped Celeste out, then came to my side of the motorcar. As soon as I stepped outside, my hair whipped into my eyes, and my long skirt flew up. I reached down to grasp my skirt with one hand and up to pull my hair back with the other. I never needed to keep my hair from flying into my eyes or my dress from revealing my legs. This was distressing, indeed. I glanced at the taxi driver, hoping he did not witness my humiliation. He took no heed of me at all. Charles noticed my discomfort and quickly guided me through the doorway. The room we entered was much smaller than the grand entryway, but it seemed comfortable and inviting despite its size.

"Welcome. You must be the Roberts." A thin, middle-aged woman with peppered gray and brown hair, dark eyes, and thin lips approached us from around a large wooden desk.

"Good evening … Miss …"

"Mrs. Scott, but please, call me Kim. Everyone here is on a first name basis. I'm the manager here at Shariton. I oversee the needs of all our guests—notice I didn't use the word patient. We don't use that word here. We want everyone who stays here to feel like they're at home, not in a hospital." Her smile appeared forced and unnatural.

"Very good of you," Charles replied stiffly. "I am Lor—Charles Roberts." He motioned to Celeste, "This is my wife … er …"

"Ruth," Celeste interjected, shaking Mrs. Scott's proffered hand.

"And my sister … Celeste," he continued slowly. I started to curtsy, then quickly shook hands and nodded instead. Such an odd custom.

"Well, let's get on with it. We have plenty of paperwork to do. Identification, please," Mrs. Scott held out her hand briskly.

I stiffened as I'd done each time I was asked for identification.

Mrs. Scott squinted at the card, then looked at Celeste. "This looks more like you."

Celeste nodded. "We get that a lot."

She walked to her desk and sat down. "Please, sit." She waved at the chairs in front of her.

"Tell me, Mrs. Scott, do the Elsegoods still own Shariton Park?" Charles asked tentatively.

"Please call me Kim. No one here uses last names," she reminded him, her smile belying the edge in her voice. "To answer your question, no. Not exactly. Moving on … Shariton Park offers a more relaxed and attentive environment for receiving treatments and holistic care." Her voice droned on in a well-rehearsed presentation of the many attributes and features of the facility. My mind wandered, and I studied the room around us. I found it odd that she would choose the old scullery as her office. *Why not choose a better room?*

My thoughts were interrupted when she asked me to sign the stack of paperwork. I concentrated on signing the name Celeste Roberts, attempting to appear natural as I directed the pen across the smooth surface many times. How many signatures does one require for a simple stay? She took down doctor information, payment information, emergency contact information, general health information, and dietary preferences. It was all so time-consuming and irritating. All I wanted was to eat a little and go right to bed.

Mrs. Scott stood. "Sorry, dear, for the mess of paperwork. Now, let's get you to your room." She came around the desk to help me up. "Since you're tired and need rest, we'll hold off on the tour until tomorrow."

"Thank you." *Bless you!*

"You may come with us and see that she's settled, but visitors may only stay until nine," she told Charles and Celeste.

They nodded, and we all followed her out of the room. Immediately, I recognized the hall we walked into, though the walls were void of most of the paintings I was used to seeing. We turned the corner and stepped through a doorway into a small lift. I covertly exchanged a look of amazement with Charles. We rode up two flights, then stopped, stepping out of the lift near the grand staircase. Not far down the hall and around a corner was my own familiar room. I wondered how much it had changed.

Mrs. Scott walked in the opposite direction to the end of the hall, up a short staircase, then down another hall. She stopped in front of one of the former guest rooms.

"Here you are. Room 304." She opened the door to reveal a room about half the size of my own. It was beautifully decorated, though some of the objects were foreign to me. A fireplace surrounded by plush armchairs offered a cozy sitting area well-lit by a tall window opposite. The four poster was invitingly made up with a plush blue comforter, pretty floral pillows, and a soft gray afghan across the foot of the bed. Opposite the door we had entered was another set of double doors. Kim walked directly across the room and opened them. Inside was a water closet as big as the bedroom. A large bathtub with steps leading down into it stood on the right, a walk-in shower beside it, and to the left was a large vanity with a sink.

"This wardrobe is where you can put your clothes. These hand bars are here for when you get weak. This cord here," she indicated a long cord next to the shower door, "is for you to pull if you ever need help while bathing. There's one on the other side by the vanity as well. It will summon any of the nurses on duty so they can assist you immediately."

She left the water closet, and I followed. Celeste and Charles sat whispering on the sofa in the other room.

"There's a map," Kim waved toward the coffee table. "The kitchen's located on the main floor. It's open from 5 a.m. to midnight. The dining room's to the right of it, and everyone who stays here eats there when they're feeling well or in their rooms when they're not. The family that owns the house wishes you to remain in the west wing. The east wing's where they reside; therefore, we must respect their wishes and give them their privacy. Tomorrow, someone will deliver your treatment schedule. Make sure you're in your room before your scheduled time so we don't have to hunt you down.

"There's a library, but it's the family's personal library, so we're only permitted to use it from 9 a.m. to 3 p.m. You may check books out from the bottom three shelves around the room. Make sure you write down your name, room number, and the book you're borrowing in the ledger. There's an indoor swimming pool, basketball court, and gym, but they're only open from 9 a.m. to 3 p.m. These are located out the back door, just beyond the first garden and the tennis courts. There's a stable for those interested and feeling well enough to ride. If you don't know how, Dolan would be willing to give you lessons. We find that keeping horses here for our guests has been rewarding in every way, and it helps with healing and overall emotional well-being."

I felt giddy at the thought of riding a horse. "I am well acquainted with riding."

"Oh, and there's a common room where you can play games and visit with the other guests. Take a look at the map if you need to know where something is before I show you around in the morning. I'll leave you to rest. Your bags were brought up already. If you like, I can have someone help you unpack your belongings in the morning."

"Thank you. I can take care of it," I said.

"Mr. and Mrs. Roberts, when you're finished with your visit, come to the office, and I'll call you a taxi." She nodded briskly and left the room.

The moment the door clicked shut, I asked, "What is a swimming pool?"

Celeste chuckled. "It's a clean pool of water that people swim in."

"Goodness. I do not even know how to swim. Pray, do people do it for fun?"

"Yes. In fact, it's a sport now. Some swim in competitions."

"How very odd," I replied.

I glanced at the wall and noticed one of those black glass squares. It was similar to the one at the inn, the same one that caused me so much curiosity. I forced myself to tear my gaze away. "What kind of person owns this place? He must be kind to open half of Shariton to the ill."

"I wonder who he is. Is he or is he not an Elsegood?" Charles leaned back in his chair and folded his arms.

Chapter Five

Present Day England, Ruth

I woke late the next morning to a knock at my door. Surprised, I sat and pulled a blanket around my shoulders. My old nightgown fell around my ankles when I stood and moved to the door. With a careful pull, the door creaked open a few inches, and I peeked out. A young woman stood at the ready with a smile.

"I apologize. I thought you'd be up. I'll come back and clean your room later," she said, then hurried away.

I blinked the haze away from my mind, I looked across the room, and found the digital clock. 9:30. How could I have slept so late? After washing and dressing in one of the few dresses Celeste had bought me, I brushed through my hair, pulled the sides away from my face, and then made my way down the hall. Right before I reached the lift, I paused. I took tentative steps toward the east wing, moving to the familiar staircase, and leaned over the banister. The grand chandelier was completely different from the one that hung there in my time. The new one was beautiful, but it did not seem to fit the elegance and architecture of my home.

The banister had also changed, with the original stone replaced with marble and iron. My heart felt heavy seeing so many changes to my home. I turned and moved further down the hall toward the off-limits area. The artwork on the walls was different, too. I covered my heart and my chin quivered. *What happened to my great grandparents' portraits? My parents'? Everyone's?*

I blinked tears away when I heard someone running up the stone staircase behind me. I turned to see a man appear at the top of the stairs. The edges of his dark hair were wet with perspiration, as was his sleeve-less shirt. His shoulders and chest rose with each quick breath and his face burned bright red. His breeches only went to his knees, leaving his legs bare, and he wore strange shoes that laced across the top. His blue eyes fell on me in surprise.

"I … I apologize, sir. I … was just admiring the art. I suppose I should be on my way." I moved my light-knit sweater higher up on my shoulder to cover the surgical tape on my collarbone and hurried past him toward the lift. I glanced at him from the corner of my eye as I passed. My steps faltered when I got a closer at his strong jaw and large shoulders. Men in my day would never show so much skin so casually.

He cleared his throat and stared at me, puzzled, then a smile crept across his face. "Well, you wouldn't want the Lord of Shariton to find you poking about his private wing, now would you?"

I paused, speechless. Why would someone I had never properly met tease me?

I raised my chin and walked to the lift, pressing the button to go down. I looked at the door, listening for his departing footsteps, which were met with silence instead. I stole another glance his way. He occupied the same place, watching me with an amused smirk. I promptly ignored him and hurried through the opening door of the lift. I knew my embarrassment showed in my behavior, which only made it worse. Before the door closed, I glanced back. He rubbed the back of his neck and watched the lift doors close. *I wonder what he was here for. What kind of cancer could he have?*

The moment the door slid open, Mrs. Scott walked up. "Oh! I was coming up to get you. Did you find the kitchen yet?"

"No, I ..."

"Well, come on, then. This way." Upon entering the kitchen, my jaw dropped. Nothing looked familiar. It was very modern, every surface was shining and pristine. It gave me an odd, empty feeling of loss. I chose my meal half-heartedly and ate at one of the dining tables while Mrs. Scott expounded upon the merits of punctuality. When I had finished, she escorted me through the house. Not one of the furnishings or paintings were original. Some appeared authentic, perhaps they were indeed from the past, but they were not from Shariton Park. Mrs. Scott pointed out the medical treatment rooms as we passed, but we did not go inside.

To my delight, the library was much the same in architectural design and layout, if not in books. It seemed someone had gone to great pains to restore this particular room to its original grandeur. I wondered once again about the family who lived here now.

After a short turn about the library, Mrs. Scott introduced me to several nurses assigned to help me during my stay. We ended the tour in the common room, where other guests were gathered. Several played cards at a table in the center of the room, and one read in a cozy corner while others talked in small groups here and there. What drew my full attention was the group sitting before the black-framed rectangle on the wall. I stepped closer, unable to take my eyes off the fascinating images floating across it. People moved, spoke, and lived upon it. How was this thing possible?

"Look, Steve, you have a visitor." An older man who appeared well into his seventies jabbed his elbow into the man beside him.

The man, Steve, was bald and possibly in his late forties. He rubbed his rib, looked at me, raised his eyebrows, then laughed. "She's not my visitor, though I wish she was." He appreciatively inspected me up and down.

I glared, wondering how he could be so bold.

"Just ignore them, sweetie." An older woman stood beside me, draping an arm around my shoulders. "They like to tease. It's what they *live* for." She smiled and maneuvered me out of their line of sight. "Who are you here to visit, dear?"

"Oh, I am not visiting. I am a guest here."

She was silent for a moment, pondering. "You're awfully young for a place like this!"

"Am I?" I glanced around self-consciously.

"Everyone who arrives here is old. In my recollection, there hasn't been anyone under forty come to stay. Why, you couldn't be more than twenty!" She scratched the back of her head, and her hat slid slightly forward, revealing a bald scalp underneath. I raised my eyebrows and looked around the room, noticing several others who were also bald— both men and women. My brow creased with worry.

"My name's Sandy," the woman went on cheerfully. She held out a frail hand, and I shook it gently. Her skin hung loosely on her bones, and dark hollows showed beneath her sparkling blue eyes.

"I'm … Ruth—er, Celeste," I replied, ducking my head and blushing.

"Ruth or Celeste?"

"Celeste." I smiled in chagrin.

"What kind of cancer do you have, Celeste?" she asked with a smile and sad eyes.

"Non-Hodgkin lymphoma." As I said the words, I noticed I had drawn a crowd. Steve, along with his elderly friend, watched me with strange expressions. Everyone stared. Some looked as though they were sorry for me. Others seemed envious.

"I would trade you cancer in a heartbeat. I imagine most of us would," she said. "Yours is one of the easiest to beat. You'll be out of here in no time," Sandy declared.

"That is my hope." I smiled a bit, though I could feel my cheeks redden.

"That's the way to think. Positive thoughts are the best way to get through this," another woman with dark eyes said.

As the novelty of youth in their midst wore off, they slowly dispersed, picking up their games, books, and conversations where they'd left off. The noise from the black box on the wall increased.

"What is that?" I asked Sandy, pointing at it.

Sandy looked at me with one eyebrow raised. "Do you mean the telly or what's on the telly?"

"What is on it, I suppose." *Was that what Celeste called it, too? I don't recall.*

"Don't tell me you've never seen a rugby game!" The old man beside Steve turned toward me in amazement. "Where have you been living? Under a rock?"

"Now, Donald, be kind. Maybe she's the only one in England who doesn't follow the game," Steve chuckled.

"You want me to pop you in the kisser?" Donald raised his voice.

"Steve, don't get him riled up again. It's not good for his heart," Sandy scolded him. She leaned toward me, adding in a low voice, "He doesn't like to be called Donald. He will only answer to Don. Best keep that in mind."

I nodded soberly. However, I do not think there will be occasion for me to address him at all.

38

"You'll love it here—well, love it when you're in between treatments, anyway. When you're feeling your best is when you'll be able to take advantage of what there is to offer. Hopefully, you'll be one of those who take to treatments well and have more good days than bad. I've been here three months already, so I know the ins and outs of what goes on. If you have any questions, you need only ask." Sandy's warm smile filled me with a sense of comradeship I had not expected to find here.

The weight of my decision lifted a little at the thought. I would have someone to depend on during my stay. I would not be alone. Now, if only I could convince Charles and Celeste to agree to my plan.

* * *

Present Day England, Celeste

"You want us to leave?" I asked Ruth in bewilderment.

"Surely you don't expect me to leave my flesh and blood behind to face this time and trial on your own?" Charles looked as hurt as I felt.

"I am sorry. I just feel that you both need to move on and live your life. I cannot expect you to sit around for months waiting for me to improve. You need to be planning for your children and be on the other side in case something happens to the portal. You two belong there. The future of Shariton Park depends on you."

"But you can't go through this alone! Please, Ruth, you must see that this will be difficult to overcome. You need us here," I pleaded.

"Celeste, I will be perfectly happy here. It is my home, after all. I have met some friends who are willing to assist me. I will not be alone." She tried to look convincing, but I could see the uncertainty in her eyes.

"No. I won't go." I folded my arms.

"Then I will refuse you as visitors. I can do that, you know," she

39

said stubbornly. She sighed when she noticed the tears pooling on my lashes. "Celeste, you can still come to visit every month. Will that be enough?"

I pulled out a handkerchief and dabbed at my eyes. "You are my best friend. How shall I live without you?"

Her eyes pooled with tears as well. "One day at a time."

"I do not like this. I promised Mama on her deathbed that I would look after you. I cannot do that from 200 years away." Charles' stood rigid with anger and frustration. I took his hand and brushed my thumb back and forth across it. After several long, silent seconds had passed, he leaned into me and whispered. "I hate it when she is right." He shifted his weight from foot to foot, then continued aloud, "We cannot stay here and abandon our duties at home. We will have to go back."

In his eyes, I read how difficult it was for him to give in.

Ruth pulled me into her arms, and we cried together. Charles put his arms around us and rested his head on Ruth's.

"I will miss you, dear brother … and you, my best friend and sister."

"I'll come back tomorrow with more clothes and some spending money. You'll need sweats for your down days, trousers for the days when you're feeling well enough to ride, and more dresses for when you go out."

"You need not fret over me, dear Celeste. I'm sure I can manage with what I already have."

"You'll need some hats as well," I continued, ignoring her protest. Suddenly, I wondered if she knew what would happen to her hair. I fidgeted and bit my lip, hesitating. "Ruth … one of the side effects of chemotherapy is … could be … hair loss."

Her expression fell, and she lowered her head in resignation. "I suspected as much. Nearly everyone I met today was bald."

"It will grow back," I assured her quickly, handing her my handkerchief. She dabbed at her watery eyes.

40

"Will it?"

"As soon as you finish your treatment."

"Then get me several hats," she tried to smile, then hugged me again.

Leaving grew harder as the minutes ticked by, knowing I would see her only once more before returning to 1812. She looked healthy enough today, but what would she look like in a month's time?

Chapter Six

Present Day England, Abbie

"Oi! Watch it!" A stranger on the street shouted angrily after we bumped into one another. He nearly spilled his coffee down my front.

"Sorry," I said. The man hurried on without acknowledging my apology. I pulled my guitar case up into my arms so that it wouldn't trip up anyone else, then weaved my way outside the crowd to a welcome bench to rest my aching feet. I sat sideways and stretched my legs across the wooden slats, leaning against my backpack.

I had planned for this trip to change my life, but not in the way it had. Ray, Mason, Grace, and I started in Ireland. We saw all the sights we had dreamed of seeing. It was great at first. But a week in, they began pressuring me to do drugs. I refused, of course. I had never tried any drug or alcohol, and I wasn't about to start now. I didn't want to turn out like my mother.

42

The day we traveled to Scotland, I learned what kind of friends they really were. I remember settling into our hostel and having dinner at a small pub. That's all I remember, but I woke up groggy, sore, and broke. They had taken everything and run. I couldn't believe Grace would do such a thing. And now, nearly two months later, after wandering the country, I found myself pregnant. Pregnant! Years of caution, watching out for myself and steering clear of the wrong crowd, planning for my future and trying to be different, yet I had still ended up like my mother.

When the shock of my discovery wore off, I felt strangely lucky—as lucky as someone could feel in my situation—that at least I had no memory of how it happened.

My solo trip began with a desperate need to earn money. I played my guitar on the streets, making my way south toward England. I relied on the kindness of strangers to supply enough money to eat, sleep in hostels, and travel south where it was warmer. Some days, I barely earned enough for one meal and a place to lay my head. My goal, of course, was to report my stolen passport and earn enough cash to get back home. But I couldn't rely on anyone else's help. When I'd scraped up enough extra coin and courage to call Kacie, she informed me that her dad had lost his job, and they were worried his health would prevent him from finding a new one. When I heard that, I kept silent about my own situation. They thought I was having the time of my life, and I didn't want to worry them any more than they already were. Besides, I could make my own way. I was stronger than my mother had been.

I can figure this out on my own.

I cleared my throat for the millionth time and tried to hold back the tears. I couldn't cry and wallow in self-pity. I needed to get over it, but it seemed my emotions had a different idea.

"Are you all right?"

I looked up to see who the sweet voice belonged to. A woman, just older than me, peered down at me. Beside her stood a very nicely dressed, very handsome man. Her wedding ring caught the light and sparkled in the sun.

"Are you all right? Is there something I can do for you?" her dark eyes were kind, emanating concern.

I shook my head. "I'm hunky dory. Only tired."

"You're American! You're a long way from home," the woman said, grinning. "Are you traveling with friends or family?"

The truth stuck in my throat, but I managed to force it out. "No. They left me high and dry."

"They left you? You don't know where they are?" the man asked.

I shook my head again, careful to keep my eyes from meeting theirs. I was too afraid of breaking down in front of them.

"Do you need a place to stay?" he asked.

"I …" I didn't want to look like I was begging. Earning money by playing beside street cafes was one thing, but accepting such a generous offer of help felt humiliating.

"Come on." The woman took me by the arm and helped me to my feet. "Our B and B is just a few doors down. You can stay there as well. I'm sure they'll have another room."

"Oh, I couldn't!"

"I insist. You're in my care now." She took me by the elbow and pulled me beside her down the street and into the lobby of the B and B. She ignored my attempts to pay for it myself—though I didn't have enough money. I thanked her repeatedly as we made our way to my room.

"What's your name?" I asked.

"Celeste."

"Your full name? When I return home, I'd like to write to you and send you a better thank you. I can pay you back when I get there."

She shook her head. "Celeste is all you need to know. What's your name?"

"Abbie. Abbie Lambert." I shook both of their hands and thanked them again. They waved goodbye, then left me to my clean room, warm shower, and soft bed. Through their kindness, I was one step closer to saving enough money to return home, and I felt better than I had in weeks. I smiled and lay on the bed with clean, wet hair. *There really are good people in the world, after all.*

* * *

Present Day England, Ruth

"How can people live in such a state?" I asked myself, following the path to the stables. I tried to scratch my leg through my jeans but could not satisfy the itch. *These jeans are too restrictive and coarse! Oh, what do they find wrong with a riding habit!* I wiped away tears of frustration and cleared my throat as I drew close to the building.

Moments ago, I had said a difficult farewell to Charles and Celeste. The fear in their eyes did little for my nerves, and I knew my gaze mirrored their unease. We did not know what the future held for any of us, and it frightened us all.

After having a good cry alone, I wiggled into a pair of jeans and a T-shirt and made my way to the stables. The familiar smell of animals blew in the wind toward me. I smiled and picked up speed. When I rounded the corner, I nearly ran into someone carrying a bucket on his shoulder.

"Watch it!" the man called. He almost dropped his load, swiftly setting the bucket down before more water sloshed over the edge. I noted his broad shoulders and dark auburn hair when he stood. When his eyes landed on me, I was stunned by how blue they were.

His eyes widened as he looked me up and down and blew a low whistle.

I narrowed my eyes and stepped back.

"You new here?" He spoke with a faint Irish accent.

"I am." I raised my chin and looked him over. He was handsome—for a stable hand.

"Just started here, then?" He held out his hand. "The name's Dolan. Let me guess, you work for Mrs. O'Doherty in the kitchens?"

I was thrown for a moment when he shook my hand instead of bowing over it. I supposed as someone who'd spent his life mucking out stables, that he did not know the proper way to greet a lady.

I pondered his question. It might be nice to know at least one person here who didn't pity me as a patient, though I felt dismayed at his assumption of my serving as a lowly scullery maid.

"How did you guess?" I replied at last.

"Easy. She's been lookin' for help." He stared me up and down again. "You out for a bit o' walk?"

"Actually, I hope to ride."

He gazed at me in surprised amazement. "That's a laugh! No one on staff is allowed. The horses are for guests only." He looked around furtively. "But if you don't snitch—and if you give me a wee bit of payment in return—I'll let you ride around inside the stable."

Snitch? "I shall not tell."

"Cross your heart and hope to die?"

"P—pardon?"

He gave me a strange look, then jerked his head toward the inside of the stable. "Let's find you a horse, then …" He paused and raised his eyebrows expectantly at me.

"Forgive me. My name is R—Celeste."

He nodded, turned, and headed inside.

At the first stall, I stepped closer to feel the warmth of horseflesh on my fingertips.

Dolan chuckled. "You don't want tha' one. He's sharp as a beach

46

ball."

This man perplexed me more and more.

He stopped and pulled open a stall door. "This here is Henrietta. She's a good little mare and will be real gentle with ya." He patted the mare on her neck.

"Who said I wanted a gentle mare?" I walked past him and halted at a stall housing a tall, elegant stallion. "What about him? Has he been properly trained?"

"O' course. Norman knows how to behave—for some. But he's no fit mount for a dainty woman."

"I shall ride him," I announced, opening the stall and patting the stallion's neck.

"You're a fiery vixen, ya are," Dolan looked me over with an approving grin and went to retrieve a saddle. In no time, he had Norman ready to go.

No mounting block could be found upon a cursory search of the indoor paddock. I would have to rely on his assistance. "Would you mind helping me up? He is a bit too tall for me." I tried not to look as self-conscious as I felt.

"O' course!" he agreed eagerly.

I held the pommel in my left hand and expectantly waited for him to offer his hands as a foothold. I jumped, feeling his hands at my waist. My breath caught as he lifted me easily into the saddle, and I held my head high, hoping he did not notice my red cheeks.

"Thank you," I said a little too loudly.

"If you keep near the stable and inside the paddock, no one will be the wiser."

I had no intention of staying inside the paddock. I flicked the reins to the left and squeezed the stallion's sides.

He leaped forward, alarmed. "No! Wait!"

Norman shot out of the stables and across the lawn. I glanced over my shoulder and saw Dolan waving his arms at me. A giggle erupted deep within when the horse cleared the fence with ease. "Let's see just how fast you can go!" I whispered to Norman. He seemed as eager as I and galloped up the hill toward the estate house. At the top, I pulled him back to a slow trot. This same hill had always been a stopping point when I rode, giving me the best view of the land my brother owned. To my dismay, I found the landscape quite altered. Small wooden houses and smooth gray roads replaced the trees and green hills I once knew. Some of the forest remained, but most of it was missing. The river still flowed not far away, but a large, ungainly bridge now traversed it.

"It's so different. It's not as peaceful and glorious. Norman, I wish you could have seen it in my day." I sighed and leaned forward to pat his neck. I turned my head at the sound of hoofbeats coming from behind. Dolan rode hard toward me.

A mischievous grin tugged at the corners of my lips, and I loosened the reins. Norman bolted to the right, along the top of the hill. Ahead of us, perfectly manicured grass spread out in unbroken emerald beauty, save for an occasional flagpole standing out upon the green. I guided Norman onto its soft, even surface, pulling him back to a slow walk when I noticed a small, boxy motorcar headed my way. Three men sat on its narrow bench seats without doors or windows to protect them.

"You shouldn't be over here!" the driver called, waving me back.

I looked behind me and saw that Dolan had stopped his horse at the edge of the trimmed grass. He waved at me furiously. Heat flushed my neck and cheeks as I realized I must have done something terribly wrong. I turned the stallion back toward Dolan, and as we approached the edge of the wide lawn, I urged him into a gallop up the hillside and to the top. There, I paused to wait.

"Were you hit with the stupid stick?" Dolan sputtered with furrowed brows.

My mouth dropped. Heat flamed my cheeks. "What did you say?"

He frowned. "I'm sorry. I shouldn't have said tha', but not only did you ride out of the stables, but you rode right out onto the golf course! The master will have my head!" He threw up his hands. "Are you trying to get us both sacked?"

Sacked? "I assure you, I had no idea I was not allowed on the … golf course." I hesitated over the unfamiliar phrase.

"The damage you've done to the course will be coming out of *your* pay—not mine." He turned his horse and started for the stables. "Come on, before we get it worse."

He would certainly be disappointed if he thought he could order me about. I waited with my head held high until I felt good and ready to return to the stables. Still, I could not believe he had called me stupid— although I had to admit, I must have come across as a bit dimwitted. Everything was so foreign to me. As I rode back to the stables, my face flushed red with embarrassment again. Dolan had already dismounted and stood waiting impatiently, his arms flexed and folded across his chest.

My insides grew hot with guilt, knowing now that his livelihood was on the line. "I truly am sorry. I will pay for any damages and will take all the blame. You may even say that I saddled my own horse and rode out without your knowledge … if you believe it would help." I gazed down at the top of his head.

He sighed and looked up at me. An unexpected smile spread across his face. "Oh, but it was jolly good to see someone ride like tha'. No one here has been able to stay on Norman long. Only Mr. Harrison rides him." I couldn't help but feel my wounded pride heal a bit at his comment.

He held up his arms to help me dismount. I swung my leg over the saddle, and he lifted me down. When my feet touched the ground, I moved to step away, but he held firmly around my waist and looked into my eyes. More heat rushed to my cheeks. I tried again to pull away, but he prevented me. I narrowed my eyes.

An impish grin spread across his face. He laughed and let go. "You're a fiery lass, you are. Maybe it would be best to wait for my payment."

"Payment?"

"A kiss is a payment from any of the girls who work for Mrs. Scott and wish to ride, but a kiss from you just might stop my heart," he said, then winked.

A kiss! He was bold as brass! I tilted my chin and watched him lead the horses into the stable. He winked at me again, then laughed when my eyes widened. I turned on my heel and walked away. When I thought of his hands around my waist, I felt the heat continuing to rise in my cheeks, and I bit back a smile.

Chapter Seven

Present Day England, Abbie

Frustrated tears filled my eyes. I had planned to find the nice couple from last night when I woke, but I was too late. The clerk at the front desk informed me that they had already checked out, but not without paying for another night for me. I left the inn feeling helpless. After lying awake the previous night, I had come to a decision … a hard decision. I couldn't take care of this baby on my own, and I knew how important it would be for this child to have both a mother and a father. Perhaps the kind couple knew someone who could help me.

Going home now wasn't an option. Truth be told, I was ashamed of my condition and I would be mortified to return. Everyone knew of my plans for an education and I had even boasted to friends that I would be top in my career before finding someone to marry. *No way could I go home like this!*

A few blocks from the B and B might be a perfect spot to play my music and earn some money. I made my way down the street, keeping my eyes on the ground in front of me. The sound of someone's voice brought my head up.

"Don't worry, my love. We'll see her soon." The voice belonged to the nice man from last night. The young woman named Celeste stood with her husband, waiting to board the bus that had pulled to a stop before them.

Sweet! I found them! I hurried to the bus before the driver could completely close the door. When he noticed me, the door swung open. The sign on the bus stated that we were heading toward London. I reached into my pocket, pulled out a few coins, and dropped them into the slot; then, I hurried to a seat near the front. The couple sat close to the middle where the man wrestled to fit a small trunk under his feet before the bus drove again. We were a good way from London, so I sat back and watched the scenery go by.

My eyes shot open when the bus jerked forward. *How long was I asleep?* I rubbed my eyes with my fingers, then looked over my shoulder in sudden anxiety. My heart stopped when I saw the nice couple no longer occupied their seats. I stood and peered out the window. They were walking toward the forest at the side of the road.

"Stop! Please stop!" I grabbed my guitar case and pack.

"Again? What's with you people! Are ya thick? Do you see a bus stop anywhere near here?" The bus driver's red cheeks and ferocious eyes burned a hole in me.

"Please. I desperately need to get off or I'll ..." I thought quickly, "I'm going to be sick!"

The driver grumbled a few choice words and slowed to a stop. I hurried off without bothering to thank the grumpy man. *Where did they go?* I ran to where I'd last seen them walking into the trees. There was no sign of them now. Without a clear direction, I made my way into the

52

forest. After several minutes, I heard someone sneeze, and quickened my pace.

Where on earth are they going? I spotted them through the thick trees, holding hands and talking in low voices as they walked with steady purpose. They appeared happy and deeply in love. The man was gentle with his wife, carefully helping her over a fallen log. I followed them silently, worrying about how to confront them, conscious of how crazy I looked following them onto the bus and through the woods. I glanced down to check my footing then found they had veered out of sight. I hurried forward, searching anxiously, and spotted them ducking under an ancient tree's tall, arched root. When they straightened, the top half of their bodies had disappeared.

I dropped my guitar and screamed, and my hand shot up to cover my mouth.

* * *

Present Day/1812 England, Celeste

I gasped. "Did you hear that?" I asked Charles.

He darted back to the arch into the future and paused under it. "Celeste. We have a problem."

I crossed through to stand at his side and saw, to my surprise, the young woman we had met on the street. She stared at us through wide, unblinking eyes, shaking her head slightly.

"How did you get here?" I asked her.

She slowly lowered her hand from her mouth, still trembling. "I—I followed you. I'm sorry. But how did you disappear like that? Just now? One minute you were there, the next ... poof!" She narrowed her eyes at the archway behind us as if trying to make out something difficult to see.

53

I sighed and cast a questioning glance at Charles.

"May I ask why you were following us?" he asked.

Her shoulders slumped. "It's a long story. I guess I was hoping you could help me."

Charles gazed at me. "I'm ready for a long story. How about you?"

I nodded. "Come here and sit, Abbie. I believe we both have a story to tell." I sat on a boulder and patted the spot next to me, indicating Charles to sit.

She hesitated for a moment, then sat on a rock across from us.

"Why don't you go first?" Charles suggested.

"First, I don't know your name," she said pointedly to Charles.

"I am Lord Elsegood," he answered. "And this is Lady Elsegood."

"But you can call me Celeste." I glanced at Charles. He hated it when I permitted people to use my given name. As if on cue, he rolled his eyes.

"Why would a lord and lady be riding a bus to the middle of no-where and then hiking through the forest?" she asked, brows raised.

Charles looked momentarily flummoxed. "We will get to that. Tell us why you are here," he huffed.

"Well …" her eyes filled with sudden tears, and her voice shook. I reached to take her hand in mine, smiling encouragingly. "About two months ago, my friends robbed me and left me behind." She gestured with air quotes and gave a sour expression. "And a few days ago, I found out I was pregnant, without memory of how it happened."

My heart ceased. "No!" *Poor girl!*

"You have no memory of it?" Charles asked.

I studied Abbie's face and thought hard. "One moment, Charles. I suspect she was drugged by these friends, who also robbed and aban-doned her. Is that right, Abbie?"

She nodded. "I guess I was. They were doing drugs. We ate and drank together before it happened."

54

"You poor, dear girl." I moved to her side, pulled her head to my shoulder, and rubbed her arm.

She cried softly for a moment, then raised her head. "I've been crying over this too much already." She wiped away her tears with a look of determination in her eyes. "I followed you to see if you could help me. I don't have the means to get back home, and I don't want to, not like this. It would be too humiliating to go back knocked up. I need to find a place to stay—somewhere they won't ship me back home—somewhere I can have my baby, then leave. I need someone to be this baby's parents—and like, since you were so kind and generous to me, I hoped *you* might be the parents this baby needs ... or something." She spoke so fast I could hardly comprehend her words.

"You want—us—to be your baby's parents?" Charles asked, his eyes moving back and forth between us.

"I know it's asking a lot. Maybe you don't want children, or maybe not yet. But if you don't want my baby, maybe you could help me find someone looking for a child," she pleaded desperately.

"Charles." Tears came to my eyes when I gazed into his, "What if ... what if our ..." I couldn't get the words out.

"What is it?" he asked.

"What if the descendants we know about didn't come from us? What if this is our child?"

"What are you saying?" His forehead creased in confusion.

"What I'm saying is, what if I truly can't have children? If we turn her away ... would it change our future—the future of our descendants?"

"I thought you were so sure about us having our own children." He paused, then added, "This child is not our flesh and blood. It could not inherit Shariton Park."

"What if no one knew it was not our child? What if we were to pretend I was carrying a child, and we accept it as our own when this baby is born?" I knew it was a far-fetched idea, but I couldn't let it go. I

55

couldn't be sure I'd have any children of my own, and I didn't want to pass up the opportunity to be a mother.

"Do you realize what you are saying? How could we fool your lady's maid? She sees you every day. She dresses you and helps you to wash."

My shoulders slumped. "Then we must ask her to swear never to reveal our secret."

"Do you honestly think it could work?" he asked. I knew the look in his eyes. It was the look of hope mixed with uncertainty.

"It is worth a try." I glanced over at Abbie. She looked bewildered as she stared back and forth between us. I smiled, "Sorry, Abbie. It's time we explained our story. It may help clear things up … or perhaps it will only confuse you further."

I told her about our desire to have children and our struggles. When I revealed how we met through time travel, her interest shifted to concern. The look on her face was easy to read. She thought I was deranged.

"I know it's unbelievable, but it's true. We live in the year 1812, and he's Viscount of Shariton Park," I waved at Charles. "I was born in the twenty-first century, two hundred years after Charles."

He chuckled. "I look young for my age."

"I found myself lost in these woods four years ago. When I emerged through that archway, I found myself in a different time. I couldn't believe it myself at first; it was utterly incomprehensible, but you saw the way we disappeared. That's the portal through which you may travel through time."

She was silent, clearly in deep thought. "Where do ya live now?"

"With Charles in the nineteenth century."

She shook her head. "This is insane!"

Charles spoke up. "The only way to convince you of the truth of what we say is for you to come with us. Shariton Park would be a safe place for you to stay while we think about what is next. I can assure you,

you will be well taken care of."

"Well …" Abbie hesitated, "If I agree to go with you—not that I believe you—but if I agree to walk through the archway, and it really takes me to the past, will you bring me back after I have the baby, so that I can go home?" she asked.

"Of course. You may leave at any time," I reassured her.

She ran her fingers through her blonde hair, catching the small braids hidden throughout its length. I watched her untangle them and waited for her answer.

"This is insane, you know. I must be out of my mind to even con-sider …" She inhaled and let her breath out slowly. "How about I go with you and see if you're telling the truth or if you're all nuts? Then, I'll decide whether or not to give you my baby." She stood before letting us agree. "We better get going, then. I'm feeling a little hungry." She picked up her pack and guitar case, eager to be moving.

"Allow me." Charles stood, took the pack from her, and pulled it on his shoulders.

"Thank you," she said.

He held his hand out for her guitar case as well.

"I'll carry it. It's my baby."

His eyebrows rose.

"She means it's dear to her as if it were a baby," I clarified.

"What is it?" he asked.

"A guitar."

"Oh! Yes! I have heard one played once or twice," he responded.

"More than once or twice. You've listened to the radio while in the modern time," I chuckled.

"Yes. Well, I would not call that noise music, and I tried not to listen to it … but it was not all bad, I suppose." He moved through the archway, and Abbie gasped beside me.

"Sorry. I forgot he'd disappear." She frowned. "I guess it is true?"

"Yes. Wait until you see what Shariton Park is like in all its past glory." I took her hand to ease the worry I saw in her eyes. "Shall we go through together?" She nodded, and we stepped through in as easily as if traveling through time were nothing. In a flash, we were through, and it was as if nothing had changed. She raised her eyebrows, doubtful once more.

"I've never seen Shariton Park," she said, her voice grim.

"That is a shame! It is a grand place," Charles lamented.

We walked on for several minutes, chatting about Shariton Park and my experiences there. I told her about our time's differences in social etiquette and manners. I described the balls, the tea, the handmaids. With each new subject, Abbie grew quieter and more sober.

At last, she paused and placed a shaky hand on a tree trunk to steady herself. "What will people think of me? I have no husband and will soon be so large I won't be able to hide that I'm pregnant and husbandless."

Charles took a breath, paused, then said, "I have been thinking of that, and I have an idea. If you enter society in your condition without a husband, you will most certainly be shunned—" Abbie grimaced, and her cheeks turned red. "—But if you are introduced as a widow in mourning, you will be welcomed easily."

Abbie nodded slowly. "I guess it's the only way. But what do I tell people? What's my story?" she asked.

I took her arm and led her forward. "Let us discuss it, and perhaps by the time we reach Shariton Park, we will know what to say."

Chapter Eight

1812 England, Abbie

Before we reached the road, Charles asked us to sit and wait for him. He went on alone to find his stable hand and the carriage he had hidden nearby so it would look like we were returning from London. After he left, Celeste and I changed our clothes. She and Charles had packed period clothing in the bottom of the trunk they carried, along with several tubes of toothpaste, toothbrushes, and packages of pencils. I was relieved to see that Celeste had an extra dress for me. It fit well enough, except for the length. She was shorter than I. After dressing, she pulled my hair up into a bun and pinned it.

"That will have to do for now." She patted my hair to check for loose strands, then stepped back to admire the effect.

I ran my fingers over the soft blue gown. "This dress is wonderful," I smiled.

"We will get you a black smock as soon as possible." Reading my puzzled expression, she explained. "Women in this time wore black dresses while in mourning, for at least a year for the death of a husband. Less time for other relatives."

"Right." I placed the back of my hand over my forehead and said in a breathy voice, "Oh, 'tis deplorable that mine husband hath been run through! How shall I ever carry on wearing only black?"

My dramatic performance did the trick, putting a smile on Celeste's lips. "Run through? Are you adding to the story we have created for you?" she teased.

"Oh, come on! Don't you think having a pretend husband who has been killed in a sword fight or lost at sea is much more romantic and exciting?"

"Illness is more believable," she replied pragmatically. "Besides, if you embellish too much, you might lose track of the details, and people could ask questions you're unprepared to answer. Also, speak of your late husband in a somber tone. Think of him as a real person," she urged.

"Okay. I get it," I said, biting my nail.

Celeste slapped my hand away. "What are you doing? You can't bite your fingernails!" She laughed when she saw the surprised look on my face. "If you were to be caught doing that in public, you'd be mocked. It's socially unacceptable to put your fingers in your mouth!"

I laughed with her. "Sorry."

"And you should say 'I apologize' or 'forgive me,' not 'I'm sorry.'"

"Wow. I guess I'll need some lessons," I said. "I'm afraid you'll have your hands full with me. I wasn't taught to keep my elbows off the table. I also have a bad habit of snorting when I laugh."

"Oh dear." She took a deep breath. "We have no time to waste." She cleared her throat. "First, you should address Charles as Lord Elsegood unless he indicates otherwise. I've permitted you to use my given name, so you need not be so formal with me. Second, when the time comes for you to reveal that you're with child, you don't say *I'm pregnant*. It sounds rather rude. Instead, you should say that you're in *a family way*, or when you are near the end, it will be said that you are *in confinement*."

"Alrighty." I bit back a laugh.

"This is serious. You must understand. Your behavior reflects on us, your generous hosts."

I stood a little taller. "You're right. I'm sorr—I mean, please forgive me."

She smiled, then explained some more proper ways of speech. I never knew things could be so different with language. When Lord Elsegood came with the carriage, I felt overwhelmed by rules and etiquette.

It was very dark by the time Shariton Park came into view. Its massive form loomed tall against the starry night, and the windows glowed with orange candlelight, giving it an ominous appearance.

"It's a perfectly spooky place to get lost in! How many rooms are there?" I asked in awe.

"More than one hundred. I can't wait for you to see it in the daylight. It's breathtaking."

"I believe you." I stuck my face against the glass of the carriage and gazed up as we pulled up to the front doors. A line of servants came filing out and stood at attention.

Lord Elsegood gently took my arm and helped me out after his wife. He then stopped me in front of an older man and a stern-looking woman with a large bundle of keys at her hip. "Herbert, Mrs. Linchner, this is Mrs. Lambert, an old friend of Lady Elsegood's. She will be staying with us for some time. You see, her husband has passed, and she has no relations here. Her family is from America, so I hope you will all give her a warm welcome."

"Welcome to Shariton Park, Mrs. Lambert. My condolences on the unfortunate passing of your husband." Herbert was formal and stiff, but his voice sounded kind. Mrs. Linchner also greeted me in much the same way.

"Thank you," I replied to them both.

"I should inform you, my lord, that Sir Garrison is here. He arrived a day ago."

"Thank you, Herbert," Lord Elsegood answered.

He briefly informed his household that Ruth would be away for medical treatments as if it were as normal as birds fluttering overhead, then escorted Celeste and I up the stairs into the house.

I couldn't hold my astonishment, staring at the large, grand entryway. "Holy crap, it's huge!" I whispered, then thought of a Micheal Scott quote that I kept to myself. Someone coughed as if trying to hold back laughter.

Celeste gave me a sharp look.

"Sorry." Then I remembered not to say sorry. "Forgive me."

She tried to hide a smile and turned to address her servants. "Mrs. Linchner, Molly, will you escort Mrs. Lambert to the large guest room on the west side? Molly, you will be her maid for the duration of her stay. Oh, and Betsy, will you have some food brought to Mrs. Lambert's room, please, as well as my own and Lord Elsegood's."

"Yes, my lady," they replied.

Mrs. Linchner locked eyes with me and nodded to indicate for me to follow. Obediently, I moved to follow her. As I walked past the line of servants, one particular man watched me with a strange expression. All the other servants kept their eyes forward in unblinking politeness. I touched my hair and glanced down at my dress self-consciously, wondering if something was out of place. Lord Elsegood cleared his throat loudly behind me, and the man's eyes quickly moved straight ahead.

When I had reached the top of the grand staircase, I looked back down and watched the line of servants file out of the room. The man peered up at me again, curiosity in his eyes. Without pause, he kept his eyes on me until he turned the corner.

What's his deal? Surely I don't look that out of place. He can't somehow tell I'm from the future, can he? I turned to find the two women waiting for me to catch up.

"Oh! Sor—I apologize." I hurried to their side and spoke to the younger of the two. "So, your name is Molly, then?"

She nodded.

"My name is Abbie." I held out my hand. She stared at it, then back at me with a bewildered expression. Mrs. Linchner watched with grim disapproval. I lowered my hand, nervously sliding it behind my back. *Oops. No handshake, then.* "Have you worked here long?"

We followed Mrs. Linchner down the hallway toward another set of stairs. "Since I was twelve," she replied.

"You had to start work when you were twelve?"

She glanced back at me with another funny expression.

"Actually, I guess it's not that young. I started babysitting at eleven."

"Babysitting?" She stopped and looked at me like I was nuts.

Oops, again. "Nothing, never mind."

She studied me with uncertainty, then began walking again. I followed at a distance. "We're not in Kansas anymore, Toto." I mumbled to myself.

* * *

Present Day England, Ruth

I watched the fluid move down a clear tube and into my arm, my heart beating faster. "Relax, Celeste. You're doing great." Barbara patted me on the shoulder and smiled.

Answering to Celeste's name had grown easier, but still, I wished to be known as Ruth. The name, this time, this place that was home but

63

not my home all at once … I felt so unlike myself here. "How much longer?"

"Not too much longer."

I glanced down at the IV again, then squeezed my eyes shut. I hated the sight of it snaking its way from my arm. Also, I hated the large tube that pushed fluid into the IV. I had already received several tubes of liquid. One medication was for infections, just in case, another for allergic reactions, just in case, and the other for nausea … just in case. I couldn't remember what the last one was for. I'd lost track once they brought out a bag of liquid with the words *Toxic* and *Biohazard* printed in red letters.

I breathed deep and long, trying to slow my beating heart. *Relax. Keep calm.* The main source of my anxiety at this moment was the nurse's watchful eyes upon the veins in my arm, ensuring the medication caused no damage upon entering. The doctor had gone over the possible side effects before we began, and the thought of what could go wrong caused me more fear than the cancer. *Why did I agree to this?*

It seemed like an eternity for the liquid to enter my body. While we waited, I read—to keep my mind occupied—and the nurse sat quietly. The magazine they had provided to keep my mind occupied was shocking, to say the least. People wore so little!

"Finished," the nurse said happily.

I blew a shaky breath and lowered the magazine to my lap, glad to be done with it.

When they had finished taking care of my IV, leaving the port under a bandage on my hand, they helped me back to my room. I didn't know what to do next, but at last, I made up my mind to walk to the library.

The room stood empty. The open curtains at the tall windows let in enough light that there was no need to light a candle—or flip a switch. A few specks of dust swam about in the rays of sunshine cast upon the settee. The smell of books calmed my agitated nerves. I moved around

64

the room, reading the titles on the spines, not recognizing any of them. Upon further inspection, I noticed the books that filled the higher shelves looked much older.

I moved to the ladder on the wall and climbed until I could reach the higher shelves. The rolling ladder glided across to the other side with one light push, and I studied the books carefully. My smile grew when I spotted a book I knew well that once belonged to my father. It looked older and more tattered than I remembered. I leaned against the ladder and opened the first page. There, inside, was an inscription my father had written. His handwriting looked shaky, but legible. Tears formed with my smile, reading my name alongside my father's words.

"The books on the higher shelves are off limits," a deep voice said behind me.

My heart leaped, and my right foot slipped off the step. I grabbed the side of the ladder with one hand and held the book tightly in the other. My body twisted around, and I found myself hanging off the side of the ladder. *Oh, bless you, ladder, for holding strong when I did not!* I could see the man move quickly to my side from the corner of my eye.

"I'm sorry. I shouldn't have startled you like that." He reached up and held onto my leg, "Just drop. I've got you."

I closed my eyes and slowly lowered my upper body until he took my arm that held the book. I lowered more until he had me around my waist with one hand, then the other. My feet touched the floor. Blue, bright, beautiful eyes greeted me, thick eyebrows furrowed when he peered back into my eyes. No sweat dripped from his brow, his breathing was steady and calm, and his hair was neatly brushed, unlike the first time I had seen him.

He looked down and took the book from my hand. "These books are very old. More than two hundred years old."

"Actually, two hundred and nine, to be exact." I remembered the date perfectly. My father had purchased the book just before he passed away. My heart stuttered thinking about how he fell ill after returning home from that trip, and memories washed over me of those few days I had read from this very book at his bedside. They were the last moments I spent with him.

The man before me looked puzzled for a moment and opened the book to the first few pages. "Hum. Are you familiar with *Lyrical Ballads*?"

"I am."

"It was printed in eighteen hundred. So that would make it two hundred and twelve years old." He smirked while he waited for my response.

"Oh. Yes. You would be right on that count, but it was purchased in the year of our Lord, eighteen hundred and three."

His head jerked back a bit, and his eyes narrowed. He stared at the book again. "How do you know that?"

I felt the blood drain from my face. I may have given myself away. "Well. Perhaps I am mistaken."

"Are you a book historian?"

"No. Though I am familiar with a few old books." I felt like my soul was being scrutinized when he looked hard into my eyes. "What is your conclusion?" I raised my head a bit.

"Conclusion?" he asked.

"Were you not examining me? Searching my soul?"

He smiled. "I haven't come to a conclusion … yet." He walked around me and started up the ladder.

"Yet?"

"You'll be here for a while. I'm sure we'll bump into each other from time to time." He put the book back on the shelf and made his way down.

"How did all these books survive over the years?" I glanced around the room.

66

"Before the war, they were packed into crates and hidden. They built a stone wall to protect them from thieves in the basement. Several paintings were found along with them … at least, that's what I was told." He leaned on the ladder while he spoke.

Tears pricked at my eyes. "Paintings?"

"Mostly family portraits. Of the Elsegood family—the family that owned the house," he replied. He seemed confused by my sudden emotion.

I turned and wiped my eyes.

"How do you like the place?" he asked.

I smiled. "It is almost like home." He could not know just how true that statement was. I looked around the room, noting that little had changed … in this room, anyway.

When I looked back, I saw him solemnly studying the bandage on my arm. "You've just had treatments?" His voice fell quiet.

"My first one."

"You should stay close to your room. The side effects can be brutal and sudden." He moved closer and leaned in, reaching past me. His wonderful, woodsy scent filled my senses. I blinked and lowered my head, hoping he would not notice the heat I felt in my cheeks. His firm, bare arm was so close, and the simple buttoned shirt fit smoothly across his chest. Seeing a man wearing but one layer of clothing was rather difficult to get used to. My only hope was that I would not blush each time he came into close proximity. When he stepped back, he held a book in his hand. It looked newer, with printed images.

"Here, try this one. These others are not off limits." He pointed above him, then held the book out to me.

"Thank you." I took the book and read the cover. *Pride and Prejudice.*

"When staying in a place like this, it fuels the imagination to read something from the past." He smiled, moved across the room, took another book from the shelf, then walked to the door.

"Oh! Ah … I apologize. I do not know your name," I called after him.

He stopped at the door. "Josh."

Unusual name. It was not what I expected. "Thank you … Josh."

"You're welcome …" He waited for my name.

I didn't want to give him my last name when he would have me use his given name. "Ruth—er, Celeste."

"Is it Ruth or Celeste?"

"Well, both. Ruth will do fine."

His brows rose. "What a coincidence. That book you were looking at was addressed to a Ruth."

"Strange," I said with a weak smile.

"You know it's after hours to be in the library. If Kim finds you in here, she'll threaten to report you." His lips pulled to one side in a teasing smile.

"Will she box my ears and lock me in my room?" I smirked, then walked to the door and followed him out.

"I wouldn't put it past her." He laughed, and we made our way down the corridor. When we reached the end, he stopped. "Well, I need to go this way." He tilted his head.

"But that's the east side. We are not allowed there." I glanced around to see if we were being watched.

"What Kim doesn't know won't hurt her." He winked, then walked away.

I watched him go. I couldn't help but notice the shape of his muscles under his lightweight shirt and the way the fabric moved against his skin. I shook my head. People in this day and age wore so little. Although I couldn't help but begin to like my own clothes—and perhaps even his. In truth, it was nice to wear less since it was summer and hot outside.

I returned to my room, opened the book he'd offered me, and curled up on the sofa. After reading for only a short time, I found my thoughts wandering to the Shariton Park I knew.

Chapter Nine

1812 England, Abbie

"Oh, good. Charles brought up your pack and guitar." Celeste walked into my spacious room and sat on my bed next to the pack. She had changed into her nightgown and robe and braided her hair to the side. "He had to be discreet in getting it up here. They don't make things like this in eighteen-twelve. Not in the same way exactly."

"I can't imagine what someone here might think if they saw it," I chuckled, looking at the modern design along the edge.

"That's why we must keep your things hidden. Charles wants you to go through your belongings and see if there's anything that might fit in or be easily hidden in your room. The rest will be taken to a hiding spot where none of the servants will find it." She opened the pack and pulled out a flip-flop. "You don't mind if I help, do you? I haven't seen things like this in some time. It's exciting."

"I don't mind," I replied. I pulled out a tablet and charger, a few feminine products—won't need those for a while—a capo for my guitar, a toiletry bag, an extra bra, and other junk to sort through. "Do I get to use my own underwear? Because it's really breezy without it."

"I'm afraid not. You'll have to get used to being without. The servants would question such garments. Be glad you don't have to wear a full corset. Pregnancy is uncomfortable enough without it."

I frowned and sighed. "Every time I think about being pregnant—I mean, in a family way—I can't help but feel … discouraged, sad, and angry. Then I feel guilty, knowing I should be a little happy to be having a miracle growing inside of me, but I can't … I can't be happy—I know that sounds horrible, but …" I sighed again and rubbed my hand down my face. "I can't imagine what you think of me. It must be hard watching someone who can't handle the burden of pregnancy when you ache for your own child."

"It's hard. But it's harder to see your heartache." Her eyes pooled with tears.

"But you hardly know me."

"When I first saw you sitting on that bench, it wasn't only the fact that you looked so forlorn that drew me to you. It was something more. I feel connected to you—like we are long-lost sisters." She smiled. "You and I need each other."

I returned the smile and wiped the tears in my eyes. "Weird. I felt drawn to you and your husband. When you left me in the hallway outside my room at the B and B, everything in me wished to see you two again."

"You see. Soul sisters." She blinked, and tears ran down her cheeks.

A thought came to me that made me hot with guilt. I lowered my head and spoke softly. "What if … what if when the time comes … what if I can't give my baby away? Will you still think of me as a sister?"

"Of course. This is *your* decision, not mine … not Charles. This brings me to something I've been thinking about. Because you have no proper clothing, we'll need to buy you some, and I don't want you to feel like we're trying to influence you in your decision. We understand you need to be cared for, and we'll help you regardless of your choice. Understand?"

I nodded.

"If you choose to keep your baby and wish to return home, we'll help you do that." Her eyes looked a little sad as she said the words. "If you choose to keep your baby and wish to stay here, you'll be given that opportunity. You and your child may stay here. I could always use a lady-in-waiting."

"You mean, get paid to keep you company?"

"It all seems a bit silly, doesn't it?"

"Everything does."

Her smile slowly melted away, and she appeared more serious. "And if you give us the honor of raising your baby, you'll still have the choice to stay or go."

"Wow. So many options."

"You're blessed to have so many options. Most women in this day and age don't."

"How so?" I asked.

"A woman's duty is to marry and procreate. If she has no dowry or opportunity to marry, she has very few choices. She can become a companion to someone wealthy or become a governess. Choosing to marry someone lower in rank is social suicide. If she's lucky, she might have a wealthy relative who could take her in and provide for her."

"Wow. Is it that bad?" I asked, dumbfounded.

"I am afraid so. I don't know if I would've stayed here without falling in love."

"I don't know if I could do that. I'd want to achieve something. Become someone important—" I covered my mouth briefly before beginning. "Not that you're not important. I mean. Sorry. Let me just yank this foot out of my mouth."

She chuckled and took something from the bag. "Deodorant. How I wish more people here could wear this."

I laughed with her as I picked up my guitar and strummed the strings.

Celeste sighed. "Oh, it has been so long since I have heard that sound."

I wiggled my brows with a playful smirk and plucked a song from the Beatles. She joined in singing with me and our voices harmonized perfectly. When I finished, Celeste clapped her hands together and smiled with tears in her eyes.

"Do you know how wonderful it is to hear that music again?"

"Well, it doesn't sound the same as the real song. My guitar is a classical guitar, so not all songs sound as good on it."

"It sounds wonderful to me. Variety is hard to come by here," she said.

"You mean you don't have any rock and roll? There is no *Stairway to Heaven*?" I asked playfully, plucking a few strings of the song.

We laughed again while we went through the rest of my pack. There wasn't anything in it I could keep. All of it would raise too many questions.

"Fortunately, we have similar guitars in this day and age, so you can keep yours as long as you do not show it off." Celeste smiled, "No playing for dinner parties."

My stomach lurched inside out at the thought of dining in a gown with other people who knew all about manners. *What had I gotten myself into?*

* * *

The next morning, I was dressed and escorted by Molly down to the breakfast room. When I entered, I found Celeste conversing with a man I didn't know.

"Good morning, Abbie! Come meet our dearest family friend."

The man stood with Celeste.

"May I present Mrs. Abbie Lambert. Abbie, this is Sir Henry Garrison," she smiled.

"Mrs. Lambert," he bowed, "it is a pleasure to meet you."

I curtsied, although it may have looked more like a stumble. "Hello," I said, feeling like a fish out of water.

Celeste cleared her throat pointedly. "*Hello,* is modern, Abbie. Perhaps try something else, like *greetings.*"

"I understand you are from Celeste's day." Sir Garrison gestured to Celeste.

My eyes grew wide. *Wait. He knows?*

"Yes, I know where you are from, though I have not had the privilege of seeing it for myself." He gave Celeste a sharp look.

"And you'll not receive such a privilege," Celeste returned primly. "Henry is one of the few who knows our secret."

"I see that Celeste is not the only beautiful young lady from her time. Hopefully we did not deprive the future of its brightest stars," he said and winked.

I laughed. "Not likely."

"Incredible! Do all young ladies have such bright, straight teeth as the two of you?" he asked, gazing at my smile in wonder.

I laughed again, then to my horror I snorted. I stopped abruptly. "Sorry," I blushed.

"Sorry?" Celeste peered at me with one eyebrow up.

"Oh! I mean, forgive me."

"Are you hungry?" she asked, deftly changing the subject.

"Starving! I could eat an elephant!" I patted my stomach and moved to the table, dropping into a seat.

"Abbie?"

"Yes?"

"An elephant?"

"Did I say something wrong?" I asked.

Henry tried to stifle a laugh.

"Well, usually people do not proclaim they're going to be eating any elephants. They simply say yes to the question, then *gently* sit down."

"Oh. I'm sor—I apologize."

Celeste *gently* sat in her chair, as if to show me how it was done. Henry held his hand over his mouth, though I could still see the laughter in his eyes. I leaned toward Celeste and whispered in her ear, "Does he know about … you know what?" I pointed discreetly to my abdomen.

She leaned back. "Yes, he does and don't worry. You can trust him not to repeat anything about it, nor will he judge you. He's the best of friends."

I smiled and let out a nervous breath.

"So, tell me Mrs. Lambert, are there really such things as motorcars?" Sir Garrison asked with a grin. "I get the impression Celeste is prone to exaggeration."

"Good morning, Henry!"

I turned to see Lord Elsegood enter the room with a smile.

"Good morning, old friend! I received your letter, and as you can see, I am here at your disposal." Sir Garrison stood to shake hands.

After they sat and shared pleasantries, the mood in the room turned somber.

"I get the feeling there is more to what is going on here," Sir Garrison stated.

"There is," Lord Shariton replied.

"In your letter, you mentioned that Ruth has fallen ill. I supposed you took her to a modern doctor. I hope she has come back with good news." Sir Garrison's eyes looked hopeful.

"I am afraid she has not returned with us."

Sir Garrison's face grew pale.

Lord Shariton held up his hand. "Now, before you come to any dire conclusions, let me assure you that she is still breathing."

Sir Garrison put a hand to his chest and breathed out heavily. "You nearly stopped my heart!"

"My apologies." Lord Elsegood went on, "She has a disease which requires medicine and treatment in the future to cure. If she were left here, she would surely die."

"Is it truly so serious?"

Both Celeste and Lord Elsegood nodded slowly.

I was dumbfounded. All this time I had never questioned why they were in the twenty-first century. I assumed they went back for toothpaste and to see the town. I had no idea of anyone staying behind with an illness. *What a selfish boob I am.* If I had only asked more questions and tried getting to know them better rather than focusing on myself, I might have done something to comfort them.

They explained the cancer, the treatment center in a future Shariton Park, and Ruth's insistence that they return without her. Celeste noticed my stunned expression and motioned for me to close my mouth, which I did, blushing furiously. Sooner than I liked, the conversation turned back to me.

"So, tell me, Abbie, where in America do you hail from?" Sir Garrison asked.

"California. It's on the western side of the continent. At this time, it isn't yet settled."

He sat up straighter. "Fascinating!"

"In my time, the whole continent is populated in every direction.

76

Roads stretch across like giant spider webs, with cars, trains, and planes taking you from one place to another."

Sir Garrison grinned at Celeste. "I get the feeling she is not going to be as secretive about the future as you are, Celeste." Everyone chuckled. "Tell me, Mrs. Lambert, what do you think of the nineteenth century thus far?"

"Well … it's a little uncomfortable."

"Uncomfortable?"

"Of course! How can anyone reduced to using chamber pots be comfortable? What you need here is some indoor plumbing." I momentarily chuckled, until I noticed the look on their faces. "I suppose I shouldn't have discussed chamber pots over breakfast?"

Chapter Ten

Present Day England, Ruth

I wish someone would come to end my life and put me out of my misery. I closed my eyes, still seeing the markings on the ceiling I had memorized. The last two weeks I spent confined to my room, mostly lying in bed. There were moments when I felt well enough to sit on the sofa, but that never lasted long. Several times, I sat on the floor next to the toilet. I had hoped the nausea would not get this bad, but fortune thus far had not favored me.

I sat up and pushed the blankets from my legs. *No quick movements.* I turned to my nightstand, searching for my book. A small black rectangular object lay beside a full glass of water. I studied it, wondering what it could be, and reached for it with numb fingers, but it slipped and fell to the floor. *Curse this debilitating disease and its enervating remedies, too!* At that moment, the large black object hanging on the wall came to life. Moving images appeared upon it, and sounds emanated from it.

Eerie music filled the room.

I gasped, and my heart raced, pulling the blankets over my head. The eerie music grew more intense. I peeked out from under the covers to see an image of a woman hunching under a table in a dark house. Suddenly, the image changed, showing a man down the hall from her. In his hands, he held a large kitchen knife.

"Run!" I called.

She did not seem to hear me. I called out again, "Run!"

The woman did not move, and the man grew closer. I stood and stumbled to the door. *I have to get help!* I ran down the hall. *I have to find my brother! He will know what to do!* I hurried across the length of the house until I came to my brother's door and pounded hard on it.

The door flew open. I stumbled back when I saw Josh staring in surprise at me. His wild hair stood on his head, and he wore the most peculiar striped trousers I had ever seen. His bare chest taking up all the space between us.

I stuttered my words, seeing a man in such a state.

"What is it, Ruth?"

I pointed down the hall and cried. "In my chamber! A woman needs help!"

He looked me up and down, and took me gently by the arm. "Where is your room?"

"Three hundred and four," I replied. "Where is my brother? Why were you in his bedchambers?"

"In his bedchamber?" he asked with a confused glance, hurrying me down the hall.

When we reached my chamber, we found the door wide open. The images on the box had changed. Motorcars rushed swiftly across the glass. *Motorcars? On the wall?* I shook my head, then regretted my action when my skull nearly split. I pointed at the telly on the wall, "There was a woman in danger only moments ago. A man was after her!"

He stared at where I pointed, then back at me. "You mean on the telly?"

I nodded. "What happened to her?"

He studied me for a long moment, then walked to the phone on the desk and put it to his ear. He spoke to someone in hushed tones, asking them to come to my room. He hung up, walked to my side, then took me by the arm.

"We need to do something! She might have been killed!" I screeched.

"It was only a show. It's not real." He helped me to my bed when someone entered the room.

My body shook. Beads of sweat dripped down my forehead. "No. Please. It was someone real, and she needed help!" *How can he be so calm and do nothing to help her?* I tried to push him away, but it did me no good in my weakened state.

"I think she's delusional. She thinks the show is real." Josh said to the nurse.

The woman took my wrist to feel my heartbeat. "It's racing, alright. I'll give her something to calm her down."

Josh took my hand in his and held me down in the bed. My eyes darted from him to the nurse, then to the telly on the wall. "Help her!"

"Shh. It will be alright. It's not real. She's safe." His voice was tender and soft in my ear.

Safe? How can she be?

The nurse stood beside me with a tube in her hand which had a needle on the end of it. Before I could protest, I felt a pinch in my arm.

"That should start working right away," she said to Josh.

"Amelia never reacted this way," he said to the nurse, keeping his eyes on me.

"I've seen this side effect only once. It's extremely rare," she replied, checking my blood pressure.

80

I started to feel lightheaded and tired. Josh stood and started to pull his hand out of mine, but I tightened my grip. "Please … do not leave. I do not want to die." My chin quivered.

"You won't die, Ruth. You will get better and live a long life." His fingers touched my forehead, and he brushed aside the hair that was plastered to my face.

I focused on his blue eyes. "I do not wish to die," I repeated weakly. My eyes drooped, then closed. I tried to open them again but instead fell into a deep sleep.

* * *

1812 England, Abbie

I had endured vigorous training on etiquette and manners over the last couple of weeks—or a fortnight, as Celeste called it. At first, I joked around a bit, pretending I was royal. I looked down my nose at everything, talked in a snobbish English accent, and said "Quite right" and "I daresay" after almost everything. Yes, I even stuck my pinky out when drinking my tea. Celeste would roll her eyes, laugh, and then kindly reprimand me for my behavior.

Sir Garrison stayed to help me with my studies. As a gentleman would, he stood in, teaching me how to do country dances. I was horrible at it. I repeatedly apologized for stepping on Sir Garrison's toes. On the bright side, it gave me enough practice at apologizing properly.

One afternoon, while practicing a country dance, I stood stunned when the song ended, and no one had called out a correction to me or winced at my bumping into them. I looked around the room and found Celeste, Sir Garrison, and Lord Elsegood smiling at me.

"Did I just complete a dance without knocking anyone over?" I asked in disbelief.

"Not only that, but you did it beautifully," Lord Elsegood stated.

I clapped my hands and spun around once. "Ow! I did it!" I started doing what is known in the States as a *touchdown dance*. I wiggled my hips and knees while I sang a victory song. I twirled my arms like a cowgirl ready to rope a bull. "I did it! I did it!" I laughed until I caught sight of the three of them gawking at me. I promptly stood straight and held my hands together in front of me with my head high.

Celeste covered her mouth and tried to hide her laughter, though her shoulders shook, giving her away. Lord Elsegood stood stunned into silence, and Sir Garrison was red-faced and bewildered.

Celeste looked at the two men and couldn't hold her laughter in any longer. I joined in, while the two men stood there … shocked.

"What was that?" Sir Garrison asked when the laughter finally died down.

"A victory dance," I said simply.

"Maybe you should hold off on that sort of dancing outside your own room," Celeste advised. "That's something we're not accustomed to." She laughed and then hugged me.

"Is that normal behavior in your time?" Sir Garrison asked.

"Very normal," Celeste responded.

"Hum," came his reply.

Chapter Eleven

Present Day England, Ruth

I woke to a mind-numbing headache, but when I finally opened my eyes, I realized that I did not feel nauseated as I had for the past two weeks. I turned my head toward a noise at the door and watched the nurse enter, pulling a machine on wheels behind her. I recognized it as one that took blood pressure and other vitals, something I'd learned from the previous doctor visit. It was strange how accustomed I was becoming to things that, before my time travel, I never could have imagined.

"Good morning, Celeste. How are you feeling today?" she asked.

"I have a bit of a headache," I responded.

"That's normal after what happened last night. Are you nauseated?"

Last night? "No."

"That's good news." She smiled and began taking my vitals.

What happened last night? I glanced around the room. When my eyes landed on the telly, the memory came flooding back to me.

"Oh no!"

"What?" the nurse asked, alarmed.

"I have made a fool of myself."

She smiled. "No, you haven't, and I wouldn't worry about it. It happens."

It happens? What did she mean? Did others see people in their telly being hurt as well?

When she had finished, she gave me some medication for my headache and advised me to take a relaxing bath. I took her advice. Afterward, I felt close to normal again. My headache was gone, and my appetite seemed on the mend, but my hands still felt numb, which made it difficult to hold onto things. After I had changed my robe for a summer dress, I moved to the mirror to brush my hair. The brush pulled away with an entire handful of hair still attached.

No! I stood there staring at the clump of hair in my hand. My chin quivered, and I slumped to the floor. My vision blurred as I tried to put the hair back on my head, pressing the strands hard against my scalp. *No! Go back on!* I let my arms drop to the floor.

A long cry later, with a new headache knocking against my skull, I sat up and stretched my stiff back. I stood, making sure not to look into the mirror again. Without brushing my hair, I carefully twisted it into a messy-looking bun and pinned it into place. I entered the closet where the wardrobe stood and pulled out one of the hats Celeste had bought me. She told me it resembled those worn by women in the 1920s. Right now, I did not care where it came from, only that it covered my entire head. I grabbed a handful of tissues and decided that staying in this room one more minute would not do. I needed fresh air and perhaps something to eat.

I made my way down to the kitchen and found a bagel. I tried to make my way back out of the kitchen before I was spotted, but I did not get my wish.

"Celeste! You're out and about, I see," Sandy hurried to my side.

"Good morning, Sandy."

"You mean afternoon," she laughed. "Sometimes it doesn't matter what time of day it is here. It all starts to blend together."

I nodded.

She bent her head to see under the brim of my hat. "Having a tough day?"

Those simple words caused tears to spring to my eyes. I nodded.

"Let me guess, you're losing your hair?"

My shoulders shook. I tried not to make a sound as the tears came pouring out.

She pulled me into her arms and rubbed my back. "I know exactly how you feel. It can be devastating."

"No one told me it would come out in clumps," I sobbed. "A whole handful came out at once!"

"I know. I will tell you, so you aren't surprised. All your hair may be gone by the end of the week."

I cried a little harder.

"Good news is, you'll get to join the club!" She laughed a little. "We're all bald here! Well, most of us. There are some with different treatments that will keep their hair." She took her hat off to reveal her bald head. "We could be twins!"

Despite my crying, I chuckled.

"When I was a kid, and my friends or siblings had the same lollipop or treat, whatever it was, we would touch them together and say "Same!" like it was the greatest thing in the world to have something similar," she laughed. "Soon, we'll get to do the same!"

I laughed again.

"Chin up. It will be okay … okay?"

85

I nodded. "Okay."

"That's a girl. Now, eat up. You look like you've lost some weight. If you keep that up, you'll blow away as soon as you step outside."

I smiled at her attempt to make me laugh. "Blowing away sounds nice right about now. I have been indoors for far too long."

"Well, I'm on my way to get my next set of treatments, so I may not see you for a few days, but if I feel well enough, you can come see me. Room 306."

"I will."

She hugged me again before I left the room and hurried through the house to get outside. The warm air felt great against my skin. The hat shielded my eyes from the sun, so I felt no need to squint in the daylight. Remembering why I needed that hat caused more tears to form. I aimlessly walked for several minutes before catching the stable's familiar scent. I breathed deeply and walked down the path toward it. Upon arriving, I found Norman in his stall, eager for a visitor.

"Norman, my friend. I've missed you." I brushed my hand down his neck. He nudged me with his nose. I leaned in, rested my head against the side of his nose, and let more tears fall.

"If you're lookin' to ride, think again."

I turned my head and found Dolan watching me with a coil of rope in his hand. I smiled. "Perhaps I *am* wishing to ride."

"After what you put me through …"

"Oh! Did you get into trouble?" I tried to wipe away my tears discreetly.

"Not too much. I told the master some new girl from the kitchens rode him, and he seemed to know who it was." He walked to the side of the stall and hung the rope on a hook on the wall.

Does that mean someone else has been punished in my place? Oh dear! I moved my head from Norman's nose and leaned it against his silky neck while Dolan went about his work. I listened to him shuffling

86

quietly about the stable and rested my hand on the horse's jaw, comforted by his steady pulse. After a time, I realized the barn had grown silent. When I lifted my head, I found Dolan right beside me. His smile slowly faded when he noticed my wet lashes and puffy red eyes.

"Now, hold on there, lass! You needn't be cryin'. He told me you wouldn't be getting into any trouble."

"It's not that—"

"Is it what I said about riding? I'll let you ride again if it's tha' important to you." He wiped a tear from my cheek, then pulled me into his arms. I stiffened when I realized this was the first time a man, other than family, had ever held me in his arms. I rather liked it … possibly? I leaned into him and rested my head against his chest.

He rubbed his hands up and down my back in a gesture of comfort. His hands stopped, and he pulled away enough for me to look up at him. He leaned down, his lips only a breath away. *Is he going to kiss me?* I panicked and pushed him away, then stepped back quickly and nearly fell. He caught me around my waist and pulled me close again.

"Now, don't tell me you're shy when I know you've got some fire inside ya," he chuckled.

I pushed away again, this time making sure I had my footing.

"Didn't you like me holdin' ya?" He took my hand with his, and wiggled his fingers between mine.

"I …" I cleared my throat, "I am a lady, sir."

He grinned. "Ladies need kissin' too." He paused and winked at me. "Have you never been kissed?"

His question took me by surprise. "How can you ask such a thing? Do you believe me to be the kind of lady to go about kissing every man I meet?"

"You've never been kissed!" His eyes grew wide with his discovery. He leaned in and whispered, "Wouldn't I like to be the lucky one to get the privilege of being your first." His breath mixed with mine for a moment, and then he moved back. "But ... you're the kind of lass that would rather give permission than have it be taken from you. Am I right?"

I almost didn't answer, but decided I better so as not to give him any ideas. "Yes. You are right to presume that."

"Then I will have to wait until you get to know me better." He lifted my hand, "And since you say you're a lady, you shall be treated as one." He kissed my hand slowly. Chills moved from my hand up my back and into my neck. My face grew hot, and I lowered my eyes.

I could tell he was grinning at me. I cleared my throat and pulled my hand away, stroking Norman's neck.

"Would you like a ride?" he asked.

"I don't think I should."

"Well, if you keep off the golf course, you won't be gettin' into trouble."

"You will not be paying for it, will you? I already told you I would." I tried to keep my distance from him.

"I don't believe Mr. Harrison was too upset. He was more impressed that someone else could ride Norman without being thrown." Dolan stood close behind me while he talked.

"What kind of person is this Mr. Harrison?" I asked.

"Have you not met him? I thought he would have interviewed you when you were hired."

"We've never met."

"He's a good chap. Usually kind. He's gone a lot. I imagine it's hard to be around so much sickness and pain. Though, he's a bit mad, in my opinion." He chuckled.

I turned to look at him. "Why do you say that?"

"Anyone who hangs hundreds of feet in the air from a bunch of strings and a chute is barking mad."

My jaw must have dropped to the ground. "Hanging from strings?"

"Have you not seen the pictures of him in the common room? They are hanging on the wall near the back by the billiard table." He smiled at me, "He's an avid Paraglider."

"Para-what?"

"Paraglider. Have you not seen it?"

I shook my head.

He retook my hand and pulled me beside him while we walked past the stalls. "I'll show ya." He turned a corner where a building had been added on and opened the door, stepping inside a room filled with tables and clutter piled about. Several doors lined one side of the wall, some closed, some open. There appeared to be private bedrooms beyond.

Dolan sat at a desk and pushed a button on a square black object similar to what the nurses used. The dark glass lit up with an image of a horse. He tapped his fingers on printed letters, and words appeared on the glass. I stood amazed. A moment later, an image appeared of a man in midair with strings attached to him and a large piece of fabric, just as Dolan had said. After a few taps on the object, the image began moving, exactly as it did on the telly.

I slowly sat on the bench beside him while I watched what was shown. A man hung in midair, flying about in the sky. I covered my mouth and laughed. I could not keep my eyes from it.

"What is this contraption? Is this like what the nurses have?" I asked him, pointing to the black square. "Or is this a telly too?"

He laughed, "Have you never seen a computer before?"

I did not answer, at the risk of feeling stupid.

"Have you been living under a rock?" he persisted.

I narrowed my eyes. "Don't be preposterous. How could anyone live under a rock?"

He looked at me as if contemplating something.

"I have lived a very different life than you," I ventured at last. "I have never seen a telly nor this thing before … whatever you called it."

"Computer."

"Yes. Well, what exactly does it do?"

"Research, watch movies … whatever you want to do with it. What do you want to know most in the world?" he asked me.

I thought for a moment. "How is the images on the tellies created?"

He pressed a few letters, then moved an oddly shaped object around the desk. A moment later, I watched what Dolan called a video clip of people making a movie. While I watched, Dolan sat beside me and placed his hand over my own. I glanced down and removed my hand. He studied me closely. I shifted away from the uncomfortable feeling I felt under his scrutiny.

The video ended, and I sat back, stunned. "It's astonishing!"

"Where did you grow up?" he asked.

I cleared my throat, feeling a bit of pain in doing so. Celeste had told me that if I were asked this question, I should say north, in the highlands. I hated to lie and I knew I was horrible at it, so I averted my eyes. "North. The highlands. In a wood."

"Let me guess, you had seven short hairy men waiting on your every whim," he said with laughter in his voice.

I held my head higher. "Of course not."

He chuckled. "You're even cuter when you do tha'."

"When I do what?" I moved to the edge of the seat.

"Hold your head high, and that look on your face, it's maddening! From the moment I saw you, I wanted to kiss you."

I stood quickly with the realization that we were alone. "Do not be absurd. You have only known me a fortnight, and we have only talked twice in that time!"

He stood beside me. "That very well may be, but I know when I held you that you wanted to be kissed as much as I wanted to kiss you."

I held my head high again. "No, I did not."

"I beg to differ."

"You are talking nonsense." I walked around him to leave and he took my hand. I shook it off.

He pulled me to a stop by my arm, leaned in, and whispered in my ear. His breath tickled my cheek, and chills ran down my back. "By the end of the week, you'll be begging to kiss me." He slowly moved back, and I peered up at him. He stopped a few inches away. "Or maybe even sooner?"

I moved a few more steps back and continued holding my head high.

He chuckled.

"You cannot kiss someone you do not see." I quickly turned around and walked out of the building with him on my heels.

"I know where to find ya. The kitchen has no hiding places!" he called after me.

I could hear him laughing as I made my way up the hill from the stables. Little did he know I would not be working in the kitchen. On my way back to my room, I took a detour through the common room. A few semi-familiar faces greeted me. An older man named Donald, or rather Don, nudged Steve again and pointed at me. Steve winked, then turned his attention back to the telly. I went to the back of the room and found three large pictures on the wall; recognizing them as photographs. I approached them, trying to make out the man's face. He wore dark glasses over his eyes and was too far away to make out his features. It amazed me that someone could have the courage to try something like that.

"Are you ready to try it for yourself?"

I jumped at the sound of a male voice and turned to find Steve had left his seat and now stood behind me. I stepped back from him to give myself more space. "I could never. I would be too terrified."

"Don't let Mr. Harrison hear you say tha'," he said. "Besides, everyone gets a chance to go along with him once their treatments are

91

over. It's a way of celebrating the end of the misery and the beginning of a new future."

"I could not. I would be too afraid."

"Fear isn't in his vocabulary. He's a man that lives life to the fullest." He chuckled, "I envy the bloke." Don called out his name, and Steve turned to leave. He paused and waved his hand toward my hat. "You should just shave it and get it done and over with. Being bald is better than the patchy look."

I swallowed hard to force the lump in my throat back down, remembering my poor hair.

Chapter Twelve

1812 England, Celeste

My dearest Ruth,

I write this letter knowing I cannot send it to you in the traditional way. I do hope to see you soon, although it may be difficult. You see, we came across an unfortunate young woman who followed us into the woods the day we left you. She accidentally discovered our secret and has come to stay with us here at Shariton Park. We could not leave her in her condition, being that she is with child and has no husband. By no means was any of it her fault. She was taken advantage of, and the scoundrel left her with no money and no one to turn to. We have offered her a home here, and we hope she may let us raise her child, as she is unsure if she is ready to be a mother.

Abbie is delightfully funny. She has many times kept me from mourning your absence. Over the last few weeks, she has been learning

93

how to live during this time period. I cannot help but laugh at times when her manners would otherwise seem appalling. I find her singing songs from a different time at the top of her lungs. She loves to play jokes as well. Your brother once found a squashed insect between the pages of his newspaper near an article on entomology. I wish you could hear her sing. Her voice is angelic and she plays the guitar beautifully.

When we first arrived, we had the pleasure of Henry's visit. He was a great help in giving Abbie the dance lessons she so desperately needed. I am pleased to say she is much improved, although she only exhibits her newfound manners when we have visitors. Sometimes, I still catch her making faces while Mrs. Cromwell's back is turned.

Henry left us this morning to return to Clair's side. She is now in confinement, and I look forward to her return to society.

I think of you often, my dear Ruth. I wonder how your treatments are getting on. I hope they are treating you well and that you have found a friend to rely on. Do not worry about your hair. I know losing it will cause you a great amount of anxiety. You will be just as beautiful without it, and it will grow back!

Charles tells me he will visit you soon, though I do not believe I will accompany him. Someone needs to stay and keep Abbie company (and keep her out of mischief). I will send this letter with him and instruct him to kiss your cheek for me. I miss you terribly, my sweet sister, and I pray for you daily.

With all my love,
Your sister, Celeste

I placed the quill on the table and blew on the paper to dry the ink. How I wanted to share my news with Ruth, but fear silenced me. Over the last two weeks, I had begun to suspect I might be with child. I had all the signs, but I kept it secret. Even Charles did not know. What if it was not so? What if I lost the baby? What if it did not survive the birth?

For the time being, I would continue to *pretend* I was with child, just as we had planned. Abbie would announce her pregnancy soon, as would I, though both Abbie and Charles would believe my pregnancy to be false.

My mind wandered into the future, and I imagined what it would be like to hold my child. I closed my eyes and leaned back in my chair. I knew I could not hide the truth for long, especially from Charles.

* * *

Present Day England, Ruth

I stood in my room, looking in the mirror. More of my hair had fallen out during the night, and I knew that if I showered, I might lose the rest. Tears streamed down my face while I carefully fingered the ends of my long, dyed brown hair. At my roots, the strawberry blond had started to grow in. *How could I let this happen? Why did I make such a choice?*

The room around me had been arranged and decorated with comfort in mind, yet all I saw was a prison. I needed to go somewhere, but I knew I might run into Dolan, if I ventured outdoors. Anywhere else, I would run into the other guests, the nurses, or the staff, whom I did not wish to see in my current state. *There was one place ... a place I had gone to cry when my father died.*

With a plan, I picked up my hat and pulled it over my ears. My hair hung down over my shoulders and back, unbrushed and tangled. I slipped on my shoes and left my room. The lift had lost its novelty briefly after I arrived, so I took the stairs instead. I walked to the second floor, down one of the greater hallways, then down another, much smaller than the previous one. Around the corner stood a large window with enough room to sit against. When I was young, the long, heavy curtains were dark and could easily hide me when I wanted solace. Here, in the future, they were almost sheer.

I glanced around, hoping this corridor was not heavily occupied then stepped into the windowsill to sit behind the curtain. I held my knees to my chest, pulled my dress down over my feet, and sniffled. The cool glass against my forehead calmed me as I carefully played with a lock of hair.

How could I return to the Shariton Park I knew with no hair to curl and pin-up? Going to balls or dinner parties would be out of the question. It was now impossible for me to marry, for who would want to marry someone as bald as their old father? I dropped my head in my hands, closed my eyes, and wept.

Hopelessness bubbled through my veins.

A shift in the air around me indicated someone stood nearby. *Josh.* I blinked up at him. How had I known it was him?

"May I join you?" he whispered.

I stared at him in shocked silence, then shrugged resignedly.

He picked up my feet and moved them onto his lap as he sat, which I thought a bit forward, though it was more comfortable than having my knees crowding my chest. He laid his hand over my ankles and looked at me. Every inch of skin warmed where he touched me, and the warmth spread throughout the rest of me. Compassion emanated from his eyes. *Does he know what it is like to lose his hair? His hair grew so perfectly upon his head. What sort of treatment was he receiving?*

"It will grow back … possibly even curlier." He smiled softly.

I looked sideways at the tangle of hair hanging over my shoulder. "It is not curly. I slept on it and made it messy." I picked up my hair gently and gazed at how the light changed the color.

"Are you afraid to brush it?"

I nodded, and my chin began to quiver.

He took my hand in his and gently pulled me closer. I bent my knees, rested my forehead on his shoulder, and cried. He placed his arm around my back and held my hand. I never felt this much compassion

96

from someone other than my family. No one ever let me cry. He sat quietly for a time, allowing me to clear my emotions.

Upon lifting my head, I spotted a wet stain. "I believe I have soiled your shirt," I said with a sniff.

"No matter," he said, pulling my head back to his shoulder.

When I felt a little better, I lifted my head, stared out the window, and wiped my tears from my cheeks. The burning in my eyes kept me from looking directly at him, convinced I appeared dreadful and swollen.

"Feel better?"

I nodded. "Thank you. Forgive me for soiling your shirt."

"It needs it once in a while. It makes a great fabric softener."

I smiled and could not help but meet his kind eyes. Embarrassment flooded through me when I remembered my behavior a few nights ago. "I am terribly sorry for waking you the other night. I am afraid I have made a cake of myself. I am not much used to tellies."

"I'm glad I could help." He smiled and looked at me with brows pulled together, "You don't watch the telly, then?"

I shook my head. "I never saw one before coming here."

"Really? That is incredible. I've never known anyone who didn't own one."

I blushed. *Did I give myself away? But surely no one could ever guess why I have not seen a telly.* I turned my head and silence fell over the two of us. I could feel him watching me. Absentmindedly, I played with the end of my hair.

"I've heard it's easier to get rid of the hair straight away than to watch it fall out in clumps over time."

I swallowed hard. "I do not know if I could do that." I paused. "Not on my own."

His voice grew softer, "Would you like me to help you?"

I pondered my answer before nodding slowly, my eyes averted.

97

Josh moved my legs off his lap and stood while he continued to hold my hand. He pulled the curtains away, helped me to my feet, and guided me down the hall and around a corner. Outside a door, he let go of my hand, pulled out a set of keys, unlocked it, and pushed it open.

Shelves lined the walls of a small space that appeared to be a storage room. Linens were folded in stacks, along with containers of soaps and other miscellaneous objects. Josh stepped into the room and began looking for something.

He moved a box and smiled. "Ah ha! I found it." He lifted it down from the shelf and showed it to me. The picture on the outside showed what was inside, I guessed. I had no idea what it was, so I only pretended, giving him a slight nod and a smile.

He left the room, shut the door, and locked it. After returning his keys to his pocket, he took my hand and led me down a few doors into what looked like a water closet. Heat burned my cheeks, and I began to back out of the room.

Amusement sparked in his eyes at my shyness. "I won't bite."

I hesitated, then stepped back into the room. *Alone with a man in a room ... again! What am I thinking?* There was safety in his eyes and I knew all would be well.

The room was larger than those at the hospitals and doctor's offices I had been to and quite a bit nicer. It was as beautifully decorated as the rest of the house. Elegant chairs stood together with a small table between them. Three wooden doors lined one wall, where I assumed the toilets were located. Next to them sat a long marble counter with several sinks and a large mirror.

Josh moved one of the chairs to the middle of the room. "Have a seat." He opened the box and pulled out an object with a long rope hanging from one end. He attached the rope to the wall, flipped a switch, and the object came to life.

I jumped. "What is that?"

He flipped it off and looked at me in confusion. "Clippers."

"What is it for?"

"To cut your hair, of course." He seemed puzzled by my reaction. I supposed I must be acting strangely. Most likely, everyone knew what clippers were, and I needed to be more careful when I reacted to things from now on.

I sat with my back to the mirror. He placed his hand on my shoulder. "Are you ready?" he asked, then removed my hat when I nodded.

"We might not even need the clippers. Your hair may fall out without them." He moved his fingers through my hair, and I turned to see the hair gathered in his hand. He reached for a rubbish bin and put the locks of hair into it. I resisted the urge to cry, pressing my lips together. He placed a bin closer and combed through my hair with both hands. His touch was so gentle that I could not help but relax. I closed my eyes and let him move my head slightly this way and that. I soon found concentrating on the calming warmth of his fingertips helped me ease into the realization that my head grew lighter with every touch.

After a short time, his fingers touched the bare skin of my head, and tears found their way down my cheeks.

He lightly brushed his hand over my scalp. "We didn't need the clippers after all." His voice was soft when he spoke. It made me wonder if he also felt sorry for my loss.

I opened my eyes, stood, and slowly turned my head to the mirror. My heart sank, and my chin quivered. Not a strand of hair remained.

"My hair," I whimpered.

He took my hand in his. "With or without hair, you're still beautiful."

A flood of joy rushed into my heart. "Beautiful?" was all I could say through my sobs.

He nodded.

I moved to him, and he pulled me into his arms. I cried once again,

99

soiling his shirt, and he gently stroked my back. Still resting against him, I gazed into the mirror at myself. *He thinks I'm beautiful?* I looked up at him in the mirror and was surprised to see his eyes full of tears. I pulled my head away and continued gazing at him. We spent several long seconds lost in one another's eyes before he glanced at my lips and quickly stepped away, clearing his throat.

My cheeks flushed, and again, I was reminded that I stood in a room, alone, with an attractive man. This was the second time in the last few days that I had come close to being kissed … by two different men! I lowered my eyes. "Thank you. I daresay I shall bear it better now." I looked at him and smiled. "And thank you for thinking me beautiful." My cheeks warmed.

He playfully touched my nose with his finger. "You *are* beautiful." He turned, packed the clippers back into the box, glanced at me, then walked to the door and opened it. I picked up my hat, carefully placed it on my head, and joined him. His eyes followed me as I left the room. He gestured toward the storage room when we both stood in the hallway. "I'd better return this, so it's not missed."

"Thank you again," I gave him a small smile.

"See you around." He turned and walked down the hall.

A million times, thank you.

Chapter Thirteen

1812 England, Abbie

Thummm. My guitar hit against the trunk of the tree when I sat down. "Oopsie." I inspected it to make sure it wasn't damaged. It showed no dents. Satisfied, I leaned back on the trunk and positioned the guitar on my lap. I strummed the strings, then began picking out a tune. I hummed for the first bit before singing. After I picked my last note I paused. I knew someone was hiding behind a tree, just like he did every time I came out in the garden to sing my songs.

I tuned in to any sound that would give him away. He was still and silent. I rolled my eyes. "You know you don't have to hide. I don't bite." I said, loud enough for him to hear.

I leaned to the side and peered behind my tree. I caught sight of the man right before he pulled his head back behind the trunk of a nearby tree. He most definitely was the same guy that had watched me the day

I arrived.

"I'm glad you're here, whoever you are. I need some help," I said. He didn't move. I sighed, "Are you unwilling to help a damsel in distress?"

"Are you in distress?" His deep, smooth voice brought a smile to my lips and warmed me through. Baritone. Possibly bass.

"I am."

He stepped out from behind the tree and slowly walked to me, stopping roughly ten feet away. His powdered wig hid any sign of his natural hair color, but given that his eyebrows were dark, I guessed his hair was, too. He stiffened and lifted his chin, looking straight ahead. "How may I be of assistance?"

"First off, relax. You don't need to be so formal with me. Second, sit down, and I'll tell you." I indicated a spot in front of me.

He hesitated a moment, then cautiously tip-toed to the spot as if he was trying not to get his clean, knee-high white stocking stained. Once settled, he shifted his attention back to me.

A smile pulled at the corner of my mouth. "I need someone to give me a beat."

"A what?"

"A beat. Like this." I slapped my hand on my guitar. It made deep thumping sounds when I kept a beat. "You try. Hit your knee."

His dark eyes watched my hand momentarily, and then he mimicked me. Once he got the rhythm, I started strumming the guitar and sang an old song my grandmother taught me. He watched me when he thought I wasn't looking, and I watched him when he had turned. His tall, thin, but strong frame was pleasing to the eye—at least, to my eyes. His only downfall was that he appeared to be in his mid-20s. Too old for me.

I finished and smiled at him, though he didn't look at me. "Hello?" I bent my head, trying to get his attention. " Yo … I'm over here."

He stared at me, but only briefly. "It is not fitting for a footman to speak to a lady, especially alone."

"That's just a bunch of bologna. You're no different than anyone else, and I would feel offended if you didn't look at me when we speak."

"Are American customs so different?" He looked me directly in the eyes. "And what is this *baloney* you speak of?"

I laughed. "It's an expression. Bologna means the same as nonsense."

"Then why not say nonsense?"

"I dunno."

"Your speech is unusual," he responded with a scowl.

"I could say the same of yours." I couldn't help the smile that continued to spread across my face. *Getting into a nice verbal banter could be fun with him.*

"I could get into trouble sitting here with you."

"Why? Can we not be friends?" *Were the rules so strict?*

He didn't answer.

"You obviously like my music. Therefore, we have something in common. Friends have common interests; therefore, you're my friend, and as my friend, I want you to stay."

"This is highly unusual," he said primly, but the glimmer in his eyes could only be amusement.

"That's my middle name," I said with a smirk.

"Your middle name is unusual?"

I laughed out loud. "No. It was a joke."

"You are not what I expected you to be." He relaxed a bit and lowered his shoulders.

"How did you expect me to be?" I plucked the strings while we spoke.

"I thought you'd be more … somber."

"Why?" I tried to frown but failed.

"You just lost a husband."

103

My face fell. I stopped playing and swallowed hard. "Um. I can understand why you would be confused."

"Your behavior would have me believe you did not care for him." He carefully watched me.

"I didn't. He was unkind."

"I am sorry … that he was unkind." He picked up a piece of grass and played with it.

"You're not sorry I didn't love him, then?"

"You would not be the first to enter an unloved marriage."

"Do you love your wife?" Yes, I was fishing for information.

He glanced up, then looked down shyly. "I am a footman; therefore, I am not attached."

"Well, I can't understand why not. You seem nice, and you're quite handsome. You should have been happily married by now."

He blushed. "Are all Americans this bold?"

"I would say most are." I laughed and started playing a song. He listened to me, but this time, he watched me without looking away. When I finished, I bowed my head. "You may applaud."

He clapped briefly, then picked up another piece of grass. "Your voice is so soft and angelic."

Now, it was my turn to blush. "Thank you."

We heard a man call in the distance.

"I should be going." He stood.

"You've not told me your name." I moved to stand as well.

"Allow me." He reached out and helped me to stand.

"Thank you, uh …" I cocked my head to the side, waiting.

"Albert Thompson." He nodded.

"Albert." I half smiled, "Can I call you Al? Or perhaps Bert?"

He blushed. Another call came. It sounded as though they called for him. "I should hasten."

Hasten, there's another old word I should use. "I hope we can do this again tomorrow, Albert." I brushed the grass off my backside.

He lifted one shoulder. "Only if I am lucky, Abbie." He smiled, then looked serious for a moment. "Please do not tell anyone I used your given name."

"My lips are sealed." I mimed zipping my lips, locking them and throwing away the key.

He appeared confused, then shook his head and laughed.

"Albert!" The man's voice sounded close.

"Good afternoon, Miss Lambert," Albert said and *hastened* away.

* * *

Present Day England, Ruth

"You're looking better, Celeste." Kaitlyn stepped into my room and tugged on the stethoscope around her neck. Her black, shoulder-length hair had been pulled back away from her face, giving her a youthful look.

"This time around was better." I quickly pulled a hat on my head. I hated not having a hat on.

Her thin eyes grew thinner when she smiled. "Then I believe we have found the right medication for you."

"That is the best news I have heard all day."

Her head bobbed in agreement. "Sometimes it takes a few tests to find the right medication to reduce the nausea."

"This one is nearly 100 percent better."

She rested her hand on my shoulder briefly and smiled. "That's good, then."

We went through our usual vital checks and conversation about the weather, movie stars I have no idea about, and traveling she was interested in. I enjoyed our conversation, but I grew anxious to return to

105

the common room and visit with the other guests, who held more lively discussions—something I had not experienced before coming here and felt drawn to.

My other incentive to stay in the common room was to speak with Josh once more. I had not seen him since the day I lost my hair, and I wondered if he was keeping to his room to recover from recent treatments.

"Will you join the rest of the guests for the activity? I believe they're having a picnic today," Kaitlyn asked as she headed to the door.

"Is that today? I thought the picnic was tomorrow."

"No. They'll be down past the stables by the stream."

I nodded and waved goodbye, quickly preparing to change my clothes to accommodate an outing. Every other week, the guests gathered for various activities. To my everlasting relief, today was not one of those days when they went *swimming*. It was a bit of a shock when I entered the pool room for the first time. I had not expected to see men and women wearing so little clothing. I did not join them that day but rather faked a headache and fled to the library before I could faint with embarrassment.

The leaves on some of the trees were beginning to change color, and the weather was perfect for a day outside. Stepping out of one of the back doors and onto the stone patio, I pulled a shawl around my shoulders and brushed at my jeans.

I hesitated, knowing I would have to walk past the stables to get to the picnic. I sighed and held my head high. I would have to face him sometime, especially if I wanted to ride again.

When I inched closer to the stable, Dolan came out with his head down, brushing the dirt off his trousers. He stopped short when he lifted his head and saw me.

He grunted. "Well, I didn't believe it possible that you could avoid me all this time. I went to the kitchens and didn't see one stitch of you.

106

I started to think you'd been sacked."

I smiled nervously.

"So, if you're not sacked, you've been avoiding me."

"Not for the reasons you might be thinking," I responded.

He turned away and walked to the outside wall of the building, then kicked the mud off his boot. "So, what is the reason?"

"Chemotherapy."

"What?"

The wind picked up and blew my hat back. In a flash, I reached up and pulled it back down. It had blown up just enough for him to see I was bald.

His eyes widened, and a look of regret crossed his features. "Why didn't you tell me?"

I glanced away, ashamed. "It's not the easiest thing to talk about." I kept one hand on my hat. I heard voices and saw a group of guests walking toward us. I smiled the best I could and waved.

"Hi, Celeste. Are you coming to the picnic?" one asked.

I nodded, then glanced at Dolan. He had turned his back to me and acted like he was busy cleaning his boot.

"I'll be there in a moment," I answered.

When they were out of earshot, Dolan turned back to face me. "When will you feel up to riding again? Now that I know you're a guest, you can ride anytime you'd like." His eyes lit up, replacing the remorse.

"I have missed Norman."

"I think he's missed you, too," he winked.

I waved goodbye and hurried to catch up to the group heading to the picnic.

After we had finished eating and wrapped up an invigorating game of Frisbee, Kim dashed across the grounds in a hurry to meet up with our group.

"Celeste! You have a visitor!" Her short, gray hair flattened against her damp forehead, but her eyes were alive with joy as she announced my first visitor in many weeks.

Everyone around me looked surprised and pleased.

"Congratulations!" Sandy said with a grin.

I suspected they all felt sorry for me. Each of the guests here received visitors regularly. I was the exception, although it did not bother me, for I knew why.

I stood quickly and hurried back up the grassy hill with Kim. I did not need to guess who had come. It could only ever be Charles and Celeste. I followed Kim down the hall toward the common room. She stopped at the door and nodded, then left me alone. I opened the door and found Charles rising to his feet, smiling at me.

"Charles!" I nearly knocked him down when I reached and threw my arms around him.

"Ruth!" He held me in a big hug, then pulled back to inspect me. "You are so thin!"

I nodded and lowered my head. "And bald."

His eyes grew moist. "Celeste has given me instructions." He kissed my cheek and hugged me tight again.

"Tell her thank you and give her a kiss in return."

He nodded and reached into his coat pocket to pull out a letter. I laughed when I noticed the clothing he wore. I had not seen nineteenth-century clothing in some time, and I would have thought he would change before making the trip to see me.

"You did not feel the need to change into modern clothes?" I ruffled his cravat around his neck.

"I am only here long enough to visit with you and give you this. A letter from Celeste. It will explain why she was not able to accompany me here."

I took it and sat down on the sofa. He sat across from me and watched me read. I was astounded at her news. "Oh dear! Is Abby truly from this time?"

He nodded. "And quite alone."

"How dreadful."

"She has grown on us. Makes us laugh more than anything."

"I hope she does not overdo it. Society can push a bit too hard. You would do well to advise her, dear brother."

"I believe she knows her limits." His smile turned somber. "How are you, Ruth? Are you tolerating living here?"

"I am doing well. Better than I could be anywhere else," I responded. "I miss you and Celeste terribly, but I am glad to see you now."

"And Celeste and I miss you, Ruth." He smiled with tears threatening to form. He cleared his throat and began asking questions about the improvements on Shariton. That was always his way. He did not like showing emotion much and always tried to change the subject when the need arose. *Oh, how I miss you.*

We talked for a time about how things were in the past. He told me the situation with Abbie and how she is known as *Mrs.* Lambert. He expressed concern about the dinner parties and how Celeste had worried over Abbie and her odd behavior.

He chuckled. "She has managed to come out of it unscathed despite her oddities. Though I believe it is because people can blame her for being American, so they do not hold her to the same high standards as everyone else in society."

Despite my smile and determination not to show my fatigue, I felt my eyes droop.

Charles sat forward in alarm. "You are tired."

I waved my hand. "It happens every afternoon."

"Well, I should return. I have a horse waiting for me at the tree, and I shan't keep him waiting long."

I nodded and stood when he did.

He embraced me, hugged me tight, and whispered in my ear. "You need to get better, Ruth. Fight your way through this so we can have you back."

I nodded, and tears sprang to my eyes. I hugged him tightly again. During our embrace, the door opened to the common room. Josh stood at the threshold with wide eyes. "Pardon—" He started to back out of the room.

"Josh, wait!"

He stopped and gazed at me with a strange expression of loss.

"Come, I would like you to meet my brother," I waved him in.

His eyes relaxed. He smiled and stepped into the room. *Was that a look of relief?*

"Josh, this is my brother, Charles. Charles, this is my friend, Josh."

I watched them shake hands and converse. Josh looked at Charles as if contemplating something important. He glanced at me with the same expression.

"Well, I should depart," Charles said.

"I will leave you to your goodbyes then." Josh nodded and made to leave.

"No, Josh. You stay. I will walk Charles out." I took Charles' arm, and we left the room.

Once we were alone, Charles spoke up. "Josh? Why did you introduce me to him as Charles? Why not Mr. Elsegood, at least?"

"Everyone goes by first names here. Besides, he could possibly know the name Elsegood as one of the families that owned Shariton. I did not want him to start asking questions about where we come from or who we truly are."

"Ah, yes. How wise of you, Ruth," he replied. "What is his last name?"

I stopped and furrowed my brow. "I do not know. He never said."

"Perhaps you should know." He stopped outside the outer door. "I will miss you, dear sister."

"And I will miss you, dearest brother." I hugged him once more. "Take care of Celeste for me. Give her my love and well wishes."

"I will." He pulled away and walked down the paved driveway toward the thinned forest.

I called after him. "Are you going to walk?"

He laughed. "It is only in the forest there!" He waved, then picked up speed.

I watched him move through the gates and over the small hill toward the forest. If we were still in the past, he would have been surrounded by the trees the instant he left the gate.

I sighed and walked back indoors. When I reached the hall to the common room, I found Josh leaning against the door jam, waiting for me.

"Will you come with me? I want to give you a tour." He stood up straight and reached for my hand.

"But I have already had a tour."

"Did Kim show you all of Shariton?" he asked.

"Well, no. Only the places where we are allowed," I answered.

"Then you should see the rest." His fingers moved between my own, and I peered down at them while we walked. A thrilling sensation ran up my arm at his warm touch. When we reached the stairway and started crossing the invisible boundary, I hesitated and stopped him.

"We should not," I said wearily.

"No one will mind." He pulled me closer to the east wing.

I shook my head. "Mr. Harrison will be angry."

"Mr. Harrison won't mind."

"Perhaps we should have someone come with us," I countered. After all, I would not want to be caught alone with him. I had already stepped over that boundary with him that day in the water closet. I do not wish to be compromised and not thought of as a true lady.

He stopped and smiled. "Do you believe I would not behave like a

111

gentleman?"

I felt my face flush. *Did he read my thoughts? No. He could not have.* "Of course not."

"Then do you trust me to be on my best behavior?"

I nodded.

"Then, let's go." He escorted me down the hall into one of my favorite sitting rooms. We stayed long enough to get a quick glance, then moved on to the view of the parlor room, the breakfast room, and the drawing room. We walked up the stairs to more rooms, and in each one, he hurried me along, never allowing me time to study the rooms. So much had changed, yet it was much the way it once had been. It was as if the person who had reconstructed the house went to great lengths to restore it to its original state.

He stopped at another door and pulled it open. He walked more slowly this time, pausing just inside the room. When I followed him in, my breath caught. The walls of the study were filled with paintings. Tears filled my eyes when I recognized my family in the portraits. My mother, father, grandparents, uncles, aunts, and great-grandparents were there and several I did not recognize, who I assumed were Charles' descendants. I covered my mouth as I walked to where my brother's portrait hung. I wiped away the tears and moved to the next one.

Celeste appeared a bit older in her portrait, though her beauty still remained. Right below the portraits on the wall stood a long glass table. Inside were objects that had belonged to members of my family. I gasped, noticing the necklace my mother had left me when she passed on. I reached out and touched the glass, wishing I could hold it again.

I heard the sound of Josh moving behind me. I stiffened, wiped my eyes, and turned to see him watching me with great curiosity. Neither of us said anything for some time.

I cleared my throat. "It's beautiful here. Forgive me for being overwhelmed. I was led to believe the family had lost the portraits of their ancestors."

"Some were lost, yes. These were found hidden away after World War II."

He stepped up to the portrait of Charles. "There are a few of them I wanted to show you. I find it interesting that you walked right to them."

I swallowed hard. "Oh?"

He held out his hand for me to take. I slowly walked forward and placed my hand in his. He pulled me closer and faced the wall. "Do you see any resemblance between this man and your brother?"

My brother's portrait had also been painted at a slightly older age, just like Celeste's. I shook my head and tried to force my body to stop trembling.

"What about this one?" He moved me to the next painting. I held my breath. *Oh, dear!* I remembered posing for the portrait only a year ago. Celeste had painted me in my favorite gown, and I wore my mother's necklace and earrings. The same necklace that now lay in the glass case.

I shook my head. "That most definitely does not look like my brother," I laughed, hoping he would not notice my nerves.

He stepped back, placed his hand under my chin, and held it up, examining my features. *Oh heavens! He's touching my face! My heart might burst!*

"Uncanny resemblance, don't you think?" he asked.

I stood still and tried not to breathe, fearing what he might say next. "What a coincidence," I squeaked.

"Does that necklace have any significant value to you?" He pointed at my mother's necklace in the glass.

I cleared my throat. "No. This is the first time I ever laid eyes on it. I was only admiring it." I hoped and prayed that he did not see the lie in my eyes, "Are we through? I am feeling a little tired and need my rest."

He did not answer but studied me silently. I moved toward the door, hoping he would not stop me. Once I was clear of the room, I hurried down to the lift. *Thank goodness he does not know my true full name.*

Chapter Fourteen

1812 England, Abbie

"Well, hello there, handsome. I see you brought a friend along," I said to Albert and Molly, my maid, as they walked toward the tree I sat against.

Molly glanced at Albert. "Handsome?"

He blushed. "She is bold with her words."

"Yes, I know. I hear it every day," Molly said. "Greetings, Mrs. Lambert."

"Molly, how many times do I have to tell you to call me Abbie?" I hated to be called Mrs. Lambert. That was my mother's name.

She looked momentarily confused. "Forgive me," she said.

"You're forgiven as long as you stop calling me that."

"We cannot stay long," Albert said. "If we are found, we shall likely receive a scolding."

"Pstch!" I batted his words away as if they hung over my head. "Not if I have anything to say about it. Please, sit."

They sat in front of me in the grass. I plucked my fingers on the strings of the guitar and hummed.

"Beautiful!" Molly cried.

"Have you never heard a guitar?" I asked.

"Never."

My stomach grumbled, and it gave me an idea. "I would like to sing you a love song. It is about a long lost love." I grinned and plucked the strings to the guitar. "A love for a particular delicacy that I miss. Ryan Shupe and the Rubberband must have known what it was like to be parted from such delicacy as I have. Here we go ..." I began the corn dog song with gusto! *Oh, how I missed junk food.* My stomach growled again just thinking of it.

Halfway through the song, I stopped and explained what a corn dog was. They thought it odd, but I made them join in the song nevertheless.

"How do you play that?" Albert asked when I finished.

"I'll teach you," I said, patting the spot beside me.

He stiffened and glanced at Molly. She waved him over. He moved to my side, and I placed the guitar in his lap. I turned a bit and helped him place his fingers in the position to play an *A* chord.

"Now, strum with your right."

He did.

"You just played a chord," I said, then moved on to explain what frets were and what fingers played where. After ten minutes he became frustrated that he couldn't remember all the different chords I'd taught him.

"I give up," he moaned, holding the guitar out to me. "My fingers are too large and bulky."

"No, they aren't. It will take time. If it will help, I can illustrate the chords for you." I took the guitar.

"He will never get it. I would much rather hear you play anyway," Molly stated.

"Thanks for the vote of confidence, Molly," Albert said sarcastically.

She stuck her tongue out at him.

"Are you two brother and sister?" I watched the two of them.

"Unfortunately," Albert replied with a grin.

Molly picked a handful of grass and flung it at him.

He picked the grass out of his wig. "If war is what you want, war is what you will get."

Instantly, they frantically picked grass, throwing it at each other.

"What about me?" I cried and joined in the fun.

The war was short-lived, for they were afraid of spoiling their work clothes and attracting the attention of anyone nearby. Once our laughter died down, they asked me to play another song from America.

"Hummm. A song from America?" I tapped my finger on my chin. I plucked out a tune and started to sing. Halfway through the song, I understood their confusion. I had chosen a song from John Denver about jet planes. When I finished, I didn't have to wait for the questions.

"What is a jet plane?" they both asked simultaneously.

I shook my head and smiled. *Now what?* Perhaps I could pass it off as simple stories of a make-believe world. "There's a place I know where I can go, full of impossible things. Would you like to hear about it?"

"You mean an imaginary place?" Molly asked.

I nodded.

"I would love a good story," she leaned forward eagerly.

I told them about the world I had come from, throwing in some crazy make-believe objects and animals that truly didn't exist to make it more unbelievable. I told them about planes, cars, trucks, and trains. I was getting on the subject of TVs when we heard someone approaching.

117

They scrambled to their feet.

"Until next time," Albert bowed and hurried off after Molly.

* * *

Present Day England, Ruth

I avoided Josh for several days following our tour, but after my initial fear of him discovering my true identity lessened, I grew restless and began looking for him in the large house. I was not successful. He seemed to have disappeared.

I rubbed my hands together. Sometimes, the numbness in my hands felt overwhelmingly irritating. Still, I was relieved that the nausea was under control.

Don reached over and took my hand in both his shaky hands. "It will go away soon enough."

His smile always made me laugh. The man had teeth that could fall out. When he smiled, they moved, and he would push them back up and wink.

I had never seen someone so old. Most people in my time only lived until their sixties. This man was nearing his eighties. His hand tightened around mine, and he leaned forward with his eyes intent on what was happening on the telly. I did not mind when he held my hand. His friendship had grown dearer to me over the last week. I understood now that people in this day and age were more casually intimate. People hugged and held hands as if it were perfectly acceptable.

"No!" Steve yelled at the telly when his team did not get the goal. I had spent the last few weeks sitting with the men on the sofa, learning about the games they watched. They were eager to teach me, and I found it fascinating.

"Ha ha! That will teach you to mess with me mates!" Don called all

118

the players on his rugby team his mates.

"Boo!" Steve waved at the telly. No matter what they watched, they always cheered for the opposite teams. When I once asked them why, I was told it made the watching all the more fun.

During the *adverts,* I gazed around the room. My eyes landed on the picture of a woman on the wall. I had seen it several times but had not asked who she was.

"Who is that?" I pointed at the photograph.

"Mrs. Harrison." Steve quickly glanced at the picture, then returned his attention to the telly.

I stepped across the room to study the picture more closely. She had dark hair and olive skin. I looked back at Steve. "Do you know her maiden name?"

"Everyone knows she's an Elsegood," he responded.

I studied her again with newfound eagerness. Yes, she did have characteristics of Celeste. I could tell there was some Elsegood in her as well. This would make her my great great great—I did not know how many greats—niece.

"Where is she? Does she ever come here?" I asked.

"Have you not heard her story?" he asked.

I shook my head and sat beside Don again, leaning into him.

"She's the reason this cancer center was opened. She was diagnosed with cancer a few years back while they were starting a remodeling job on the place. She got the idea to turn the place into a cancer center for people who needed a place to stay while going through treatments." Steve stopped and grinned. "She hated hospitals." He returned his attention back to the telly and continued, "Sadly, she passed away before it was completed."

"That was almost two years ago," Don added.

"How sad," I whispered, "Poor Mr. Harrison. Are there any pictures of him?"

"Sure. All over—NO!" Steve yelled at the telly again. He used a few choice words that I had come to learn to block out. It seemed to be common use for most people.

"It's just not your day," Don said with a grin that made his teeth slip. He pushed them back in.

All over? I stood and walked from the room. Down the hall, I walked in and out of rooms, searching for pictures on the walls. Most featured the mysterious paraglider I had seen before. His face was not visible. When I reached the ballroom, I opened the door and stepped inside. When was the last time this room was used? It looked clean, but it had a distinctly vacant feeling. *How long has it been since someone danced in here?* I lifted my head and curtsied to an imaginary man. I stepped forward *one, two, three, four* ... I turned on my toes, then held my hands out as if taking someone's hand. I closed my eyes and twirled to the music in my mind. I moved backward, then forward with my arms up, and suddenly felt someone's hand in mine.

My eyes flew open. "Oh!"

"May I have this dance?" Josh asked with a dashingly handsome smile.

My heart quickened. *How often I have imagined being in his arms again!* "It is customary for the gentleman to ask a lady *before* he takes her in his arms to dance. And again, it is even more customary for him not to hold her so close. At least, the dances I am used to."

"What dances would those be?" he asked without stepping away.

"Well ... there are quadrilles and reels and ..." the heat in my cheeks intensified with each second that went by as he held me close to him. Our bodies nearly touched.

"Ah ha. The Regency Era. Are you so interested in that era that you've learned the dances?"

"I suppose I am."

His fingers moved between my own, and he lowered our hands

against his shoulder. "Will you teach me?"

"If—" my voice squeaked, and I cleared my throat. "If you wish me to."

"I do," he smiled. "How does it start?"

"Well, for me to show you, you must let go of me."

He released me and moved back a bit. "Now what?"

Much better. Now I can think. "It starts with a bow."

He demonstrated a nice bow.

"Very good," I said. "Now take three quick steps to me and lightly take my hand. A gentleman never clings to a lady. He only touches her ever so lightly." I demonstrated how to take a lady's hand. "When he must touch her waist, he does so in an elegant and soft manner—and only briefly." I again demonstrated it for him. He grinned at me when I touched his waist.

Oh, he is beastly!

I bit both my lips to hide the smile from my expression. I gave the first few steps, then stopped. "Oh, dear. I can never properly teach you with only the two of us. Let me go find someone to join us." Before he could respond, I hurried from the room and found Sandy, Carol, and William chatting nearby. I waved them over. Sandy was most eager to learn a new dance.

I instructed them for nearly an hour until they had it mostly put to memory. Had they not been so eager, I might have ended our impromptu lesson earlier, but they were engaged and seemed to enjoy themselves.

When we finished, Sandy clapped her hands with glee. "We should throw a ball! Just like in the olden days. Ruth can teach everyone to dance, and we can dress up and buy some wigs."

"We would need Mr. Harrison's permission," I stated, hoping she would not get her hopes up. After all, I had no idea what he would think of it.

Sandy looked to Josh. "What do you think? Would *Mr. Harrison* mind?"

"I believe he would think it a good idea," he winked at her.

She clapped her hands again. "Wonderful! When should we have it?"

"Christmas would be the perfect time, I think."

"Oooh, and with the lights, it would look so heavenly," Carol sighed.

"Watch out, Josh, soon these women will have you doing all kinds of things here at Shariton," William laughed.

I wondered why they assumed Josh would have any say in the matter.

He glanced at me, then smiled at Sandy's enthusiasm over the ball. She carried on and on about the decorations and the costumes we could wear.

Carol sidled up to me and leaned in. "Sandy used to be a professional decorator. I understand she may have even done party planning. Allowing her to plan this would help her spirits considerably."

"Has she been feeling down lately?" I asked.

"A little," she replied. "Everyone has their moments of frustration with treatments."

"Come on, Carol, I have some websites we can look at for ideas," Sandy waved to her, and the group departed, excitedly chatting as they went.

Seeing them so overjoyed in anticipation of the ball made me smile. I turned back to find Josh's attention drawn to me. I touched my hat, feeling self-conscious.

"I hope Mr. Harrison will give his permission. I would hate to see Sandy disappointed."

He nodded. "I hope so, too." He paused, then asked thoughtfully, "How many dances do you know from the Regency Era?"

"All of them," I answered.

"I find it interesting that you could know so much. What other things do you know about the era?" He moved closer.

"I am not sure." The heat rose in my cheeks, and my heart quickened.

"I wonder, could you identify something for me?" He took my hand in his.

"I can try."

He guided me to a room across the hall. "This room has a few objects from over 200 years ago." He stopped at a sofa table and picked up a bowl. "This is a bowl, but I don't understand why it has this funny curve on one side?" He held it out for me to look at.

"That is a bowl used mainly for bleeding or blood-letting." Emotion crept into my voice. It was the exact bowl they had used on my own father.

"Bleeding?"

"Yes. When someone was ill, they would place the person's arm in this curve, cut their arm, and let a small amount of blood drain from the wound."

"Really? And to think, we used it as a candy dish."

I laughed.

His eyes brightened at my laughter. "Thank you. I've been wondering about that for some time." He placed his hand on the small of my back, and familiar warmth spread through me. He led me to another object, "What about this?"

The item looked completely foreign to me. I shook my head, "I do not know."

"Hum." He looked at me quizzically. "I was told it was an extremely old camera. Perhaps from the turn of the twentieth century. Strange you don't know it." He reached into his pocket and pulled out the same mobile phone I had seen other guests carry. He placed it in my hand, "Can you look up on the internet what an old camera might look like during that time? I'd do it myself if it weren't for my eyesight."

I looked at the phone and felt helpless to know what to do. "How do you work it?"

He pushed the side, and it lit up.

I stared at it. Symbols stared back. I reached up and touched a symbol. A noise came from it, and I held it further from me. I looked up and found Josh watching me curiously. He always did that. Why did he find me so fascinating? I touched another symbol, and the picture changed. I pushed another symbol, and suddenly, it started to make a ringing sound. Josh reached out and took the phone from me, touching something to stop the ringing. He looked at me with the same look. I lowered my head.

"Do you know how to work a mobile?" he asked.

"Please forgive me. I am unfamiliar with them. You see, we did not have such luxuries where I lived."

"Interesting."

"I suppose my life seems interesting to some." I moved to the door. "Are we through, or is there something else you wish me to identify?"

"None that I can think of at the moment. This house is full of forgotten objects, so I may come to find you another day." He still had that look as if he were searching for something.

"I will be happy to assist you then." I smiled weakly and left the room. I had the sneaking suspicion he was working out my secrets.

Chapter Fifteen

1812 England, Abbie

It rained buckets outside while I sat in the windowsill of the parlor room. I liked this room the best because it was hardly used, and indoor alone time sometimes proved difficult. I leaned back against the pillow, placed my guitar on my lap, and started to play a song. I noticed movement from the corner of my eyes and saw Celeste enter the room.

"Hey, howdy, hey, Celeste."

She chuckled at my greeting. "Good afternoon, Abbie." She moved a chair beside me and sat. "Will you play for me?"

"But of course, my lady," I answered. She almost always found me when I had my guitar in hand. She had even once joined Albert and Molly in the garden to listen to me play. At first, Albert and Molly were terrified of being caught interacting with me, but Celeste didn't mind in the least. She seemed pleased that I'd found friends. She did advise us not to mention it to anyone else. It would be frowned upon.

I played a few songs she might know, then a few that had become popular after she left. She sang along when she knew the songs. I sang soprano, and she sang the harmony. It was the perfect way to spend an afternoon.

"That's beautiful," Celeste said about a tune I'd plucked out.

"Thank you."

"Are there lyrics to it?"

"Not yet. I know how I feel and think when I play it, but I can't seem to put it into words."

"What is it you're thinking of?"

I touched my belly and whispered, "The baby."

"Oh," she whispered back. "Then that is something that comes from the heart and is sacred."

I nodded. "I'll find the words in time."

"How are you feeling?" she asked.

"I don't understand how I could've been so lucky not to have morning sickness. I guess I'm blessed. You've been pretending to have it well enough for the both of us."

She nodded and blushed. "I guess I have. It will not be long before we'll have to break the news."

"No. Not long," I said solemnly.

* * *

1812 England, Abbie

I wanted to hide away after we made the announcement. It was far too embarrassing to face visitors now that the news of my pregnancy was out. Celeste announced her false pregnancy the same day, which thankfully took some of the attention away from me. The difference in how our news was received was staggering. Celeste was married to a wealthy Viscount. She had every reason to be happy about having a baby. I, on the other hand, was a penniless, pregnant *widow*, and I had no one to share my joy with. Therefore, I was looked upon with pity.

I gazed at myself in the mirror and sighed. It was well into October, halfway through my pregnancy, and my belly had grown too large to hide.

Since the announcement, I had been avoiding Albert. I didn't want to know what he thought of me, and I didn't want to see the pity in his eyes. We had become great friends, he and I. During good weather, we met out by our tree and sang songs. At times, Molly would join us. Sometimes, our visits would only last a few minutes, as they were kept busy with their work. Sometimes, they could last for over an hour.

On the day of my announcement, I used the gloomy weather as my excuse not to venture outside. It worked for a few days, but I knew it couldn't last much longer.

A knock sounded at the door.

"I beg your pardon, Abbie, I was sent to fetch you," Molly curtsied.

"Oh! Right. I'm keeping them, aren't I?"

She nodded. "They are in the drawing room."

"Thank you."

Another dreadful dinner party. I disliked dinner parties, dances, and social calls. But they were a break in the monotony. Truthfully, if I didn't have my guitar to haul around, I would go completely bonkers. *How can people sit for hours reading and sewing or strolling about the gardens?*

The moment I entered the drawing room, my stomach turned to knots. The party guests appeared annoyed at my lack of punctuality. Celeste and Lord Elsegood, on the other hand, didn't seem to mind in the least.

"Mrs. Lambert, you remember the Cromwells," Lord Elsegood

said.

I nodded and curtsied. "Good evening, Mr. and Mrs. Cromwell."

"Good evening," Mr. Cromwell replied. Mrs. Cromwell nodded primly.

"And this is their guest, Mr. Baily from Sussex. Mr. Baily, this is Mrs. Lambert."

"It's a pleasure to meet you, Mr. Baily," I curtsied again.

The man barely nodded in my direction. He was somewhat handsome, but I instantly knew I disliked him because he looked down at me as if I were trash. I wished there were such things as cars in this day and age. If there were, these people would have no excuse to stay the night. I already dreaded having to socialize with them tomorrow as well.

"And you know our other neighbors, Mr. and Mrs. Foster."

"Good evening," I smiled. Out of all the people invited, the Fosters were the kindest.

"Please forgive my tardiness." Only the Elsegoods and the Fosters acknowledged my apology.

Herbert stepped into the room and announced that dinner was ready. I quickly did a head count and found an equal number of women and men. *Oh, snap!* That meant I'd be escorted into the dining room. I resisted the urge to sigh out loud. *Stupid old English customs.*

Mr. Baily stepped to my side without a sideward glance and held his arm out for me to take. I touched him only with the tips of my fingers and moved into the room with him. We sat beside each other and hardly spoke a word through much of the meal. Those around the room chatted happily with one another but not with me. Those closest to me wouldn't give me the time of day, let alone chat about the weather.

This is so boring! I glanced at Mr. Baily and noticed he had the same look of boredom. At least I wasn't alone in my annoyance.

"Have you ever been to America, Mr. Baily?" I asked, feeling there was nothing to do but open the can of worms this conversation would bring.

"No."

"You should go there sometime. It's beautiful," I persisted.

"England is beautiful," he replied.

"Yes, but I would say that England, though it has its beauty, isn't as diverse in landscape as America."

"That is not what I have heard," he grumbled.

"Then your source couldn't have seen much of the continent."

"And you have?"

"A good portion of it, yes."

He finally looked at me. "Really? So you are a traveler, are you?"

"It's my favorite occupation," I grinned.

"Well then, tell me what is so very beautiful to see there." He held his head high and poked his nose down at me.

It was a challenge, and I wasn't going to pass it up. I raised my head, "The northeast in the fall is breathtaking with the rolling hills of red and orange trees. The Appalachian Mountains stretching across the east and the Rocky Mountains in the west are spectacular to behold. The red rock in the southwest is stunning, with the arches and natural shapes carved into the sandstone, and the Grand Canyon ... to see it could make one speechless."

He scowled, then lowered his fork. "Tell me, Mrs. Lambert, how can someone so young and delicate possibly travel to such wild and out-of-the-way places?"

My face flushed. *Oops. I might have dug myself into a hole.* I hadn't paid enough attention in my history classes to remember when places were discovered. I also didn't think about the fact that I couldn't travel easily to these areas. To top it off, I was a woman, and women didn't go exploring.

"You look ill, Mrs. Lambert, or is it simply that you've been found out?" His smug gaze made my insides boil.

129

I felt hot and angry that I couldn't prove what I knew. "I have been to some of those places, though not all. I've heard and seen photos—paintings of the rest."

"Shall we gather in the drawing room?" Celeste stood abruptly, giving me a sharp look.

"Paintings?" Mr. Baily continued, ignoring the interruption.

"Yes. People paint, you know." I stood and moved toward the door. The men stayed to indulge in their disgusting habit of drinks and cigars while the women shuffled into the drawing room for gossip, games, and embroidery.

Heat rolled through me. I wanted to put Mr. Baily in his place and wipe that smugness off his face. It might not be possible to do so, at least not without a good punch. I walked to the window, wishing I could have internet access to show him pictures of the places I knew.

"Come sit with us, Mrs. Lambert," Mrs. Foster called. I obliged, listening to the talk of new bonnets, illness, balls, and weather until the men rejoined the group. Not wanting to be near them, I stood and moved to the window to watch the sunset. To my discomfort, Mr. Baily joined me. *Stinkin' jerk! Go away!*

"Tell me, Mrs. Lambert, what other stories of America have you concocted in that interesting mind of yours?"

I decided I wouldn't give him the pleasure of continuing his game, so I changed the subject. "How long have you known the Cromwells?"

"From childhood. Mrs. Cromwell and my mother are friends," he replied. "Mr. Cromwell was married to my mother's older sister for a short time before she died, and he married again."

"It's a blessing that he was able to marry again. They seem a perfect fit for each other." I watched the hoity-toity couple chatter on and on about themselves. I shifted, annoyed at how my joints didn't seem to fit together like they used to.

"Quite right. Of course, everyone knew he would marry again;

most widowers do, though I cannot say the same for a widow. I do not believe it is right for women to marry twice."

I couldn't help but glower at him. "So, you believe women shouldn't have the same happiness of a second companionship after the first is taken from them?"

"Precisely. All they can hope for is an," he leaned in closer and lowered his voice, "illicit love affair from time to time."

Was he offering? The pig! "So, what you're saying is someone young, like me, has no chance for happiness compared to a middle-aged man, well past his prime?" I balled my hands into fists and held them behind my back to avoid lashing out.

"It is unfortunate. You have some good qualities that might catch a man's eye but not enough to tempt him to marry a woman in your condition," he gestured toward my growing belly. "I flatter myself on my ability to know the opinions of others, and I am quite sure those of the *ton* would agree. Do you not think, Mrs. Lambert, that one should know what is or is not possible so as not to get one's hopes up?"

My eyes darted to the iron poker at the fireplace, wishing it closer so I might bash it over his gigantic, inflated head. I huffed, clenched my fists tighter, turned and stomped—yes, I stomped away, right into the edge of one of the small tables in the room. My pinky toe crashed and bent on the wooden leg. I cursed out loud and hopped with my foot in the air.

"Damn table!" I cried and then froze when I saw the shocked expressions on every face in the room.

Celeste's eyes were wide, as was her mouth.

Oh, crap. "Forgive me. I think I need to lie down." I hurried from the room before another word could be said. Angry, hot tears filled my eyes as I hurried up the stairs. *I don't belong here.*

Chapter Sixteen

1812 England, Celeste

I knocked on Abbie's chamber door and waited for her to answer.
When she didn't, I opened it and peeked in. Her muffled weeping drew
me closer to the bed, where I sat and rested a hand on her shoulder.

"What happened?" I asked.

"The sexist pig insulted me—right to my face!" she cried.

"What did he say?"

She sat up and let the blanket fall from her upper body. "Is it true a
woman doesn't remarry if she becomes a widow?"

"Some women do, though not as many as in our time," I responded.
"What did he tell you?"

"Basically, I have nothing to offer and will live the rest of my life
miserably alone. Oh, but I can take a lover," she said, rolling her eyes.

"It sounds like you have it about right, then. He most definitely is a sexist pig," I huffed. "He deserves a knuckle sandwich."

"I would have given him one had I not run from the room. I didn't want to upset you by punching your dinner guest in the nose."

"Part of me wishes you had," I chuckled.

"Sorry for cursing when I stubbed my toe."

I tilted my head. "That probably didn't help the situation."

She smiled and leaned into me. I put my arm around her shoulders and rested my head on hers. "I hope you don't believe everyone here are like Mr. Baily and the Cromwells."

"I hope they aren't." She wiped her tears. "Do you think I could sneak into his room and leave a snake or two hidden in his bed?"

I laughed. "I'm not sure which would be considered worse, the snakes or your entering his bedchamber."

"Well ... it would be awesome to get even with him."

To satisfy Abbie's pride, we talked and chuckled about all the pranks we could pull on Mr. Baily. Her ideas were very clever. My favorite was putting dye into his bath. Of course, we wouldn't have the chance to pull any pranks, so we imagined them and laughed over them instead.

After saying good night, I retired to my room and found Charles waiting for me, still in his evening attire. I stiffened. Over the last week, I'd been coming up with excuses not to sleep in the same chambers as him. We had our own rooms, as was customary for the time, but up until recently, we had spent our nights together. When my belly began growing larger, I excused myself, retiring alone with a headache or other ailment in order to avoid his scrutiny. I didn't want him to know about the pregnancy too soon. Now, I knew I could not keep the ruse up any longer.

"Is Abbie feeling well?" he asked while he fought to untie his cravat.

"She's well. She was insulted by Mr. Baily." I made a face to show my dissatisfaction, then proceeded to tell him what was discussed between the two.

Charles looked upset and expressed his desire to land Mr. Baily a facer. After he cooled down a bit, he began helping me unbutton my evening gown. He stood behind me, slipped his arms around my waist, kissed the back of my neck, and paused. I held my breath in anticipation of his reaction.

He took hold of my shoulders and spun me around, placing his hands on my belly. His eyes grew wide, and I could see the question in them.

I bit my lip, smiled, and nodded. I placed my hand over his and held it against my belly. "There's life in there. I don't need to pretend."

"Wh—why did you not tell me sooner?"

"I was afraid it wouldn't last. I was afraid of losing him."

"Him?"

"Or her." I shrugged.

He laughed and hugged me tight, then kissed me repeatedly. He placed both hands on my belly again, knelt down, and kissed my abdomen.

His reaction brought a smile to my lips that I couldn't erase. I giggled and cried tears of joy. He stood again, picked me up, carried me to the bed, laid beside me, and held his ear against my belly. "Does Abbie know?"

"No. I have been afraid to tell her, too."

He lifted his head to look at me, his eyes alight. "Life is a wonder, is it not?"

* * *

Present Day England, Ruth

"What's the score?"

134

The words cut through the haze and confused me. *Who is that?* The deep voice did not match my brother, who stood beside me.

"10–12."

"Hold on, is this an old game?"

I knew that voice. I tried to lift my head toward the voice, but could not.

"Shh. I think she's asleep." The one shaky voice had to belong to Don. *Who is the other voice?*

Don was right and wrong. I hovered on the verge of sleep and wake, where dreams mix with reality. Charles standing in his traveling coat did not match the voices around me, neither did the sounds of a large crowd cheering, whistles being blown, and the commentary.

"Is this the game from last season?" the voice sounded nearer as the movement beside me brought me closer to reality.

Wait.

"Reds and sharks."

That smooth voice was the same one that warmed my heart and filled my dreams. My eyes shot open. *Josh!*

I woke in a different position from the one I had fallen asleep in, my head resting on Josh's shoulder and my hand in his. I inhaled too quickly and coughed as I sat up.

"Sorry for waking you," he whispered.

A lady does not sit so close to a man. I carefully shifted my weight away from him.

My mind muddled into an incoherent mess. I did not know what else I should do. Should I apologize? Should I get up and walk away? If I did, would I offend Josh?

While I thought about what to do, I continued to cough. Josh began to pat my back, continuing to rub it once my coughing had subsided. "Are you well?"

I nodded. "Yes, thank you." I glanced at the clock. I had only been

135

asleep for ten minutes.

"I'm sorry for startling you," he repeated, turning his attention to the game on the telly when Don called out about an unlucky hit.

"Oh, come on! That's a load of rubbish!" Josh joined in the commotion beside me. "Where's Steve?"

"Treatments," Don answered without pulling his attention away from the game. He pointed at the telly. "Watch this next hit."

"Brilliant!" With his arm still around me, Josh leaned over to ask Don a question about the game, therefore getting even closer. I held my breath. His smooth cheek was inches away. An unfamiliar, clean scent floated around me. His wavy hair had grown just past his ears, and upon seeing it unruly and disheveled, I wished to reach out and run my fingers through it to tidy it up for him—and to feel its softness. I should have stopped staring, but my eyes never left his handsome face. As he began to sit back, he turned his head and caught me watching him. My whole body warmed at his shy smile.

If only I had my hand fan to hide behind.

The sofas of this modern time were deeper and softer. I could practically disappear within its depths. Getting myself up and out of it proved challenging. My exit was far from graceful and added to my embarrassment as I stood.

"Where are you going? The game's not over," Don said with a quick glance in my direction.

"Forgive me, Don. I must beg you to excuse me. I am afraid it was not sensible of me to fall asleep next to you in such an undignified manner. I shall rest in my chambers."

Both Don and Josh peered up at me with foreheads creased and brows up.

"No need to get stuffy with us. Go, have your nap," Don waved me off.

Heavens! What could he have found in that to be offensive? "I didn't mean to say that I did not—that is—" I exhaled and tried again, "Do you wish me to stay?"

He winked. "Go on, me lassie. But I expect you to watch with me tomorrow. Maybe I can talk you into a little wager?"

"Oh, no. Steve warned me about you," I frowned.

He laughed briefly along with Josh, before shouting at the game again. Seeing that I was no longer his focus, I headed out of the room. I had only made it a little down the hall before hearing my name.

"Ruth, wait." Josh hurried to stand before me. "I'm sorry for waking you in there. My mother always told me I am louder than I realize."

The heat from my embarrassment returned. "Oh, you do not need to apologize. I should not have fallen asleep."

"You can nap any place you like here. It's meant to feel like home."

I nodded once, then turned to walk away.

"Ruth, can I ask you something?"

I turned back to see the curiosity in his eyes. "Yes."

"Why do you speak the way you do?"

Oh dear. I tried to act as though I knew not what he was saying. "I do not understand."

"Never mind." He lowered his head and scowled. "Enjoy your rest."

I watched him return to the common room, shaking his head as he went.

Belonging and blending into this age is more difficult than I thought.

Chapter Seventeen

1812 England, Abbie

I didn't get out of bed until well past breakfast. After Molly helped me bathe, I sat at the vanity in my room while she brushed my hair. My puffy red eyes reminded me of the reason why I had stayed up late.

"Molly, can I ask you a question?"

"You may." She took hold of my hair and began to twist.

"Do you know of any widows that have remarried?"

"Oh no, miss."

She did my hair up into curls while she tried to get me to talk about America and the imaginary place I had spoken of before, but I wasn't in the mood.

After she finished, I headed out into the corridor. The rain tapped heavily against the windows, so I wandered the halls and avoided the rooms where I knew the servants and guests would be. After turning down several hallways, I spotted a panel of curtains hanging from ceiling to floor. I moved toward them and pulled the curtains back to reveal a wonderful deep windowsill along a beautiful window overlooking the gardens and the stables beyond, perfect for sitting in secret. I sat with my back against the window frame, pulling my knees up—as far as I could with a growing belly—and folding my arms around them. Then, I slid the curtains back into place.

I looked out the window down toward the stables and watched the rain drip down the window. I could almost get lost counting each spark of light reflected on the raindrops. Almost. I was so overwhelmed with emotions. When I first arrived, I felt like a princess in a fairytale. I began to believe I could stay here and live the life of royalty in a peaceful place. But after hearing that someone like me had no chance of marrying and would most likely become a nobody, my hopes for this future were splattered against the wall.

It wasn't so much that I wanted marriage right away—maybe a year or two down the road, after college. But having the option of a serious relationship that would lead to a family was something I wanted open to me. Most girls my age would want to have that option. To someday be held and give my heart to someone who would treasure me would be a dream come true. Here, that dream didn't seem to exist.

My tears mimicked the rain on the paned glass. I had difficulty keeping my sobbing quiet, so I covered my face in my arms. My breath caught at the sound of someone clearing their throat. A hand holding a handkerchief reached through the curtain. I moved the curtain aside. Albert stood straight and tall with a worried expression.

I suppose he thought my opening the curtain was an invitation to join me because he sat with his back against the glass. He still held out the handkerchief, so I took it and dried my tears.

"I heard what Mr. Baily said to you. He is cruel and unfeeling. Do not believe a word of it."

I cleared my throat. "Albert, why do you and your sister talk with a different accent than the other servants? You speak more like Lord Elsegood or Celeste."

He smiled weakly and looked down at his hands. "My mother raised me. She was a noblewoman, disowned by her family, and my father is a lord."

"But why do you work as a footman then?" I didn't understand much about this time, but noblemen didn't seem to become servants.

"Molly and I are … illegitimate children of an earl. My father fell in love with my mother after he had married someone of his father's choosing. My father kept us secret and took care of us for some time. When my mother died, I was sent to be educated while Molly stayed with a friend of the family. When I was old enough, my father arranged for us to find work here. We are fortunate to serve the Elsegoods."

I sighed. *So there really is no hope for my child to achieve his dreams of becoming anything he—or she—wants to be here.*

He looked at my hand resting on my belly. "Is this the reason why you have been avoiding me?"

I lowered my eyes and nodded, then whispered. "I figured you wouldn't want to be around me once you knew I was with child."

He lifted my chin and gazed hard into my eyes. "I will always be your friend, no matter what may come."

Tears flooded my eyes, and joy filled my heart like a hot air balloon. My body felt like a wave of warm electricity moved through me with enough jolt to make me sigh. I took his hand in mine, kissed his palm, and laid my cheek against it. His hands were warm and wonderful.

"Thank you," I whispered. *I think I'm in love with you.*

My baby kicked hard inside me as if to agree with my thoughts. I'd felt the baby move before, but never this hard. I gasped and peered up at Albert in awe.

"What is it?" he asked breathlessly.

With a smile, I placed his hand against my abdomen. I giggled and rolled my eyes when I saw his ears and cheeks go scarlet. I pushed his hand onto the place where the baby had kicked. The baby leaned and moved slowly across the spot, then gave a good hard kick as if to say, "Stop pushing or I'll push back!"

Albert's eyes widened. "Is that …"

I nodded. "It's the baby."

His eyes moistened and his smile grew. "Incredible! I've never felt anything like it!" He moved his other hand to press against my belly. He bent down. "Greetings, little one."

The baby kicked as if in response. We both laughed, and Albert raised his head. He was closer than he'd ever been before. His smile faded, and he pulled back. The moment was so brief, but at that moment, I sorely wished I could kiss him, hold him in my arms, and be held in his.

He cleared his throat and stood. "I apologize for being so forward." He turned to go, turned back as if he would speak, then shifted his weight from side to side. "I … I wish you would not avoid me any longer, Abbie. I have missed hearing your songs." He smiled and stepped back, letting the curtain cover my hiding place. His footsteps faded.

I sighed. *He's my light in the darkness.*

* * *

Present day, Ruth

My sweet Celeste,

Thank you, dear sister, for the letter. Oh, how I wish I could have visited with you. I hope Charles will return soon so I may give him this letter.

It was quite surprising to hear about the young woman who now lives with you. Mind you, I am not surprised to hear you took her in to

141

care for her; rather, I am surprised she followed you in the first place. I am sorry to hear of her misfortune, but I know she is in good hands.

I wish now to express my deepest gratitude to you for bringing me here. Although this Shariton Park is vastly different from the one in which I grew up, I must say the improvements are growing on me. Now that the weather is growing colder, I am especially fond of warm water and electric heat. The modern conveniences truly make life easier and more comfortable!

I have made several friends here and enjoy time with them. I spend my days riding horses, playing card games, reading, watching the telly with friends, and napping. The side effects of my treatments are usually only a nuisance, but there are days when I feel worse and I fear I shall never get better, but enough of that. I have good news. I was asked to teach my new friends to dance, and we are to have a ball! I suppose I am the best person to teach them. After all, I taught you, and you dance divinely! We gather in the ballroom for our lessons twice a week to prepare for the Christmas ball. It is fortunate that Mr. Harrison gave us permission to use the ballroom. He must be kindhearted, though I do not know that firsthand, as I have yet to meet him.

I hope you are not worried about me, Celeste. I am doing quite well and looking forward to the day when I can come home. I wish you well and miss you terribly.

With all my love,
Ruth

My brother's visit was the highlight of my day. I could not stop smiling at the news he brought of Celeste in the family way. I still giggled as I waved goodbye and watched him walk past the great gate and over the hill.

I clapped my hands and spun around, "Oh, how happy I am for Celeste!" I exclaimed. I turned to make my way back toward the house when I caught Kim watching me from her office window. She waved when our eyes met, and I returned her wave.

She opened the window and stuck her head out. "You seem happy."

"As do you," I replied evasively.

"Well, seeing a man in breeches and a fine coat always makes my day!" she laughed. "Was that your brother?"

"It was. He is working on a historical film nearby and stays in costume when he visits. Sort of an inside joke," I said, giving the excuse Celeste had suggested.

"Does he always walk?" she asked.

"Yes. It's not far."

"Well, I hope he comes again soon," she winked and closed the window.

Instead of going back inside and getting my coat, I decided to walk around the building and enjoy the autumn weather. I skipped down the hill around the west side and walked the path leading to the stables. I plucked a leaf from the nearest tree and thought of Celeste and her marvelous growing belly. Oh, how I would have loved to jump for joy with her at that moment of discovery.

"What's got you so happy, my little vixen? Up to no good?" Dolan stood near the stable, leaning on a shovel, his eyes traveling over me from head to toe.

I slowed my steps and held my hat to my head so the wind would not claim it. "Good afternoon, Dolan."

"Are you ready for another ride, or has yesterday's ride done you in?" He let the shovel drop and stepped closer to me.

I stepped back and then began walking toward the stable. "I am wearing a dress, and last I checked, you do not have a sidesaddle."

"I told Mr. Harrison about tha' and he ordered one."

I stopped short inside the stable. "Has he? Whatever for?"

"I suppose he'd not considered owning one until someone brought it to his attention. I think he likes that someone else can ride ol' Norman here." He gestured toward the stallion.

"Oh."

"Come on, tell me. Why are you in such good spirits?" He followed me to Norman's stall and stood close while I greeted the horse.

"I have had good news from my sister-in-law. She is in a family way."

He looked puzzled for a moment, then understanding dawned. "Oh. She's got a bun in the ol' oven."

My brows raced up at his choice of words. "Yes ... she has." I nuzzled my nose into Norman's fur.

"Well, I'm glad because I get the privilege of seeing your smile." He moved closer to me, and I stepped back. He continued to step forward until my back hit the wall.

"Why do you insist on getting so close?" I pushed against his chest. "We should not be alone together, and here you are, breaking all the bounds and getting too close ... to ..."

His breath tickled my nose and lips. His arms blocked me at either side. I had nowhere to go. I scowled at him. "We should not be alone, Dolan. I am a lady." I glanced at his lips, then at his eyes.

"There it is ... that sign. You want to kiss me, don't you?" He did not allow me to answer before his lips pressed firmly on my own, and his arms pulled me against him.

I simultaneously pushed against his chest and felt his lips part. The tip of his tongue brushed against my lower lip. I tried to pull back to protest and tell him this was not what a lady should do, but he pulled me harder against him and kissed me more fervently.

There was no emotion, no sigh building deep inside as I thought there would be. His kiss was nothing.

I turned my head, which led to his lips upon my neck. "Stop. Dolan, stop." It was difficult to push away, for he held me tightly. Hot, angry tears burst from my eyes. If someone found us like this, I would be ruined and forced to marry him. That was something I could not allow to happen. I pushed against him with all my might and cried, "Get off!"

He stepped back, looking surprised at first, then anger took over. "Don't play with me." His expression turned hard. "I know you want it."

I hurried for the door. "A lady never wishes to be forced into circumstances that could condemn her good character. If I did anything to give you the impression—"

He took hold of my arm, stopping me so suddenly that I nearly lost my footing. His fingers dug into my arm. He reached to pull me to him again, but I reacted so fast that I surprised even myself. I slapped him hard across the side of his face. My hand stung at the blow. His grip slackened, and I pulled myself loose. I ran as fast as my shaking legs could carry me back to the house. One quick glance over my shoulder told me he had not chosen to follow. The moment I reached the door, I began to weep. I flung the door open and bumped into someone's chest.

Josh held a mobile phone to his ear, stopping mid-sentence. He gently took my arm as I tried to hurry past, and he spoke into the phone. "I'll have to call you back, Bill. Book the flight, and I'll see you there. I've got to go."

I pulled my arm free, feeling a little tired of men holding me against my will.

"Ruth, what happened? What's wrong?" He slipped his phone into his pocket.

"I …" I had almost told him exactly what happened, then paused. What would be the consequence of him knowing? Would I be forced to marry Dolan now that I had been disgraced? Or does that even apply in this century? I wiped my tears and held my head up. "Nothing happened. I am just being silly."

"Oh." He looked me over as if to determine the truth of my words.

I knew he could see the lie in my eyes. "Are you sure?"

"There is nothing wrong."

"Then where is your hat?" His eyes rested on my head.

My hands shot up in dismay. I had not realized I'd lost my hat in the scuffle. My face warmed at the thought of him seeing my bare scalp.

He shook his head. "You look just as lovely without your hat, Ruth." He opened the door and held it. "Shall we go look for it?"

I hesitated silently, wondering if he could see the panic in my eyes.

He narrowed his brows and took my hand to guide me out the door. I stumbled, and he took hold of my waist to steady me. "So, where did you come from?"

I stiffened. "Why?"

"Most likely, that would be where you lost your hat." His smile turned mischievous. "Unless it grew legs and walked off into the woods. If that is the case, then I'm afraid nothing can be done."

I could feel his eyes on me, waiting for me to smile at his joke. I looked down at my feet, trying to hold back more tears.

"So?"

I peered up at him and frowned. "The stables."

He glanced toward the stables, then continued to study me. I looked away, struggling to control my emotions, taking deep breaths and clearing my throat. My emotions proved harder to gather the closer we got to the stables. I stopped short when I saw Dolan shoveling manure nearby, and worked as though nothing had happened. Josh walked on, and Dolan lifted his head and waved. Dolan had not seen me yet because I waited further up the path. How could he behave in such a casual way after taking advantage of me as he did?

Josh stopped and looked at me quizzically when I paused. I stepped forward in a hurry without looking in Dolan's direction. I loudly exhaled once we were out of Dolan's sight. Josh studied me again, and his eyes narrowed slightly as we made our way through the stable doors. There on the ground lay my hat. Josh picked it up, then stopped and studied the ground. In the dirt were several distinct footprints matching two different shoes. One set was small and smooth. The other belonged to a pair of large boots. I looked down at my shoes, as did Josh. My face grew red, and my control over my emotions weakened. *I should not have come in here with him. I should have insisted nothing was wrong and hurried back to my room.*

"Nothing happened?" Josh appeared upset, almost hurt.

"Nothing."

"Is there something going on with you and Dolan?" A look in his eyes made me believe he regretted the question.

"No! Of course not! He's a—" I choked back a sob.

"What happened, Ruth?"

I shook my head and turned, running swiftly back up the hillside. What would he think of me if Josh found out what had happened? Would he force me into marriage? If Charles were here, he would most certainly call Dolan out. Josh and I hardly knew one another, and it was not his duty to defend my honor, but something in me wished he would do just that.

I pushed all thoughts of Josh from my mind as I made my way through the house. Whenever I grew upset, my legs seemed to know where to take me. I pulled my cardigan sweater over my head to cover my baldness and sank into the windowsill to cry.

Chapter Eighteen

1812 England, Abbie

I shook from lack of nutrition. I missed breakfast and didn't want to wait until tea time, so I went to the kitchen. This wasn't the place for me, but I had visited often enough to befriend the cook, who often allowed me to take a pastry or two between meals.

"Good afternoon, Gwen," I greeted her with a smile.

"Abbie, me dear. Just in time. I am in need of an extra hand." She waved toward a pot, "Would you mind stirring that, dear?"

When I last visited her, I insisted she allow me to help her cook. Lucy, the young girl who normally helped, was retrieving more herbs, so I rolled up my sleeves to show Gwen that I wasn't afraid of a little work.

"Not at all," I responded, taking the handle to stir the savory stew. Only a few minutes later, we started a conversation about pies versus cakes and which was better while we chopped vegetables. Lucy soon joined us, and I found myself feeling at home. I asked several questions about servants' roles and daily chores. I felt sorry for the whole lot of them simply because of their lack of choices.

Our conversation paused when a young girl walked into the room and stopped to stare at me.

"Hello," I smiled.

Her eyes narrowed, and without a word, she hurried from the room, carrying a wooden bucket.

"Who was that? I've not seen her before."

"Martha. She's the scullery maid. Don't mind her. She's a wee bit jealous of you." Lucy shook her head. "She's jealous of anyone who so much as looks or speaks to Albert."

Heat rushed to my ears at the mention of Albert, and at the exact moment, an older man walked into the kitchen. After recovering from the shock of seeing a lady in the kitchen, he moved to a bucket full of water to wash up.

"Paul! You go wash up somewhere else! You're covered in dirt!" Gwen waved her knife at the man.

He rolled his eyes, "It's only sulfur! A little sulfur won't 'urt nobody."

My ears perked up. "Sulfur?"

Paul nodded. "Out back, there's a pile of it." He waved toward the door.

I quickly searched the kitchen and found a small iron pot. "Gwen, do you have any vinegar?"

"That bottle, there," she quickly pointed above my head, then returned to kneading her bread. I reached for the bottle and grabbed the iron pot and a spoon. "If you'll excuse me, I have something to take care of. It's been great helping you."

Gwen smiled while she kneaded the bread. "Thank you for your help, me dear."

I hurried out of the room by way of the back door. Once outside, I carried the pot to a pile of earth and found what I was searching for. Yellow chunks of sulfur were mixed in with the dark soil. I laughed deep in my throat while I gathered a few chunks, placed them in the pot, and then hurried back inside. I wandered to the third floor and down the corridor where I knew Mr. Baily had stayed. *Which room is his?*

Footsteps sounded down the corridor, so I hid behind a potted plant. It wasn't much of a hiding place, so I wasn't surprised when the person stopped.

"Abbie. What are you doing?"

My shoulders relaxed when I heard Albert's deep voice. I moved out from behind the plant. "What does it look like I'm doing?"

He glanced at the pot in my hand and shook his head. "I have not the slightest."

I smiled with one eyebrow raised. "I'm up to no good and need your help."

He chuckled. "I am not sure I should."

"What room is Mr. Baily staying in?"

He hesitated.

I tilted my head and grinned. "It's a harmless little prank, and as long as you keep watch, he won't know who did it."

His lips spread into a wickedly perfect grin that made me want to kiss them. "This way." He walked a few paces away, stopped, and opened the door. He held it open, and I moved inside.

Mr. Baily's clothes were on the bed, ready to be packed into his trunk. I giggled and moved to the fireplace to set the pot over the hot coals. I glanced over my shoulder and winked at Albert. He looked nervously out the door, then back at me.

"What are you doing, Abbie? Making him a stew?" he whispered.

"I'm making him new cologne," I grinned. I broke up the sulfur and stirred it around. When the pot was hot, I poured a little vinegar over the sulfur and hurried out of the room, leaving the pot behind and carrying the vinegar bottle. I waved Albert out of the room, then held my nose.

He quickly shut the door behind me and uncovered his nose. "What was that stench?"

"His new cologne." I laughed and took his hand to pull him away from the door. When I looked back at him, I noticed his attention on our hands. I let go and blushed. Did he like holding my hand, or did it repulse him?

I held the bottle of vinegar out to him. "Could you return this to the kitchen, preferably without Gwen knowing?"

He straightened as he always did when asked to do something. "Of course, but if anyone finds out about this ..." He took the bottle and frowned.

"I'll take the blame. Don't worry. Celeste will understand. Thank you for your help, my friend."

He bowed and hurried down the corridor.

* * *

Present Day England, Ruth

"Ruth. Wake up."

I woke with a start and instantly felt the sharp pain of having slept wrong on my neck. I quickly assessed where I sat and instantly understood that I had fallen asleep in the window. My cardigan sweater that hid my baldness still lay on my head and nearly covered my line of vision. I pulled it back and found Josh's head poking through the curtains.

He held my hand in both of his and patted it as he woke me. I pulled my hand free and felt the heat in my cheeks.

"I've been looking for you." He paused. "I suppose this is your

151

sanctuary, then?"

"At times," I whispered and rubbed my neck.

He reached for my legs and lifted them when he sat down and held my feet on his lap while studying me as he always had. He sat in silence for a moment, then he spoke softly. "I talked with Dolan."

My eyes grew and fear crept into my soul. I waited for him to speak.

"He said you …" He huffed. "He said you flirted with him and kissed …"

I choked in surprise. "He said what?" Tears sprung to my eyes, "I did nothing of the sort! I am a lady! Ladies do not go about flirting and kissing men! He advanced on me! He forced himself on me! I repeatedly told him to keep his distance, and he ignored my requests!"

Anger flashed in Josh's eyes, and he stiffened. "He forced himself on you?"

I covered my mouth to keep my cries muffled. I had not meant for him to know. My voice broke as I took his hand and pleaded with him. "Please do not make me marry him! I know it might be disreputable after what has happened, but I cannot marry someone I do not respect or love."

He looked momentarily confused, and then his anger returned. "Why would you be forced to marry him?"

"He had me in his arms … he kissed me rather scandalously," I replied, feeling a little hopeful by his response.

"He only kissed you, then?" He squeezed my hand in his.

"Is that not enough?" Beads of sweat gathered on my forehead.

He sighed, and his shoulders relaxed. "Why would you have to marry someone just because you kissed?"

"Does it not happen that way now?"

"Now?" His eyes narrowed.

"I apologize, I am confused, I …" my voice trailed off weakly.

His eyes softened. "You won't need to worry over him any longer.

152

He won't be around to cause you distress again." He stood and pulled me up and out of the window beside him.

I covered my mouth with my cardigan and wiped my eyes. My shoulders shook, and I cried with relief. Josh bent down, picked up my hat, which he must have brought with him, and gently placed it on my head. He smiled and pulled it down over my eyes. I laughed through my tears and pushed the hat back. I felt the sudden urge to step into his arms and bury my head in his chest as I had done before. Before I could act on that impulse, he stepped away and cleared his throat.

"You must be hungry. It's past dinner, and I believe you may have skipped lunch too." He began moving down the corridor, and I walked beside him. "If you like, I can get someone to bring a tray of food to your room."

"Thank you." His suggestion made me wonder. "Josh?"

"Hum?" He kept his eyes forward.

"What is your last name?"

He hesitated a moment, then cleared his throat. "My name is Joshua David Harrison."

I stopped, as did he, though he did not look at me. "But I thought Mr. Harrison was someone else entirely. Why did you never tell me when we spoke of him? I thought you were a guest here, like me."

"I like being the same as everyone else," he replied.

I stepped closer and peered directly into his eyes. "Did you believe I would treat you differently if I knew you were Mr. Harrison?"

He slowly nodded.

"I would not have," I whispered earnestly. "You are my friend, the same as all my friends here." At that moment, I knew it was a lie. I was his friend, but it was not the same. There was something more between us. We stood gazing into each other's eyes for a long moment. I did not want to look away for fear he would find me insincere. From the corner of my eye, I saw his hand slowly rise almost to my face, then stop

153

abruptly. He stepped back and hesitated, then gave a small smile. His behavior confused me. Was he reaching for me? Did he feel that same pull to be close to me? Did he, too, feel that there was something more?

"I'm truly sorry Dolan behaved the way he did, Ruth. I wouldn't want any of my guests to be treated that way, and I hope it won't reflect badly on your stay here. I promise it won't happen again." He tried to smile, but it fell flat. He appeared worried.

"Thank you," I whispered.

Chapter Nineteen

1812 England, Celeste

"What could be taking him so long?" Mrs. Cromwell asked impatiently. We had finished afternoon tea with our guests and then made our way into the hall to say goodbye when Mr. Baily discovered his trunk was not among the rest of their belongings. He looked quite put out when he excused himself to discover its whereabouts. He took longer than necessary, and I wondered what could keep him. He already missed saying goodbye to the Fosters.

"Perhaps he needs to freshen up," Abbie suggested with a hint of laughter.

From the stairs, I heard footsteps and saw Mr. Baily holding a handkerchief to his face. Following behind him were two of our footmen carrying his trunk. The footmen looked as though they were holding their breath as they descended the stairs. Almost at once, I understood why. I covered my mouth and started to gag. The smell felt like a slap in the face. It was so strong. Everyone in the room had nearly the same reaction. I looked at Abbie, and even though she, too, was gagging, I could also hear quiet giggles.

"What is that repulsive stench?" Mr. Cromwell asked under his handkerchief.

"Why, I do believe it is Mr. Baily," Abbie said in a rather affronted voice.

"What happened to you, Mr. Baily?" Mrs. Cromwell moved out the door in a hurry. Everyone followed, including Mr. Baily and his noxious trunk. Charles tried to stay farthest away and held his breath.

"It was nothing of my doing, Mrs. Cromwell. I assure you," he said, then gagged once. "It seems we have a witch in our midst." His eyes darted toward Abbie.

She shot him a deathly stare.

Mr. Baily stepped up to me, and I held my breath as politely as I could. "Lady Elsegood, I would seriously reconsider the invitation you have extended to your house guest." He nodded toward Abbie. "I fear she may disgrace your household if allowed to remain."

I narrowed my eyes and held my head high. "It sounds as though you blame poor Mrs. Lambert, Mr. Baily, for your … unfortunate odor. Let me assure you, she is not to blame, and I, for one, am not concerned by her behavior, but as for you, I am not so certain."

He huffed and stepped into the waiting carriage without so much as a goodbye. Mr. and Mrs. Cromwell said farewells with handkerchiefs held over their noses and reluctantly stepped into the carriage with Mr. Baily. The carriage jerked, and Mrs. Cromwell's head appeared out the carriage window. The sight reminded me of a dog on a joy ride, and I laughed out loud. My laughter was muffled under my hands, but it did not go unnoticed. Abbie joined in, and as soon as the carriage passed through the gate, Charles and the footmen let out their breath with a bout of uproarious laughter.

I turned to Abbie with a questioning look.

She held her head high and grinned. "What?"

"Now, do not deny it, Abbie. We know it was you," Charles laughed.

"He deserved it," she said smugly.

"That he did!" called Albert from behind her.

"He may have deserved it, Abbie, but you must be careful. It could reflect badly on us as hosts." Charles tried to appear stern, but his laughter won out and we could not help but continue laughing at Abbie's joke.

* * *

Present Day England, Ruth

The waltz I had first heard on Celeste's MP3 player sounded beautifully sweet over the loudspeaker as I taught my fellow guests the familiar steps of the quadrille.

While they practiced, I walked the ballroom, correcting those who needed help. Spouses had been invited to learn the dances for the Christmas Ball. It was a pleasure to watch the couples dancing and enjoying time together.

"Josh! You're back!" Sandy said excitedly. I paused and turned to see Josh entering the room. He slipped the pack from his shoulder and looked over the group. His eyes stopped when they met mine. We both smiled.

He waved to everyone and moved closer to Sandy and me. "How are the lessons going?"

"They are doing well," I said, trying to hide my delight at seeing him.

"They would be doing loads better if everyone showed up for classes," Sandy replied. "You especially need the lessons," she added pointedly.

"Why me?" he protested.

"You are our host, Josh. You must lead the first dance, as, I under-stand, is customary." Sandy looked at me.

"Is it?" he asked feebly.

I nodded and gestured for everyone to continue their practice.

"You've been gone for some time, Josh. We've missed you," Krista said reproachfully, leaning heavily on her cane as she joined the three of us.

"It's been almost a month," Sandy agreed, one hand on her hip and her eyebrows raised. "I've had quite a time trying to plan this ball with-out you, young man. I hope you won't be leaving again anytime soon."

"What kept you away?" Krista put in.

He glanced at me briefly before answering. "Oh, you know. Work."

"That and your crazy flying trips!" Sandy laughed.

"Oh! I had forgotten you fly," I said without realizing I had spoken out loud. I blushed at my outburst, then chastised myself for feeling bashful. I had never felt embarrassed about speaking to someone. Why was I so shy around Josh?

"If you ask me, he's looney," Sandy laughed again.

"Don't mock it, Sandy. Before long, you'll be riding the wind right along with me," Josh teased.

"That's right," I said thoughtfully. "I was told you take those who finish treatment up with you in that ... that ... thing."

"That *thing* is actually a wing. Not to be confused with a parachute," he smiled. "I hope you'll soon have your chance as well."

My eyes widened. "Oh, no! I could never do such a thing!" I pro-tested.

"Well, enough chatting," Sandy sighed. "Josh needs to learn the dances before time runs out. We only have three weeks until the Christ-mas Ball."

158

"Would you mind being Josh's partner? I need to check on Don," I said, moving across the room to stand beside Don's wheelchair. Over the last week, he had grown increasingly frail. My heart ached for him. I could not understand why the treatments did not work the same for everyone.

"How is my favorite dance student?" I asked brightly, taking his hand in mine.

"It would cheer me considerably if I could get you to sit on my lap," he winked. If any other man said that to me, I would be appalled. But coming from Don, it was endearing. I did not mind in the least.

I laughed and took his other hand. "Now, it is not customary for a lady to ask a gentleman to dance, but I couldn't help myself. Would you do me the honor?"

"Gentleman! Ha!" He laughed and let me help him stand. I could tell by the way he clung to me that he struggled to stay upright. Despite this, his grin curved upward, and his eyes twinkled brighter. I knew he needed this. He danced with me for a few minutes before asking for his wheelchair, and he sat back down, breathing heavily with his eyes closed.

"Forgive me, Don. This is too much exertion for you." I knelt at his side in concern.

"Don't worry about me. I only need to rest a bit. Next time, *I'll* ask *you.*" He waved one of the nurses over, and she pushed him out of the room.

"Ruth! We're in desperate need of help," Sandy called.

"What is it?"

She laughed and waved at Josh. "He's hopeless!"

He covered his heart, as if wounded. "I'm not that bad."

"You'd do better to teach him yourself." Sandy took my hand and pulled me closer.

His eyes softened as he looked at me. Something was different about him. His gaze reminded me of Charles when he looked upon Celeste.

I swallowed and took his hand, pushing the thought of Charles, Celeste, and any idea of love out of my mind. The music played on repeat while the group continued to practice. After thirty minutes, Steve stopped and peered at me with pleading eyes. "Please, Ruth. Can we listen to a different song?"

I laughed and nodded. He hurried to the MP3 player and switched on a modern tune. Before he returned to his wife, Steve took my hand, spun me around merrily, then left me standing with Josh. Steve pulled his wife close so that their cheeks pressed together and danced her around the room, spinning her out then in again, his arm around her waist and one hand holding hers against his chest. The back of my neck warmed as I watched them, yet I could not pull my eyes away. I had never seen anyone dance so close.

I was shaken from my reverie by the feel of a hand in mine. Josh pulled me to him, laying his hand lightly upon the small of my back and holding my hand at shoulder level. He did not hold me as close as Steve did his wife, for which I was grateful. Nevertheless, I felt the heat of his body near mine. He stepped to the beat and guided me around the other dancing couples. My feet did not seem to want to cooperate.

"I am afraid I only know how to dance the older dances. I have not danced like this before." I knew my cheeks must be crimson by now.

"Move with the beat, and I will guide you." He pulled away from me, lifted my arm above my head, gently turned me around. I spun once, twice, and then he pulled me back into his arms.

"That was thrilling," I said breathlessly.

He chuckled and turned us around in a half circle. He spun me one way, then the other. I squeaked out a laugh each time I turned. I could not help myself. The dance ended quite suddenly, and another began. In no time, four songs had come and gone, and we had danced to everyone. At the beginning of the fifth song, my attention was torn from

160

his handsome face.

"Good night, you two," Steve called and waved.

"Good night, Steve and Sherry," Josh called over my shoulder.

"Good night," I turned with a smile, noticing we were the last ones in the ballroom. I gazed back into Josh's smiling eyes and blushed. "Everyone has already left?"

"I suppose being the youngest couple counts for something. We can outlast them all!" He winked and spun me around once more.

The next song was slow, and the words caused my face to flush. I lowered my gaze to hide my embarrassment but could feel his eyes on me. Slowly, I lifted my head, lingering for a moment on his lips before meeting his beautiful eyes. His expression confused me. He appeared conflicted. He pulled me closer until I was pressed against him. Our bodies swayed together to the music. I could only breathe shallow, rapid breaths. The end of the song grew near, and he spun me one last time, then suddenly dipped me backward, his arm supporting me as he leaned in close. I gasped and held tightly around his neck so I would not fall. He laughed and lifted me upright.

My blush deepened, realizing my arms were still around his neck. I hastily lowered them, and he reluctantly let me go. I stepped back and studied the windows, feeling the loss of his warm hands upon my back and his body pressed close to mine. "Forgive me. I should not have … that is … we should not be alone. It is not proper."

"Are you always so old-fashioned?" His smile caused my heart to flutter.

"I suppose I am." The smile faded from my lips, "I hope being old-fashioned is not a problem."

He touched my cheek with his fingertips and looked into my eyes. "Not at all."

I watched his eyes glance quickly at my lips and suddenly felt myself in danger of being kissed. My first thought was how much I wanted

161

him to kiss me, but then a warning went off deep inside—the fear of not knowing what would come after forced me to step back.

"I should go." I hurried to the MP3 player and began pushing buttons, trying to get it to stop. I only managed to change the songs at a rapid rate.

I heard Josh chuckle behind me. "When it comes to electronics, you're completely lost, aren't you?" He reached around me and pushed a button on the side of the machine.

"Oh. Thank you." I turned around and found him looking at me with the same conflicted gaze. I stepped back and curtsied out of habit. "Good evening, Josh. I hope you rest well."

"Good night, Ruth. Sweet dreams." His smile was small and wistful before he turned away from me just as I turned from him and walked to the door. I glanced back while stepping from the room. I saw a look of anguish wash over his features as he ran his hands through his hair.

Had I caused that?

Chapter Twenty

1812 England, Abbie

Ugh! I was so tired of sitting. My hips were screaming at me, but that wasn't new. They pinched and cried nearly every day now. Walking only helped for a short time, and then I had nothing better to do than sit. Every evening, it was the same. "How on earth can people live like this?" I voiced my thoughts aloud without realizing it.

Charles' eyes rose from the book he was reading. "May I ask what you are referring to, Abbie?"

I sighed. "Nothing. I guess I'm bored stiff."

"Do you prefer staring at a telly for hours until you become stiff?" Celeste asked with a slight smile.

No matter what I do, I'm stiff. "At least then my mind would be distracted," I replied.

"You should try reading a book." Charles returned his attention to the page before him.

"You don't have the kind of books I like to read." I stood with slumped shoulders. "I'll just turn in for the night."

They bid me goodnight, but spending the evening alone in my room didn't appeal to me. I wandered the corridors restlessly. In the vicinity of the kitchens, my ears caught deep baritone voices singing a tune, and a moment later, a tenor and a bass joined in. Intrigued, I walked to the door, which stood ajar. I pushed it open a little further to see who sang the unfamiliar song. The door squeaked terribly, and the singing stopped abruptly. Around a large table sat some of the servants, several with forks frozen before their mouths, others with embroidery needles paused above their work. They all stared at me momentarily, then hastened to stand at attention.

The housekeeper, Mrs. Burke, was the only one who looked me in the eyes. "Is there something we can do for you, Mrs. Lambert?"

"Oh, you all don't need to stand for me. Please sit and act like I'm not here." I smiled and waved for them to sit. A few of them glanced at each other, and their heads still bowed, as if they didn't know what to do. Mrs. Burke cleared her throat. "Can we bring some tea to your room, perhaps?"

I peered around the door and noticed Albert standing there as well. It was evident I didn't belong. I took a step back. "Uh, no. I'll go now." I backed away, then spun around and hurried down the hall. *Awkward!*

Back in my room, I sat down on my bed. It was too early to sleep. Only children went to bed so early. Stepping to the window to view the sky, I discovered a full moon rising in the east. *Someone might as well enjoy it.* I picked up my spencer, pulled it on, leaving the room again.

Tiptoeing had been my specialty growing up. I silently slipped through the ballroom and out into the cool night air. A shiver ran down my back as I made my way through the hedges. I didn't get far when I heard a deep male voice. "Young ladies should not be out at night, unaccompanied."

I spun around and held my hand over my heart. I lowered my hand at the sight of Albert leaning against a tree. I sighed with relief. "Then accompany me."

Albert straightened. "I … uh … it would be … that is to say, I should not. You should go back inside."

"Why?" I asked with my hand on my hip.

"You could come to some harm out at night alone." He stared at me as if to say, "You're a smart girl, can't you figure that out?"

"Do you think someone would dare to mess with me?" I stood straighter.

He looked momentarily confused. "I believe you could easily be 'messed with,' as you put it."

"I'll have you know," I held my bare fists in front of me, bent my knees, and rocked back and forth on the balls of my feet. "I can hold my own in a fight."

His eyes nearly bugged from their sockets. "Mrs. Lambert!"

I danced around him like a prize boxer, ready for the fight of my life. "Oh yes, I can even take you on." I tried to keep my expression stern and disagreeable, but I found a smile pulling at the corners of my mouth. "I can fight you with my eyes closed." I closed my eyes tight, then peeked one open.

"Abbie, I do believe you are toying with me." His deep laughter made its way from behind the ceremonious stance he always held.

"Am not." I continued to move about, dodging an imaginary foe. "You don't believe me?"

"I cannot say. You almost have me convinced you could cut down any bloke that threatened you." He laughed. "You move about as if you know the art of boxing. I sincerely hope, Abbie, that a lovely lady, such as yourself, has never taken part in watching such things as men dancing about and beating each other senseless."

I stopped abruptly and looked at him. "You think I'm lovely?"

He lowered his head and rubbed the back of his neck, which caused his wig to wiggle.

It's so cute when he's shy. "Are you supposed to wear that all the time?" I asked, pointing to his white wig.

"Of course." He stood straight.

"May I see you with it off?" I moved closer to him.

"I should not take it off." He frowned.

Before he could suspect anything, I stood on my toes and reached for his wig, pulling it from his head and running just out of reach. "There. You do look nicer with it off, even if your hair is messy."

He ran his fingers through his dark, wavy hair. *Oh, how I'd love to do that.* He stood tall and straightened the collar of his coat. "You, Abbie, must be the most unabashed young lady I have ever had the privilege to know."

"Ah, but it is a privilege to know me, then?" I winked.

He leaped forward with such force it surprised me. I shrieked and ran, holding his wig high in the air. Of course, I knew his long legs could outrun me, and I would stand no chance against his reach to keep the wig from him, but I ran nevertheless.

I darted around a tree, keeping it between us. He stopped, smiled mischievously, and moved to his right. I moved to my right. He quickly darted left. I moved left and then right. *Ha! I faked him out!* I ran toward the bridge and had almost made it there when his large hand pulled at my side and spun me around. I nearly lost my balance but found I had been corrected by his right arm gently around my waist with my back against him. I still held his wig out before me, just out of his reach. I could hear his laughter in my ears. *Sweet music!*

"Abbie, give it back." His breath moved my hair and tickled my neck.

"Never." I lifted my legs so my body weight would work against him. I slipped from his arms, and he stumbled forward, trying hard not to step on me. I watched him stumble when I stood, lifting my skirts with my free hand, and started to run. I laughed a good maniacal laugh and glanced behind me. My heart leaped to see him already within arm's reach. I squealed, and he caught me once again. This time he had my left arm pinned to my side with his arm around my waist, just above my baby bump. I had my other arm with the wig out of his reach again.. I could tell he had difficulty holding me so he wouldn't push against my belly. I used that to my advantage. I wiggled to get free and turned my body around in his arms. The moment our eyes met, we both paused. I still held my hand up and arched behind me. His arm still held me against his body. His smile faded when he looked at me.

My heart seemed to increase in speed even though I had stopped running. Many thoughts were fighting for dominance in my head, most of which was how much I enjoyed being in his arms and how much I wanted to taste his lips.

He abruptly let go. "Very well, Abbie. You win." He smiled shyly, stepped away, and bowed.

"Giving up so soon?" I laughed to try to hide my disappointment.

"I know when I have been bested." His smile broadened.

"Is this wig all that important?" I held it up and brushed at its loose strands.

"Immensely."

"Would you lose your job over it?" I asked with one brow raised.

"If employed by someone other than Lord Elsegood, I might. Our master is quite forgiving, but you can be sure the price of such a wig would come out of my wages."

"Then perhaps I should take pity on you?" I asked, taking one step closer.

"Perhaps."

I stepped closer to him, lifted the wig, and placed it on his head, purposely upside down. I fiddled with it as long as possible to be near him again. His arms stayed stiff at his sides. I stepped back. "There. Perfect."

He rolled his eyes and reached for the wig, brushed back his hair and replaced it correctly. "Unabashed," he mumbled. He stood at attention once again. "Now that you have had your fun, may I beg you to return to the house?"

"Yes. You may beg." I folded my arms and lifted my chin.

"Abbie," he said sternly.

"Oh, all right." I rolled my eyes, took hold of his hand, slipped my fingers between his, and pulled him toward the house.

He stumbled along beside me, looking down at his hand in mine. "Perhaps you should not ... we should not be found holding hands like this, Abbie. Especially walking into the house at night ... alone. One might think ..."

I let go of his hand. "You could get into trouble?"

He hesitated, looking at me oddly, then nodded.

"Well, I wouldn't want that." I smiled and gave him a swift peck on the cheek, then hurried to my bedchambers, still wishing I could have tasted his lips, instead.

* * *

1812 England, Abbie

It was a snowy day, so I decided to pass the time by writing a song. It would be great to take my mind off my worries, at least. I was tired of sitting with Celeste while she received visitors for tea and went on calls to her neighbors. Not that I had anything against Celeste; she was wonderful to be around. It was all those snobby, pigheaded people she was forced to mingle with. Every last one of them irritated me. Over the last month, I made numerous excuses for missing afternoon tea. Today, I wouldn't give them the chance to ask.

I dropped a sheet of paper and one of Celeste's pencils onto the windowsill, and leaned against the glass, my feet dangling and my toes touching the closed curtain. I plucked my guitar and thought about a subject for my song. My guitar moved slightly to the kicking of my baby.

"Do you want me to sing you a lullaby?" I asked aloud.

I plucked a tune, testing out words to match. After about an hour, I had nearly completed my song. I started from the beginning and sang as I played.

> *Will I be the lucky one*
> *To whisper in your ear?*
> *Will I be the one*
> *To wipe away the tears?*
>
> *Baby in my womb*
> *You hear the whispers of my voice*
> *Will you recognize me*
> *When you see my face?*
>
> *Whispers to my darling*
> *Whispers in the night*
> *Whispers to my darling*
> *When I hold you tight*
>
> *When you are older*
> *Will I be the one*
> *To whisper I love yous*
> *At each rising sun?*

A baritone voice joined in during the last two lines, singing the lyrics in perfect harmony. I slowed to a stop and poked my head out of the curtain to find Albert sitting on the floor beside the window.

My heart quickened. "What are you doing?"

"Listening to you play," he responded.

"How long have you been there?"

"Long enough to learn some of the words." He stood. "I hope you do not feel I have intruded on your solitude. I apologize. I should go …" He rose to leave, but I caught the end of his coat.

"Don't be silly. Sit down." I moved over to make room. He sat beside me and smiled sheepishly. I smiled in return. "This is a rare treat to have you here. You've been far too busy lately to join me when I play." I continued plucking on the strings.

"Forgive me for that. I get busier when we have guests visiting. Plus, one of the other footmen has been ill, and I have needed to take over his work."

"Well, I'm glad you're here now." I started singing a soft country love song. Though I didn't know all the right cords, I played the best I could.

When I stopped, Albert looked at me as if pondering something.

"What?" I smiled

"You always sing songs about love. Why?"

I shrugged. "Maybe all the songwriters believe love is the most important thing to sing about. It's the most powerful of all emotions."

He didn't respond, so I began another love song, then stopped in the middle of it when I realized what the next words were. Singing something of *that* nature to someone with such old-fashioned views of romance and virtue would cause us to blush.

"That one was beautiful. Why did you stop?" he asked.

I blushed just thinking about it. "My fingers needed a rest." I placed

170

my guitar on the floor between my legs and leaned against the glass again, feeling his shoulder against mine.

"Do you ever think about the future and what it will be like in a hundred years, or two hundred years from now?" I asked.

"Sometimes," he said quietly, as if deep in thought. "When I think of it, I cannot help but think of the fantasy world you told me about. Maybe the future is like that."

"I believe it will be." I squeezed his hand, meaning to let go right away, but he held it tight. I glanced down at our hands. His thumb moved gently back and forth across my knuckles.

His attention had moved to my lips. I waited, holding my breath, hoping he would kiss me. He seemed to be frozen with a look of longing in his eyes. I smiled and whispered, "Albert?"

"Yes?"

"Kiss me, please."

He leaned down and turned so his shoulder wouldn't get in the way. Our lips met softly at first, then while his hand rested on the small of my back, he pulled me close and pressed his lips a little firmer against mine. A tingling sensation moved down to my toes, then back up again. My eyes closed in elation. Never had I been kissed like this before, like he cherished me. His warm, inviting embrace held more genuine emotion than anything I could dream up. It spoke directly to my heart, and my heart screamed back for more. *This is what I've been waiting for. This is what I've been singing about.*

I let go of my guitar, pushed back his wig, and ran my fingers through his hair while our lips moved together. My guitar slipped across my shins and crashed on the hard floor. He jumped and pulled away. Wide-eyed, he scrambled to his feet.

"Forgive me!" He grabbed his wig and stepped around the curtains.

I stood and slid them aside. Albert stepped back from me, looking like a deer caught in the headlights. "Albert?"

171

"I should not have kissed you." He looked around as if he would be struck by lightning at any moment.

"Why not?" My head still spun from the taste of him.

"You are a lady in mourning—and I am just a footman."

"Do you think I care about you being a footman?"

He closed his eyes and breathed deeply. "You are a widow with child, and I have nothing to offer." He looked as though he would cry. "I am so sorry." He hastily walked away.

"Albert!" My voice cracked with emotion.

He didn't stop, but disappeared around the corner. It felt as if he stomped on my heart with every footstep. I hung my head and sat heavily in the window, letting the tears fall.

Chapter Twenty-One

Present Day England, Ruth

The slap of my shoes echoed down the hall as I ran to the common room. I had to know for myself if he truly was gone. I flew around the corner into a rather large and unhappy man in uniform. Ignoring his protests, I hurried past to our sofa. Steve spotted me right before I reached the crowded couch. He took hold of my arm and pulled me toward the door. "You shouldn't be in here, Ruth."

"He cannot be gone. He just danced with me last night. He was fine then. Tell me he is well!" I tried to pull free, but he held my shoulders firm, moving me into the hall.

"Don is gone, Ruth. He knew it was going to happen. That's why he was here."

I stopped struggling as his words set in. "He knew? What do you mean he knew?"

"He's been through treatments three times already. It wasn't getting any better, and he knew it was only a matter of time, so he came here, where he could die among friends and not alone in his empty home. He wanted it this way."

My vision blurred with tears. "Is that why you are here, too? Are you dying?" *Is everyone dying? Is there no hope for any of us?*

"Me? Dying? Ha! I'm almost in the clear. I'll be going home soon." He sounded confident in his statement, but the hollowness in his eyes said otherwise.

"Why did you come here then?"

"Same as you. To get better without burdening the family. I know my wife couldn't handle watching me deal with the side effects of chemo. She's sensitive to such things." He looked me over, "Are you all right?"

I did not answer either way. I stood there in shock. My next words came out quiet and weak, "Why did you not tell me Don would …" I pushed Steve's hand away and hurried back down the hall where I had come from. I walked outside and ran down the small hill to the stable. I was greeted by a new stable hand and helped into a sidesaddle atop Norman, and the moment we were free of the stable, I urged him into a fast gallop.

He cannot be gone! He cannot!

I wanted to ride far, so far that I could get lost and be free of the emotions that threatened to strangle me. I rode to the east side of the property, only to be reminded that hundreds of other people now own most of it. I rode to the south and found the golf course and more houses. West was the river and more homes, along with the Shariton church and its graveyard. The stone grave markers stole a few heartbeats from my already aching soul. *Death is everywhere here.*

I rode north around the estate until I reached the gate beyond the boundaries. I paused and looked to the sky. It was late afternoon. If I left, I would most certainly be missed, but I needed to talk to someone I knew. I again urged Norman into a full gallop, riding hard for several miles until I came to the large tree that would take me home. I slid easily from the saddle, clipped the lead rope to Norman's bridle, and tied him securely to a tree trunk.

"Be a good boy while I am gone, okay Norman?" I smiled, and he neighed in response. He seemed uneasy, but I would not be gone long, and he would be safe in this quiet, out-of-the-way place.

I slipped through the arch from the tree root and continued on by foot to Shariton Park, pulling the hood of my wool jacket tightly over my ears as I went. I arrived well after dark and gasping for breath. My legs were weak and shaky when I climbed the steps to the front door. I froze mid-step when I noticed a figure sitting against the stone steps. He noticed me at the same moment.

"Who goes there?" the man called out, jumping to his feet.

I exhaled in relief. "Albert. You startled me."

"Miss Elsegood? Is that you?" He stepped closer to see my face in the moonlight.

"It is I."

"How did you get here? Were you not in London? How did you arrive?" He looked around as if searching for my mode of transportation.

"I am sorry, Albert. I have not the time or energy to discuss it with you now. I have only come to speak with Lord Elsegood, and I am in a hurry."

"Oh. Of course," He opened the door open and examined my odd clothing and hat.

"Why were you sitting out on the steps in the dark, Albert?" I stepped into the entry hall.

"I was walking the grounds and paused to rest on the steps for a moment," he answered. "Would you like to wait in the sitting room while I fetch Lord and Lady—"

"No. I can get them on my own." Both legs shook with each step up the stairs. *Please let me get to the top before I collapse.* At last I leaned heavily on the chamber door frame and knocked. Charles pulled the door open, his hair a mess, wearing only a nightshirt and breeches.

"Ruth! Lud, what are you doing here?" He pulled me into the room and shut the door.

"Ruth!" Celeste rushed to me and nearly knocked me to the floor. She held me so tight I feared she would crush her unborn child. She pulled away and examined me. "What are you doing here?"

I burst into tears before I could explain myself. Charles guided me to a sofa and sat me down. They sat on either side of me and held onto my hands.

"What is it, dear? What has happened?"

"Don passed away," I said through my tears.

"Don?" Celeste asked in confusion.

I nodded. "He is a friend of mine. He knew he was dying, so he came to Shariton Park to die among friends. You see, he did not want to be alone. He was the oldest man I have ever known and one of the funniest and most kind-hearted." I rambled on about Don and how I would watch sports with him and Steve while he held my hand and made me feel like I had a grandfather. I found myself laughing and crying as I reminisced.

"He sounds like someone worth knowing." Celeste rubbed my back as I lay with my head in her lap. My energy was spent.

"He *is* worth knowing."

"So why did you come, Ruth? Was it only to tell us of his passing?" Charles asked.

"No … I … I had to come because … I am afraid. I am afraid I will be next." I held my hands over my face as I sobbed harder.

Celeste chuckled. "You? Never." She poked me in the ribs. "You are a fighter, Ruth. You will get better and be back with us in no time at all."

"But what are the chances of my getting better? What if the cancer comes back?" I lifted my head and wiped my eyes.

"From what I understand, the chances of recovery are very good." Celeste's confidence comforted me some.

I sighed and focused on the patterned slate floor. "I was able to dance with Don last night before he passed on. The Christmas ball we have planned is going to be grand. Sandy said she is going to fill the room with white lights. I do not have any idea how she will accomplish such a feat." *And Don will not be there to see it.*

"Just wait. You will *love* the Christmas season, Ruth! The lights, the decorations … it will astound you! Please feel free to purchase gifts for your friends. We can certainly afford it."

"Good heavens! I had not even thought about gifts! What should I get for them?"

"Slippers and ties," Celeste laughed.

I grew quiet and thought hard about what I could possibly get for Josh. Why he suddenly consumed my thoughts, I could not say. I only knew I did not want to fail at getting him something grand.

"Can you stay the night, Ruth? Or will you be missed?" Charles' voice broke through my preoccupied mind.

I stood abruptly. "I most certainly will be missed. I have a horse tied to the tree beside the arch."

"I will accompany you back." Charles made his way to the door, which separated his and Celeste's chambers. "Meet me downstairs."

I nodded and watched him close the door behind him. I hugged Celeste and sighed. "I have missed you."

"And I've missed you," she smiled. "I thought it would be months before seeing you again."

"When I learned of your condition, I was thrilled." I touched her growing belly lightly. "How I wish I could have giggled and cried joyfully with you when you realized."

She gestured toward the door, "Come. We must not keep Charles waiting." She pulled on a dressing gown, and we walked out into the corridor together.

"Damn!" A young woman appeared around the corner dressed in a nightgown, her blond hair hanging loose over her shoulders. "Oh!" Her tears glistened in the dim moonlight shining through the nearby window.

"Abbie! Why are you out of your bed?" Celeste reached out for her. "Are you unwell?"

"Oh. No. I'm fine—hunky dory. My legs get restless at night, and walking the halls helps. It can be annoying at times." She wiped her tears and glanced at me, her eyes lingering on my hat and the bare head beneath it.

"Abbie, this is Charles' sister, Ruth. Ruth, this is Abbie, the young lady I wrote about."

"Oh! Ruth! I'm so happy to meet you," Abbie rushed up and squeezed me in a quick but secure embrace. I didn't have the time to react before she pulled away. "I feel like I know you already. I'm guessing you just returned from our time?" she gestured toward Celeste.

I nodded and gave a weak smile.

"You didn't happen to bring any chocolate with you, did you?" she asked, grinning hopefully.

I laughed. "Forgive me. My visit was unplanned. Perhaps next time." I immediately felt at ease with Abbie and found her completely adorable and full of spirit.

Her shoulders slumped. "I've been craving that stuff for months, that and peanut butter. Chocolate here is not the same." She sighed. "C'est la vie."

"I hear you are learning the life of the elite?"

She rolled her eyes. "Trying."

"Well, do keep Celeste on her toes. We would not want her to be bored," I smiled.

Celeste rolled her eyes and laughed. "Do not encourage her."

I jumped at the sound of a man clearing his throat behind me. I caught Abbie's pained expression before I turned to find Albert standing at the top of the stairs. "Miss Elsegood, my lord, is waiting outside with the horses."

"Thank you, Albert. Please tell him I will be there presently."

He nodded and slipped away.

An idea formed in my mind and I looked to Celeste for help. "Do you know that painting you did of Shariton Park? The one in the yellow room?"

She nodded.

"May I give it to Josh for Christmas? He is quite fond of old paintings."

Her face brightened. "Of course! I have painted so many of Shariton Park. Pick whichever you like best."

I curtsied to Abbie. "It was a pleasure to meet you. I hope we will see each other again soon."

"I'm sure we will." She smiled and glanced nervously at Albert, then leaned in and whispered, "I wish you well with your treatments."

"Thank you." I smiled and hurried down the corridor toward my room with Celeste close behind. I reached my vanity and opened the box that held my most treasured belongings.

"What are you doing?" Celeste asked.

I held up the necklace that had once belonged to my mother, which now lay in a glass case in Josh's study. "This necklace, along with a few books and some paintings, is all that is left of our family heirlooms. Put it in a safe place where it cannot be stolen or damaged." I held up the matching earrings, "These will complete the set."

Chapter Twenty-Two

1812 England, Abbie

I stood there feeling like a fool. I had walked the halls to find relief from my aching legs and my broken heart. I hadn't seen Albert since we'd kissed in the window yesterday until he came upon the three of us in the hall. He had walked away without a word to me. I stood at the top of the stairs peering toward the entryway. Seeing him only caused me pain, and my entire body ached to be in his arms again. I stood there staring off into the darkness, wishing.

"Abbie?"

I jumped at the sound of Albert's voice. I didn't realize he had come back inside.

"Are you unwell?" His eyes looked sad. His hand moved toward me, then paused.

Tears pooled in my eyes, and the words of rejection pierced my heart once more. "I am well enough," I whispered.

"Please forgive me, Abbie. I did not mean to hurt you." His voice cracked.

I turned my head and wiped away the sudden tears. "Do you always work so late?"

"No. Not usually. I happened upon Ruth outside." He paused. "It seems a bit unusual, her showing up like this … dressed that way, and her hair … it seems to have fallen out."

I shrugged. I didn't know what to say.

"You seem less surprised by this than I am," he pressed.

I remained silent. What could I possibly say to explain this away?

"What treatments is she having? What ails her, Abbie?"

I ducked my head uncomfortably. *Did he hear what I said to Ruth?* "It's not my place to say."

He nodded slowly. "I understand. You should go back to your chambers and get some rest."

"As should you," I responded.

He gave a curt nod, then turned and walked briskly away. I felt my heart being drawn after him as if a thread connected us. I wanted to throw my arms around him and never let go. I shook my head to rid it of such thoughts. *Don't be stupid, Abbie.*

* * *

1812 England, Ruth

I pulled on the reins of my beautiful horse and patted his neck. "Do you suppose someone might have found my horse I left and will be waiting?"

Charles pulled his horse to a stop and looked toward the tree ahead. The cloud of his breath lit up in the light of the moon. "If they found him there, they could be waiting nearby or possibly searching in close proximity."

"Then I should go the rest of the way on foot." I slid off my horse, as did Charles. I was dismayed when my feet hit the ground, and my knees almost gave way. I had weakened rather quickly. I held onto the saddle momentarily, trying to gather the strength I needed to continue. I took a steady breath, then turned and handed the reins to Charles.

I continued with the painting tucked under my arm. Charles followed with careful steps behind me. I stopped next to the portal and peeked around the tree. A silhouette of a man sitting astride a horse had his back to us; only the lower half of his body was visible through the arch.

Now or never. If his back remained turned and he did not see us suddenly appear, the man would not suspect anything of this old tree. I reached back and pulled Charles through the portal with me. Once we made it through, the man turned.

"Ruth!" Josh appeared surprised, then relieved. He slid off his horse and took me by the shoulders, almost knocking the painting out from under my arm. He looked ready to pull me to him until he noticed Charles behind me. He paused and let his arms drop. "Are you okay?"

"I am well."

"She was a little shaken up over the death of a friend and needed someone to comfort her," Charles stated. My brother inspected Josh up and down as if evaluating him. Josh did the same in return, with a look of curiosity, most likely from the odd clothing Charles wore … again. I could not imagine what he must think of Charles.

"You've been gone for hours. I thought the worst had happened," his voice wavered.

"Forgive me, Josh. I did not mean to cause you distress." I shifted my weight and tightened my hold on Charles' arm. "It was wrong of me to disappear without telling anyone where I had gone."

182

"Where *did* you go?" He glanced around. "Did you hear me calling you?"

"I am staying close by. She did not need to travel far," Charles explained.

"Why did you leave Norman?" Josh asked me.

"He was tired, and I needed to move my legs." I hoped my excuse was good enough. The wind picked up at that moment and caused us all to shiver.

"We should be heading back. A snowstorm is coming." He looked at the sky and pulled an odd object from his coat pocket. He pushed the side and spoke into it. "George, Blake, Robby, do you copy? Over."

Instantly, several voices sounded from the object. Both Charles and I stared in a state of awe.

"I have found her in good order and we are heading back to the house. Over." He slipped the object back into his pocket. I let the look of wonder fall from my face and nudged Charles, hoping he would do the same. Charles cleared his throat and resumed a look of disinterest.

"Will you come back with us and stay … uh … Charles, was it?"

Charles hesitated. "Of course."

"Celeste may worry, Charles," I stated.

"Celeste?" Josh looked back and forth between the two of us.

"My wife," Charles said to him, then leaned toward me, lowering his voice. "I do not believe it would be wise to let an unmarried man escort you through the forest alone."

Heat warmed my neck at the thought of all that had already occurred between Josh and me, of which my brother had no idea.

Josh chuckled. "Boy, you two are old-fashioned." His laughter faded at the sight of Charles' stern expression. Josh cleared his throat and held up his hand. "Upon my honor, no harm will come to Ruth while she is in my care."

Charles stiffened and looked Josh up and down once more.

"I trust him, Charles." I whispered in his ear, "You must remember what time we are in."

"Very well. I trust my sister's good sense." He narrowed his eyes at Josh. "But I will pay a call soon to see that she is being well looked after."

"Point taken. You will find her well when you do come to visit. She doesn't receive many guests, so I'm sure she'd be happy to see you." Josh's voice rang with accusation. I glanced at Charles nervously and read the anger in his eyes.

He nodded curtly, then took my hand and kissed my cheek.

I smiled and hugged him with my free arm. The other still held the painting. Charles helped me mount Norman, and I smiled in amusement as he eyed the stallion. I could tell he approved of the horse but he looked leery of my riding him.

"Are you sure this stallion will not throw you? He seems rather skittish." He held Norman's bridle and patted his neck.

"Norman is a little spirited, but your sister likes him, and he in turn, seems to like her," Josh smiled wistfully.

After I had situated myself in the saddle, Charles handed the painting up to me. I tucked it under my arm and smiled at him before the tears flooded my lashes, "Thank you, dear brother."

He held my hand. "I will see you soon."

"Goodbye," I whispered.

Josh and Charles nodded at each other, then we turned the horses around and trotted away. I glanced back and waved before Charles disappeared through the arch. The wind threatened to blow my hat off, so I opened my coat, tucked the painting inside, then held tight to my hat.

"What is that? A painting?" Josh asked.

"Yes."

"I'd like to see it when we get back."

"Maybe someday you will." I smiled.

184

We were silent as we rode on. He seemed deep in thought. There were moments when I thought he might be crying. My thoughts turned to Don. I half expected to find him in the common room, saving a spot on the couch, welcoming me back with a joke and a wink.

As the minutes passed, I found it hard to stay in the saddle. I could not let my body lean forward. The framed painting kept me from slouching, and the energy it took to remain upright was draining.

"How is everyone dealing with … Don's … death?" I asked slowly.

"Huh? Oh … all right, I suppose. Death always seems to rattle everyone around there … understandably so." His voice grew somber and deep that I could barely discern what he said.

"I suppose you have seen enough of it. Is that why you are always gone?"

He nodded slowly. "Partially."

Just when we reached the road, several other men on horseback joined us, asking where I had gone. I gave vague answers, as always, and tried to keep silent when I could. When we reached the manor, I handed someone the painting, slid off my horse, and instantly crumbled to the ground. My legs refused to hold me up.

"Ruth!" Josh knelt at my side. "Are you hurt?"

"Just weak." My vision darkened, then returned to normal. He wrapped his arms around my waist, pulled me to my feet, and held me at his side. I put one arm around his neck and looked at the man holding the painting. "Please, do not let anyone see that."

He nodded and held the painting to his chest.

"Can you take it to her room, Robby?" Josh asked him. He nodded and hurried inside.

A few large snowflakes floated past my eyes and landed on my coat sleeve. I blinked at the sky to watch the white flakes floating down to earth. I looked at Josh and smiled. "It's snowing."

He smiled in return. "So it is."

185

I tried to let go of him and stand on my two feet but my legs were about to give out. At the same time, my vision darkened again, then returned just as quickly. I turned to Josh, "I feel fa …" Josh's grip tightened around me, and he lifted my legs into his arms. Everything grew dark, but I could hear voices and feel Josh's footsteps as he carried me. Cold air touched my head when my hat slipped off. Josh asked someone to retrieve it.

I kept my eyes shut tight and clutched his coat collar with my head resting against his chest. His smell soothed my senses. Once in my room, he placed me on my bed. I missed being in his arms and reached for his hand. He held it for a moment before he was shooed away by the many nurses hovering around me, checking my vitals and asking me questions. When the nurses were satisfied I was well, I looked around the room for Josh, but he had left. My heart constricted, remembering the pained expression on his face as he'd retreated from the room.

* * *

1812 England, Celeste

"Good afternoon, Mrs. Russel, Miss Russel, Miss Caroline. I am pleased you could come." I greeted my neighbors with a curtsy. *Why did they have to come today?* I didn't feel well. I avoided visits with this particular family as much as possible. Today, however, they had caught me off guard.

"Lady Elsegood! We are delighted to come—we were beginning to think you were avoiding us!" Mrs. Russel's eyes nearly disappeared when she smiled. "Of course, it was not easy for us to come over the last week, you know, with the weather and what."

"Yes, the weather has improved today." I looked at Abbie. "You remember Mrs. Lambert."

186

"Yes." Mrs. Russel's voice grew icy, and she hardly glanced at Abbie. She moved into the room and sat down. Her two young daughters followed suit, which surprised me. Mrs. Russel should have let me introduce her daughters to Abbie. I looked at Abbie, who stood there waiting to be introduced. She shrugged, then moved to sit across from the woman on the sofa. I joined her and paused to see if Mrs. Russel would recognize her blunder, but she began talking as if nothing had been missed.

When the opportunity arose, I turned to Albert and asked him to inform the cook to prepare tea for our guests. Before Mrs. Russel could start up again, I spoke. "Miss Russel, Miss Caroline, may I introduce my dear friend from America, Mrs. Abbie Lambert."

Miss Russel gave a curt nod. Miss Caroline smiled. "I am pleased to make your acquaintance, Mrs. Lambert. I have always wanted to meet someone from America. I hear so little about—"

"Caroline." The tone in Mrs. Russel's voice caused her daughter to shy away and sit silently with her eyes averted from us.

Mrs. Russel began clucking away as if nothing had happened. She completely ignored Abbie's questions or comments and shot menacing stares at Miss Caroline when she tried to answer Abbie. I began to feel quite fed up with Mrs. Russel's behavior and was about to convey my distress when Abbie stood, sighed, and excused herself from the room.

"She gets tired in the afternoons," I told the women as they watched Abbie leave.

"Well," Mrs. Russel held her head high, "I, for one, am quite relieved she is so easily fatigued. Now I can speak to you about the real reason we came."

I stiffened. "Pray, what would you need to speak to me about, Mrs. Russel, that cannot be said in front of Mrs. Lambert?"

"Now you know I do not like to speak ill of others, especially the unfortunate …"

187

Yeah, right. Mrs. Russel was well known as the town gossip. Therein lay the reason for my dislike of her.

"Well, everyone is talking—and I would not have come to you if I were not concerned for you, my dear Lady Elsegood—as you know, I am very attentive when assisting where I can."

Her arrogance was making me sick. "You are indeed, Mrs. Russel." Miss Caroline rolled her eyes, and I barely resisted a smile.

Mrs. Russel smiled and continued. "When I heard what all the talk was about, I knew I had to come and warn you, my dear Lady Elsegood—for I would not want any harm to come to you or your growing family."

Get to the point.

"Proceed, Mother." Miss Russel echoed my thoughts. She sighed as if she were the most bored woman alive.

Mrs. Russel shot her a look of annoyance, then smiled at me. "I have heard that Mrs. Lambert is, in fact, a witch, Lady Elsegood."

My eyes widened.

"Oh, you may well be surprised. I was, too! I could not believe such a thing, but when I heard the report of all she had done, I could not help but believe." She leaned forward with enthusiasm, eyes wide and lips twitching. "I have heard she uses live chickens in her spells to curse her enemies. She sneaks about at night, poisoning their livestock—"

I held up my hand. "Mrs. Russel, please. I do not wish to hear such foolishness."

"But it is true. I heard she concocted some spell that greatly decreased the size of Mr. Baily's wardrobe!"

I had difficulty holding back my smile at the mention of "the spell" Mrs. Russel spoke of.

"She has also been seen roaming the countryside in her—"

"Mother!" Miss Caroline stood abruptly. "We have trespassed on Lady Elsegood's time long enough. Besides, I am feeling a little unwell.

188

We should be going." She smiled sweetly at me. "Thank you, Lady Elsegood. It was a delight to see you again, as always."

Mrs. Russel appeared appalled at her daughter's outburst but rose to her feet along with Miss Russel.

"I suppose I should not neglect my daughter's health, Lady Elsegood. I hope you will take heed of my warning and get rid of the nuisance so you may rest well knowing your family will be safe."

"Mother, please." Miss Caroline's tone was that of a scolding mother. Mrs. Russel gave her daughter a venomous look as they walked out the door.

Miss Caroline paused before she slipped out and leaned closer to me. "I hope my mother has not upset you, Lady Elsegood. I am afraid she takes things too far at times."

"Thank you for your concern, Miss Caroline. You're a good daughter to Mrs. Russel and a great comfort to me." I smiled and squeezed her hand in gratitude.

"Goodbye, Lady Elsegood."

"Goodbye, Miss Caroline." I watched the women load into the waiting carriage to take them home. *At least one person in the family has their head on straight.*

Chapter Twenty-Three

1812 England, Abbie

"I thought you might be here." Celeste's feet made a path through the blanket of snow on the ground.

I raised my hand to block the sun that nearly blinded me when I looked up. "Hey."

She chuckled, most likely at my use of the more modern form of greeting. She bent to clear the snow from the bench, sat beside me, and looked at my guitar. "Serenading the trees, I see."

I shrugged. "Actually, I'm having difficulty feeling up to it." I had sat on the bench for some time without playing an entire song. Most songs I knew were love songs. My heart felt too heavy to play anything of the sort.

Celeste placed her hand on my shoulder to comfort me. "I'm sorry about Mrs. Russel's witch accusation. Now you see why I have tried to avoid her."

"Her daughter didn't seem that bad," I said, trying to find the positive.

"Yes. I believe she has more sense than her mother."

I nodded in agreement.

"There's something more than Mrs. Russel that's bothering you, isn't there?"

I stiffened. "What do you mean?"

"You have been moping around for days. It's not like you."

Celeste was too perceptive.

"I ..." I sighed. "I don't know. I guess it's this place. I had hoped I'd find friends, and this would be a happy place to stay for a while, but it's a lot different than I expected."

Celeste looked confused. "I thought you had made friends, Abbie. I'm your friend—even more than a friend. I think of you as a sister."

"I didn't mean you. You feel like a sister to me as well. I ... I hoped with so many people here I could enjoy many friendships."

"You mean friendships with the servants?"

I nodded.

"It's not common to have friends among the servants, Abbie. It's not in their character to befriend those they serve. I respect them and treat them with kindness, but to be buddy buddy with them is ... well, odd. They respect us, but anything beyond that is viewed as improper. They're taught to know their place, so to speak." She studied me. "I thought you had befriended Molly and her brother, at least, despite the fact that they are servants."

"I thought so, too. I don't see them much anymore." I examined the snow on the ground while I talked.

"They work hard, and for them to have a moment of free time is extremely rare."

I knew the real reason why I didn't see Albert, but I didn't want to admit it to anyone, especially with the heavy feeling of rejection hanging over me. I sat up straight and breathed deeply.

"Is there something else bothering you?" she asked.

"You are too perceptive, Celeste."

"One of my faults." She smiled and waited for me to speak.

"It frustrates me the way people are treated in this day. With social class and titles, family histories, land you may or may not own, how many servants you have, and blardy blah blah blah! How do you keep from going insane and punching everyone in the nose for their pride and stupidity?"

She chuckled. "There are times it irritates me as well, but I think I was better prepared for it than you when I first arrived. I had studied the culture of the era and read many novels."

"I suppose being a Jane Austen nut—er, fan—has benefits."

She laughed and nodded. "You know, much of that same pride still thrives in our day. Pride has run rampant since time began."

"I suppose you're right. There's no escaping it."

The wind picked up, and Celeste shivered. "Well, I'm going to head back in. Would you like to join me?" She stood and brushed off her coat.

"I'm going to stay out here for a few more minutes." I wasn't done thinking through the song I'd been struggling to write.

"Do not stay out too long. It's almost time to dress for dinner." She smiled and strolled back down the garden path.

I sat for a few more minutes until the cold wind drove me inside. It had started to rain before I reached the edge of the garden. I tucked my head in and hovered over my guitar to protect it, not watching where I was heading. I collided with a large man who seemed to be expecting the collision, for he held my shoulders to keep me from falling, then hurried me under a stone arch against the wall. My eyes met Albert's handsome face when I lifted my chin.

"You should be more careful, Abbie."

I smiled at the sound of my name and felt happy he still used it. "If it means bumping into you, I think I will continue to be reckless."

He smiled back, but his eyes remained solemn. "You have been playing?"

I nodded. "Not well, I'm afraid. I've not had a friend to play for, you see."

His smile fell completely.

"Can't we still be friends?" I tried not to sound too desperate.

"Back to how it used to be?" he whispered.

I nodded. I didn't know if it could ever be the way it used to be. I knew I would always look at Albert's strong arms, wish I were in them, and study his lips hoping I could kiss them. Going back to how it used to be would be tough, but if it meant talking to him once again, I'd do anything.

"I would like that, Abbie," he said.

* * *

Present Day England, Ruth

If I had known my trip into the woods and through time would cause me to be completely fatigued, I would not have gone. I slept for twenty-four hours and woke feeling rested but weakened from lack of food. Even after eating a large meal, I still felt drained.

There was little time to mourn before I woke on the morning of Don's funeral. I dragged my feet as I readied myself, fearing what the day might bring.

I dressed in my only black dress, which Celeste had chosen for me. It hung just below my knees, leaving my bare legs exposed. I felt awkward and vulnerable in it. The only nice pair of shoes Celeste had picked out were high heels. I wondered if I would be able to walk in them.

Most of the snow had blown away or melted over the last day, so I hoped I would not slip or fall during the funeral. I wobbled a little on my way down to breakfast and found several others dressed in black, waiting and eating.

"Celeste. What happened to you the other night? We heard you took off out into the woods." Sandy slid into the chair beside me with a plate full of food.

"Yes, I did, but only to visit my brother."

"Your brother resides in the woods?" She looked ready to laugh as if it were a good joke.

"On the other side of the wood." *Time to change the subject.* "How are you?"

Her eyes filled with tears, "Oh … you know. It's hard to see those around us die."

Perhaps this subject was not the best choice. We both started to weep and found ourselves without tissues or handkerchiefs.

"They should put boxes of tissues out on every table, in every corner, in every room when someone passes away here," Sandy shook her head and tried wiping her tears away with her fingers.

"We should stop behaving like a couple of water pots and think of the happier, more delightful things we remember about him." I wiped away my tears and smiled as we reminisced over the funny things Don had said or done. He was quite the character, and it was not hard to laugh when remembering him.

After the services and arriving at the cemetery, I found it difficult to think of happier times. Seeing his family—or lack thereof—caused heartache. Standing among the grave markers of people who had been born decades after me was surreal, yet I still stood there living and breathing. I hovered at the edges of the gathering, allowing the family the space and time to grieve together.

194

Ironically, the sun shone brightly and warmed our bodies, yet I felt so cold inside. *Will I end up like him soon, or will I live a long life?* The weight of my own mortality crushed down on me and made it challenging to keep my breathing even and my tears to a minimum. *I do not want to die.*

When the last prayer was said, and people began moving away from the open grave, I lifted my head to find Josh watching me with his arms folded. My heart instantly lightened and fluttered like it had been turned into a million butterflies. He gave a small smile and waved his hand in greeting. I moved to step toward him but found my high heels had sunk into the earth. I tried to jerk them free and nearly toppled over. My arms frantically waved around in circles while I tried to right myself. Josh stepped to my side instantly and took hold of my arm with one hand and my waist with the other.

"Not the best shoes for a place like this," he said.

"I wish I had another choice."

"Let me help you." He bent down and placed one warm hand on my leg right above my foot and the other at my heel. A warm sensation ran through my body at his touch, and heat rose in my cheeks. My legs felt entirely naked at the moment, and a man—a handsome and extremely attractive man—was touching them. He pulled the heel out of the ground and did the same with the other.

He stood, keeping his head down and looking at my shoes. "Try keeping your weight on your toes."

I shifted my weight forward and nearly fell again. Josh held me up by holding my arm.

"Are you blushing, Ruth?" There was laughter in his voice.

I raised my eyes and saw him grinning at me. I glanced around at the people slowly leaving the graveside and held my chin up. "Laugh if you must, but I have never had a man touch my leg before." *Why did I just admit that to him?* The look on his face did not help my embarrassment.

"Never?" He smiled. "I don't believe I've ever met anyone as virtuous as you, Ruth. I find it refreshing."

I lowered my head to hide my smile, peering at my feet again. *Is the world so bad that my virtue is an oddity?* I tried to walk away on my toes, but the ground still held the night's moisture, and the traction on my shoes was nonexistent. I slipped on my first step. Luckily, Josh still had my hand.

"How did you get out here with those on?" He held me tighter around my waist and began slowly walking with me.

"I ..." My head buzzed at his touch. I could not think straight, "I ... believe the ground was not quite as soft then, and Steve had my arm. They did stick a little." Every few steps, I was slipping or sticking, needing saving. Each time, Josh helped free my shoes from the soft earth. I blushed further with each touch of his hand, and my heart nearly flew out of my chest. Halfway back to where the cars were parked, the driver that shuttled everyone from Shariton stood waiting for us.

"Go on without her. I'll take her back." Josh called to him while he still held me tight to his side. The man waved, then stepped into the shuttle and drove away. The only people left were close relatives who had stayed behind at Don's grave.

We finally made it to Josh's car, and he helped me inside. When we pulled out onto the busy street, he turned the wrong direction.

"Is not our home back that way?" I pointed.

"Home?" He smiled at me.

"Shariton," I corrected myself. I stiffened when a car rushed past, too close for comfort.

"I'm glad you think of it as home."

I smiled inwardly. *You have no idea.*

Chapter Twenty-Four

Present Day England, Ruth

"I thought we could take you shopping and get better shoes."

"But I do not have any money with me," I protested and clung to my seat as we passed a rather large motor car.

"Don't worry about that. It's only a pair of shoes." Josh drove into the shopping center parking lot where I'd come with Celeste and Charles during our first days here. He helped me out of the car and led me into a shoe store where he assisted me in picking out some slippers. After paying for them, he knelt and replaced my shoes with new ones. I blushed again at his gentle touch. He led me around the shopping center, observing clothes, hats, books, and more. He was shocked when some of the books we looked at were unfamiliar to me, and he vowed he would not rest until I read the copies he had in his library. When we made it back to the car, I was disturbed by the late hour.

"Well, it's almost dinner time. How about I take you to my favorite place to eat in London?" he asked.

London? Can we really get to London soon enough to dine tonight? "Will they not expect me back?"

"No. Do you want to go back?"

I hesitated. I was tired but hungry, and spending time with Josh was always appealing. I wondered what sort of outing this was and what my brother would think. After all, for me, spending time alone with a man was unheard of, and taking a meal alone together seemed positively scandalous. Still, my conversations and telly viewing had taught me that intimate friendships between a man and a woman were nothing to raise an eyebrow about now. But I wondered if he meant to court me. Did he expect something romantic to come of this?

My mind and heart debated for only a moment before I agreed to accompany him. We drove to a train stop and boarded a long moving box. I tried to portray some sort of familiarity with the things around me, but my racing heart and the anxious jerks revealed my inward turmoil. I gazed out the window, watching the land fly by as my knuckles grew white from gripping the seat. I had never traveled so fast in all my life.

Josh's soft chuckle took my attention away from the window. He took my hand in his and squeezed it. "Your nails might just cut the seat to shreds if you're not careful."

"Forgive me."

"Do you dislike trains?" He peered at me quizzically.

I shook my head. "Oh, no. Trains are delightful. I ride them all the time." From the look of doubt in his eyes, I could see my lie was not convincing. "I mean, I did when I was younger." I returned to the window, striving to appear calm and at ease.

Josh remained silent, his hand still holding mine. My hand tingled with every movement his thumb made as it moved back and forth. My heart thumped hard in my chest. I wished I could let go of the façade I had been living and tell him everything true about myself, then let him wrap his arms around me and never let go. Did he feel the same? Did his heart pound in his ears at the nearness of me, too?

The bigger question that had continued to return to my mind for days, consuming my thoughts, was whether I loved him? Was it love I felt? Did this reaction to his touch mean love? I had thought of him every second of each day for several weeks. I wondered if he would be home. I wondered if he thought of me. I wondered if he ached to be near me as I ached to be near him—to understand and listen to him.

Was all this love?

He, too, gazed thoughtfully out the window. When I focused not on the view outside but on the reflection of us in the window, I could see the sun highlighting his hair and giving it a red tint. The sad look I caught in his eyes forced my breath to halt.

"Why did you open your home and turn it into a cancer center?" The question came to me, and without a thought, it had found its way out of my lips.

He cleared his throat and watched his thumb rub mine. "It was my late wife's idea, and I saw it through after she passed on."

I bit my lip. I'd wondered about his wife at times, but never wanted to press him to share. "I am truly sorry for your loss. I'm sure it is difficult."

He turned and looked directly into my eyes. "It hasn't been difficult … not until you arrived."

I swallowed hard. "Why is that?"

He shook his head and raised his brows. "It's strange, but … you remind me of her. You have the same smile."

"Well, we are—" I almost said *related,* but caught myself in time.

He looked at me, confused. "Are what?"

I shook my head. "Nothing." We were silent for a moment, then I glanced back at him, "I am sorry I have made it harder on you."

His hand tightened on mine, and he gave me the smallest of smiles, one that held so many conflicting emotions.

I could not know what went on in his heart. It must be broken after losing someone so dear. My desire to learn more about his late wife grew, but how could I ask about her without letting my own secrets slip? Even more important, how could I entertain the idea that something romantic could happen between us? Or that he would even want that?

My thoughts swirled around the possibilities of what might lie ahead. I daydreamed of dancing with him the way Steven and his wife had danced with each other. How thrilling it would be …

"Ruth."

My eyes fluttered open when his breath tickled my ear, and he shifted his weight. "Dear me. Did I fall asleep?"

"It's all right. You slept for fifteen minutes. I think you needed it."

"Did I really?" My cheeks flamed.

The sun had set, and the city lights flew by. The train entered a stone ravine, stopping in a grand building. Josh escorted me off the loud metal beast and into the waiting throng. He seemed to know where to go. The words King's Cross Station appeared at every turn, and metal and brick surrounded me everywhere. The doomed crisscrossing of it over my head gave me a feeling of apprehension. What if it all came tumbling down?

Josh continued to follow the crowds of people toward the strangest set of staircases I had ever laid eyes on. People stepped on, and without moving their legs, they were taken up or down, depending on the stairs they stood upon. "A moving staircase?"

Josh tilted his head to the side. "What was that?"

I shook my head and paused when he stepped onto the moving stair that grew from the ground and made its way down. His hand tightened on mine as his body moved away from me. He took two steps back up the changing stairs to take hold of my hand, which had slipped out of his. My heart tightened with fear at the foreign experience.

From behind, someone shoved my body forward. My feet stepped onto the metal step and half of the step instantly fell away, causing me to tip forward into Josh's arms.

"Watch it!" Josh scowled at the man, pulling me tighter against him.

The man's words came out in a rush of foreign language. Those on the staircase beside us passed us going up, making my head spin. The motion from the moving stair stirred my stomach in a most unpleasant way.

"Are you all right?" Josh asked when I hesitated before stepping off onto stable ground once again.

"Quite." Looking around, I found myself in a room filled with strange objects and even stranger people. Arched tunnels led from the room in different directions. Josh paid a man who gave us slips of paper, which Josh then put through a machine. A metal bar moved, allowing us to continue on into one of the tunnels. The noise bouncing off the walls made speaking difficult without raising our voices, so I remained silent. My eyes must have been as large as teacups.

At last, Josh stopped beside a track. "Another train?" I asked.

He tilted his head again and narrowed his eyes. "Have you never been on the Tube?"

Oh, dash it. At the rate I am going I will expose my secrets before the day is out. At that moment, a great noise came from a dark tunnel. It grew louder and louder.

"Hold onto your hat," Josh warned.

I did as he instructed and held my hat just in time. A train rushed by, bringing a surge of wind along with it, and my dress lifted and waved, which brought on the burning in my cheeks. Doors slid open in front of us, and Josh, with his arm around my waist, helped me onto a train much like the one we had ridden into London.

"Mind the gap between the train and the platform," said an invisible woman from somewhere above our heads.

The ride on the Tube was very different from the train where far more people moved on and off. It sped forward much faster, with shorter distances between stops. I had no place to sit. Thankfully, Josh helped to keep my footing.

When we finally stepped out of the noisy underground tunnel, I first noticed the smell. The London I knew had the scent of soot, animal dung, and sometimes human waste. This London smelled only of rain and food cooking nearby. Everything seemed much larger, brighter, and busier, completely different from my time.

"Have you ever had sushi?" Josh asked, taking my hand.

"Sushi? Pray tell, what is sushi?"

He chuckled. "Raw fish."

I wrinkled up my nose in disgust.

He laughed harder and quickly touched the end of my nose. "I figured you hadn't."

He led me into a building with tables, chairs, people, and round paper lanterns. Glasses and silverware clinked together and mingled with quiet chatter. A beautiful waitress led us to a table with a soft bench on one side and two chairs on the other. Josh gestured for me to sit on the bench and slid in next to me. I had not expected him to sit beside me, but I did not protest.

We had an enjoyable time laughing and talking during dinner. Every new flavor elicited a reaction from me, delighting Josh. "I rather like sushi. At least some of it."

Josh kept his arm around the back of the bench and smiled at me. "I'm glad. We should come again so you can learn how to eat with chopsticks." He then told me stories of his years at university and how he ate sushi as often as he could. The conversation turned to what he'd learned in school. I envied every bit of it.

"Did you attend university?" Josh asked.

"Of course not. I am a woman."

"What does being a woman have to do with it?"

Oh, dear. "I was taught at home by a governess."

"You should go to university. I bet you'd make a smashing great history teacher. You know so much of it."

"Perhaps I should." *I need to change the subject.*

"So, tell me," he leaned back against the seat and put his arm around me. "How are the preparations for the Christmas Ball going?"

Oh, bless you. "They are going well. We have been given permission to use the costumes from the local theater group, and we have all purchased wigs. They will fit into the old time period perfectly." I smiled, then jumped in my seat, "Oh no!" My shoulders dropped.

"What?" Josh stiffened.

"I forgot. Everyone was planning to have a practice dance tonight. I told them it might be best to take a break, but they disagreed, wishing to have something to look forward to after the funeral."

"Then we should be going." He waved the server over and quickly paid for our meal, then escorted me back through the streets, onto the Tube to Kingscross, then aboard the train heading home. When we were back in his car, driving through the countryside, he asked me several questions about my family and childhood. I had to change my answers so they did not sound strange. I tried to avoid some questions and some I had to outright lie about. When we arrived, he pulled around to the back of the estate and into a building where the whole side of the wall opened. He drove right inside it and parked next to several other motorcars.

"Amazing," I whispered.

"Let me guess, you've never been inside a garage before either?" he asked dryly.

I did not answer.

He led the way to the ballroom, where music flowed but no one danced. Not a soul was around.

"I guess they're finished for the night," Josh stated.

"Why would they leave the music playing?"

Josh shrugged and pulled me into the room. He pressed a button on the MP3 player, then slid his hand onto the small of my back. He held me close … really close. *Charles most definitely would not approve.*

"I wasn't entirely honest with you, Ruth."

"About what?" My voice was so quiet I could hardly hear it. I was sure he could feel my heart beating against his chest. My head spun, and my legs weakened.

"The real reason it's been so hard on me with you here is … well, it's because … from the moment I saw you, I've felt something for you. It scared me, so I left. When I came back, the feeling returned. Each time I left, I thought I could get a handle on it, but with each return I found myself falling more and more … in love with you."

"Oh," I sighed.

"I didn't want to love you, Ruth. I know that's a horrible thing to say, but you must understand. I didn't want to fall in love with someone who …" Tears filled his eyes. "I can't bear to lose you as well—that's not to say that you'll … forgive me, Ruth. I'm making a muddle of this."

"Oh, Josh." My voice shook, and tears filled my own eyes when I saw the pain in his.

"I love you, Ruth."

Warmth filled my soul, and a smile spread while the tears rolled down my cheeks. My heart leaped from my body and soared around the room. "I love you, Josh." In that instant, I knew the words were true.

He let go of my hand, touched my cheek, and leaned his head closer. His hand moved along my jaw and back around my neck. His lips touched lightly against mine, then pressed a little more. Warm shockwaves ran through my body and my brain fogged like winter in London. All I could think about were his lips and hands. My arms acted of their own accord, wrapping around his neck and holding him tight. *Now, this is the kiss I have been waiting for all my life.*

We kissed and held each other for some time. His hands moved about my back, then caressed my face and neck. When our lips parted, I smiled and sighed. "I love you."

"I love you, my sweet Ruth," he smiled. "For weeks now, I've wondered what your lips would taste like."

I giggled. "Oh?"

"So sweet." He kissed me again and sighed.

"Perhaps we should retire for the night," I said breathlessly.

He pulled away abruptly and stared at me with surprise.

I blushed. "Separately."

He grinned impishly. "I wasn't sure what you meant for a minute there."

"I am a lady—a lady in love—but still a lady. That is why we should not stay here alone together any longer."

I took a step back. He bent to the floor and picked up my hat.

"I didn't know it fell off." I quickly took it from him and pulled it down over my head.

"You don't need to feel self-conscious about that with me, my love."

I smiled at his choice of words. *My love.*

"I've said it once, and I'll say it many times over ... you look just as beautiful with no hair." He kissed me again, then took my hand and led me from the room.

Chapter Twenty-Five

1812 England, Celeste

I stormed up the stairs. Charles followed right behind me with his hand supporting my back.

"Calm yourself, my dear, or you will make yourself ill—or possibly harm the baby."

"Oh, please. My getting upset is not going to hurt the baby one stitch."

"What's goin' on?" Abbie asked from the top of the stairs. She stood there in her nightdress, looking worried.

"Nothing terribly concerning, Abbie," Charles waved her away.

"Nothing? I wouldn't call it nothing. Those beastly, meddling, pretentious …" I growled in frustration. "Those stupid gits. How can they say such things? Abbie is the sweetest, most loving person I know. How can they ruin her with those ridiculous stories they're spreading?"

"What did they say?" Abbie asked, alarmed.

My shoulders slumped. *Oh dear. I shouldn't have said anything in front of her.* "I dare not tell you. It would be best to return to your bed, Abbie."

Charles guided me away. "Come, my dear. You need to calm yourself."

I rolled my eyes. "I *am* calm." Peering back at Abbie, I saw the worry on her brow. "I apologize, Abbie. I shouldn't have worried you."

"I'm more worried about *you*," she replied.

"I get a little hot-headed at times. I will be right as rain by morning," I said reassuringly. I made my way to my chambers and let Charles help me into bed. "How *can* they say such things? Do they not know how utterly absurd those accusations are?"

Charles sighed. "I believe they do. Perhaps it is entertaining for them, making up such rot," Charles replied, pulling me into his arms.

"If it wasn't women spreading those lies, I would demand you call them out."

He chuckled. "How I would love to see Mrs. Thornton brandishing a sword and vowing to run me through."

I couldn't help but laugh at the thought. "She would likely stick herself at the first swing." We laughed harder. My smile fell when I thought of the cruel things they had said. "How can anyone believe she would harm a baby?"

"I do not think anyone believed it, dear." Charles caressed my cheek and neck and played with my hair, attempting to distract me. He rested his forehead against mine and pulled me closer. "Especially after the tongue lashing you gave them. Everyone will think twice before crossing the Viscountess of Shariton Park again."

I sighed and let Charles distract me fully.

* * *

A knock sounded at my door, so I quickly buttoned the last button of my cardigan, pulled my hat over my head, and opened the door. Josh immediately had me in his arms. He kissed me tenderly, then moved his newly shaven cheek against mine and buried his face in my neck. Those same heart-pounding, dizzying feelings from last night swept through me again.

"Good morning, my sweet Ruth." His breath tickled my neck.

I sighed aloud.

He straightened and gazed at me. "Will you spend the day with me?"

"You wish me to?"

"Always." He took me by the hand, led me from the room, then stopped and looked me up and down. "Perhaps you should change into some trousers. And get your jumper."

"Where are we going?" I asked doubtfully.

He pulled me closer. "I've been dying to see you ride Norman. I have a feeling you're a fierce rider."

I smirked and lifted my chin. "Perhaps."

He kissed me again, sending tingles down my back. I pulled away, quickly changed my clothes, then met him back in the corridor. He had an odd grin on his face which gave me pause.

"What?" I asked.

His grin grew. "I've only ever seen you in skirts and dresses. You look rather inviting in jeans."

By the sound of his voice and the expression on his face, I could only assume that inviting meant something that would make me blush … and smile. He led me to the other side of the house, where the guests weren't permitted.

"First, we should eat a good, hearty breakfast." He smiled and led me into the breakfast room, where I was used to sharing my morning meals with my family.

"It is almost exactly the same," I said, taking in the room around me.

"You've been here before?"

"Uh …"

"I don't remember the family ever giving tours."

"Perhaps I am mistaken." I avoided his eyes, feigning interest in the familiar molded plaster on the ceiling.

We ate quickly, both eager to get out into the countryside. We hurried hand-in-hand to the stables to saddle Norman and another powerful stallion, Horace.

The stable hand pulled the mounting block out for me. "There you are, Celeste. Norman has been eager for your visit."

"Thank you. I have been eager as well."

We mounted, and I rode out ahead of Josh. Once clear of the stables, I shot off at a full gallop, with Josh at my heels. I could hear him whooping and laughing behind me, urging his horse faster. I slowed to a stop at the top of the hill and peered down upon the scenery before us.

"Beautiful isn't it?" he said with reverence.

"I wish you could have seen it two hundred years ago," I smiled and looked over the land.

"You speak as if you have." He studied me again. "Sometimes I get this crazy feeling you *are* from the past."

I lowered my head.

"Even now, your reaction to the idea disturbs me." He shook his head, "The things you say and the things you know—even the things you don't know or that are new to you—make me wonder."

I remained silent as a battle waged in my mind. I knew I should shrug it off and call the idea absurd, but I ached to tell him the truth. I loved him and wanted him to know everything about me, even the crazy, absurd truth, but if I did would he dismiss it? Would he shun me? Would he call me crazy and leave? He continued to study me closely. I turned and let Norman meander away. He guided his horse alongside me.

"What if time travel were possible?" I asked without looking at him.

"What a mess it could create," he said.

"Yes. It does," I said, too softly for him to hear.

"Ruth?"

I stopped and stared at him.

"What is your last name? I heard the stable hand call you Celeste. I've heard others use that name as well. I guess ..."

My hands started to sweat. "Roberts."

His eyes rose. "Is your name Ruth or Celeste?"

"I go by both." *Oh, this is getting confusing.*

"Are you related to a Damian Roberts, by chance?"

I thought of Celeste's late father. *I suppose I am to pretend he is my father.* "Yes."

His eyes widened. He quickly dismounted, hurrying to the side of my horse, and pulled me out of my saddle. My feet didn't touch the ground before he embraced me tightly, his face buried in my neck.

"I can't believe it!" His shoulders shook from his cries.

"What is it, Josh? You're scaring me."

"I can't believe it!" He kissed me up my neck, then on the lips, "All this time ... I didn't know your name ... who your family was. I didn't bother to ask."

"What are you talking about?" I asked

He gazed at me with tear-filled eyes. "Your family. They donated substantial money to rebuild Shariton Park, giving my late wife the dream of seeing its restoration. Not only that, but it gave us the chance to open this cancer treatment center." He cried and pulled me closer, then kissed my cheek.

"Oh. I had forgotten about that."

"Forgotten?" He looked at me and laughed. "How can you forget such a thing? If not for your family, you wouldn't receive treatments here."

I smiled and wiped at my tears. "I had not thought of that."

"How is Damian related? I must thank him in person. When can I meet him?"

My heart pounded. "Uh ... I am not sure when he will be around."

"Then let's go to him." He kissed me and lifted me back into my saddle.

"Josh ... I am not sure that is a good idea." I struggled to find a good reason to avoid the meeting.

He laughed and mounted Horace. "Why? I'll eventually meet them, so why not now?"

"Please, Josh. Give me some time."

His smile faded. He must've noticed the panic in my voice. "If time's what you need ... but not too long. I want to express my gratitude."

"It will not be long," I whispered. *Now what am I to do?*

My thoughts deepened while we rode slowly along the top of the hill. Josh must have also been deep in thought, for he remained quiet. I tried to turn my thoughts to less stressful things and instead gazed out over the land full of houses. "When did the land get sold?"

"What land?"

I pointed at the homes. "The land that belonged to the Elsegood family. It used to stretch out over acres and acres, beyond the road you see there in the distance."

"Really?" He glanced across the land, then back at me, "How do you know this?"

"Uh ... I studied it." I looked down, then away. *Why does my mouth*

211

insist on setting traps?

"Really?" He moved his horse closer, "And how does one do that with no resources?"

"Books." I held my chin high. "Quite a lot of books."

He chuckled. "I didn't know they had such books about Shariton Park. Most of it was destroyed."

I began to fidget under his searching eyes, not that I did not enjoy him looking at me, but I feared what he might find. There were too many lies just below the surface. I kicked my horse to go a little faster, and we made our way around the grounds. I paused when we reached the church at the edge of the property. In the churchyard stood several statues and tombstones. There were a great many more than when I last saw them back in 1812. I watched Josh ride forward toward the church. He stopped when he noticed I had not followed. I could not get any closer to that churchyard for fear of what I might see. I did not wish to know what would happen and when my loved ones would die.

I turned my horse and nudged him into a canter back toward the house.

"Hold up, Ruth!" Josh called.

I slowed Norman and glanced back.

"Head to the group of trees … there by the gazebo." He pointed and we both rode toward it. When I arrived, a small metal table with chairs sat in the middle of the gazebo. A light green cloth covered the table with a vase of red roses arranged in the middle. Two sets of plates and silverware sat across from each other, along with a folded cloth to resemble a swan. Josh took my hand and helped me dismount. He wrapped his arms around me, pressed his forehead against mine, and smiled.

"You have planned a picnic?" I asked, my worries melted away.

He nodded and took my hand to guide me to a chair. The combination of being in the shade and the cold metal chair caused me to shiver despite my warm coat. Josh walked to the side of the gazebo and picked up a blanket then placed it around my shoulders.

"You thought of everything," I said and kissed his hand.

He reached under the table, grabbed a wicker basket, opened it, and began unloading bread, cheeses, fruits, nuts, a log of salami, and drinks. We talked while we ate, mostly discussing Josh's life history. He told me stories about all the trouble he had gotten into at school as a boy. It seemed he was quite mischievous. He spoke of his brother and his parents. I envied him that his parents were still alive. He promised to take me to meet them one day. He even spoke of his late wife.

"What was she like?" I found myself yearning to know about her.

"Amelia was quiet and well-mannered but fierce when someone crossed her. She was intelligent and quite good at playing the piano." His peaceful smile pulled at my heart. He had just described Celeste.

"You loved her deeply."

He nodded. "I still do."

"I am happy to hear that. I do not believe love dies after death." I squeezed his hand tighter.

He brought my hand to his lips and kissed it tenderly. "I never thought I could love another." He smiled at me. "I'm glad I was wrong."

My heart fluttered. "Me too." I paused, then asked, "What was her favorite food? Did she like sushi as much as you?"

He chuckled. "No. It repulsed her. She wouldn't go near fish if she could help it."

I laughed. Another characteristic of Celeste. It seemed Amelia had received several of Celeste's traits. "Did she paraglide with you?"

He shook his head. "No. I didn't start doing that until after her death. I expressed interest before, but she never felt comfortable with me doing something so daring."

"Does it bother you to talk about her?"

"Not with you. Somehow it's … soothing." He pulled a flower from the vase and moved his chair closer. He pulled my hat from my head, and I quickly covered my baldness. He frowned. "You shouldn't be embarrassed about that, Ruth."

"I am not so much with you anymore. It is cold without a hat." I shivered.

He tucked the rose in my hat, replaced it on my head, and covered my eyes.

"Ha. Ha." I pushed it back up.

He chuckled, kissed my hand, and pulled me to my feet. We rode back to the stables and hurried inside just as the wind picked up and the rain fell. Leaving the horses in the care of the stable hand, we ran up the hill to the house in the downpour. "We need to get changed. I don't want you to catch cold." Josh kissed me and led me to my room, leaving me at the door. Inside, I nearly stumbled over a trunk in the middle of the room.

"What is this?" I asked the empty room. I reached down and opened the envelope on top. Inside was a letter from Celeste with a note attached.

May you be the belle of the ball.
Love, Charles

My heart fell. I had missed a visit from my dear brother? I wanted to cry in frustration. *I need to talk with him!* I desperately needed advice, now more than ever. I had to know what to do about Josh. I wanted to know if Charles thought I could have a future with Josh, and if that future could exist in the past or now … or both. I needed to know if I could even tell Josh the truth.

I could sense in Celeste's writing her dissatisfaction with the trials she was undergoing with the gossip and hateful rumors running through society. She worried that Abbie's dislike of the time would sway her decision, and she would not stay long enough to birth her baby at Shariton. At the end of the letter, she explained the trunk, noting she had sent some things for the Christmas ball.

I knelt and opened the trunk to find she had packed two of my dresses, my white evening dress used for dining and my favorite light blue gown and undergarments. I pulled out my gown and held it up under my chin. Hiding under the gown were the matching slippers and gloves.

"Oh, Celeste. How thoughtful you are." I choked back my tears and quickly undressed to try on the clothes, fearing they would not fit properly after all the weight I had lost. I put the underthings on as best I could, then pulled the blue dress over my head, only to find that it hung slightly loose. I sighed. *It will do for one night.* I removed the dress and put my evening gown on. It, too, fit well enough. After all, we were only playing dress-up. I reached for the ties at the back when a knock sounded on my door.

I hesitated, then opened it a few inches and peeked through. Josh stood in a nice button-up shirt and slacks, a smile on his face. "Are you still changing?"

I blushed. "Uh … I was distracted."

"Distracted?"

"My brother came to visit while we were out this afternoon. He left behind a trunk of some of my old dresses."

"Are you wearing one now?"

I nodded.

He gently pushed the door open. "May I see?"

I sighed and let him in, biting my lip.

His eyes widened. "Wow! Is that what you're wearing to the ball?" He lifted my hand to guide me into a slow spin under his arm.

"No. This is an evening gown. He brought me a different one for the ball."

"May I see it?"

215

"No. Not until the ball." I smiled when he pulled me into his arms. "Now you must leave, for it is not prudent for you to be in a lady's chamber, especially with that look in your eyes."

His fingers moved across my back. "Are you wearing old-fashioned underwear as well?"

"Joshua David Harrison!" My cheeks flamed, and I pushed him out into the hall. "It is not gentlemanly of you to ask such things!" I started to shut the door, but he put his foot in the way.

"You are entirely too old-fashioned, Ruth."

"Not entirely. I let you kiss me."

"*Let* me kiss you? It seems to me you kiss back with equal dedication." He leaned in and kissed me softly, trying to open the door again. I pulled my head back, pressed against the door, and frowned at him.

"Entirely too old-fashioned," he pouted.

"And proud to be," I said with my head held high. "Now, if you will excuse me, I need to change."

"Why don't you keep it on? I'll change into something nice, and we'll dine and be old-fashioned together." He wiggled his eyebrows.

I inspected him, wondering what he might look like in an old jacket, breeches, and cravat. I doubted he would have anything like it in his wardrobe, but I would love to see him dressed up. I tilted my head to the side. "Very well. I will meet you in the drawing room. If we are to do this, it must be done properly—the same as they once would in old times—but it was not common for an unwed man and woman to dine alone. So find someone to dine with us."

"Will do, Miss Roberts."

I shut the door before he could advance on me yet again. *Technically, it is Miss Elsegood* ... but I could not tell him that.

Chapter Twenty-Six

1812 England, Abbie

I waddled into the kitchen to find a bite to eat and avoid sitting with Celeste's neighbors for tea. When I arrived, I noticed Gwen teetering as she tip-toed on top of a stool. Her height impaired her ability to reach the highest shelves. "Let me help." I took hold of the pot she was reaching for and handed it to her.

Her eyes narrowed. She didn't say a word but turned back to her work preparing dinner.

Odd. "Can I help you with anything?"

"No. Do not be getting any ideas about taking any more of my ingredients to make your heathen concoctions. I will not put up with it in *my* kitchen." She waved her finger at me, then watched me like a hawk as she began to chop potatoes and slide them into the pot.

"You don't believe all that nonsense that's been going around, do you?" I tried to smile to lighten the anger that emanated from her.

"All I know is that you took some vinegar from my kitchen, and the next moment Mr. Baily's room stinks to high heaven. So, the way I see it, there is some truth to what some folks say. I also know that you sing heathen songs—of course, I don't believe you'd go so far as to sacrifice a baby. That rumor has gone a bit too far."

Her words pierced me through the gut. My jaw dropped and heat rose in my chest. How could they spread such lies? My fist balled up and I shook. "I didn't think a person could believe such things of a friend." Tears stung my eyes. "I would never believe it of you." I turned and fled quickly out of the kitchen and down the corridor.

Things were going from bad to worse. Not only were the ladies of high rank believing and spreading such lies, but now those among my friends were doing the same. How could I continue living here among these arrogant and malicious people? I wanted to go home. The only thing keeping me here was Celeste, Charles, and—"Albert!" I hadn't been looking where I stormed, and I ran right into him—again. I glanced around the corridor to see if anyone else was nearby.

"Abbie, what's wrong?" He took my hand in both of his. "You are shaking. You look upset."

"Do you believe the rumors going around about me?"

His eyes narrowed. "What rumors?"

My shoulders relaxed, but only slightly. "Please don't lie and say you've not heard."

"I would be lying if I told you I did. I do not typically listen to gossip if I can help it." He took my other hand in his. "What is so terrible that you are this upset?"

"Horrible, moronic people are spreading rumors about me. What's worse is my friends are starting to believe them."

"Do not tell me Lady Elsegood—"

"No. Not Lady Elsegood. In fact, I believe she's more upset about it than I am." I wiped at an angry tear that had escaped, despite my efforts.

"Do not be upset, Abbie." He wiped at another tear. "You should not listen to the lies. You know they are untrue, so do not give them a second thought."

"I wouldn't if everyone didn't treat me differently because of them," I huffed.

"Well, I will not—" He abruptly stopped when someone approached. The scullery maid I'd seen not long ago in the kitchen stepped around the corner. *Mary or Martha? I can't remember.* She stopped and narrowed her eyes when she noticed my hands in Albert's. He instantly straightened and held his hands behind his back. If looks could kill, I'd be dead.

I lifted my chin. "Is there something you need?" I asked her.

"No, miss." Her lips tightened and she breathed heavily through her nose. She moved to walk back the way she had come. When she was out of sight, I turned back to Albert to find that he had already walked away to the end of the corridor. I disliked Mary or Martha—whoever she was—even more.

* * *

Present Day England, Ruth

December twenty-third, the night of the Christmas Ball, Sandy stepped up beside me and giggled. "Are you ready to see the ballroom?" She led me down the corridor, "We've been working on it all day. You're going to love it!" When we turned the corner into the entry hall, I breathed deeply and covered my heart with both hands.

The largest pine tree I had ever beheld indoors stood in the middle of the large entry. Even more stunning were the soft glowing lights and objects of red and white hanging from its branches. Around the room, lights and ribbons draped the columns and doors, and evergreens wrapped the banisters going up the stairs. From the chandelier, holly and lights hung. Never had I seen such lavish decorations in all my life.

"I see you like this tree. Wait until you see the one in the ballroom!" She pulled me down the corridor and into the ballroom. "What do you think?"

The ballroom was equally breathtaking, with more lights and evergreen wrapped around the room. The tree stood just as tall as the other, decorated all in white with shining snowflakes filling its branches, and the top held a large glowing star. "It is the most beautiful sight I have ever seen." I walked across the room and touched the tree.

A high whistle brought my head around to see Josh heading toward us. His eyes glanced at the tree, then lingered on me. He smiled, put his arm around my waist, and pulled me into his side.

I shyly dropped my head at his attention. "I was just telling Sandy that it is the most beautiful sight I have ever seen."

"I know it isn't quite right with the décor and all. Traditionally, they put candles in the tree, but I don't believe in burning down Shariton Park for the sake of authenticity," Sandy smiled.

I laughed. "In the early eighteen hundreds, it was not tradition to have a tree at all."

"Really? I should have done my research better."

"Well, we couldn't very well go without one, could we?" Josh said.

"No, we could not." I glanced at both Josh and Sandy. They stood there with eyes squinted, looking at the tree.

"Is it too bright for you?" I asked with a laugh.

They shook their heads. Josh squinted again. "Try it. If you squint, it looks like it's glowing more."

I closed my eyes enough to see the lights glow brighter. "Amazing."

Sandy clapped her hands together. "Well, I'd better go get dressed for the ball. And you, Josh, are the party host, so you need to start the dance. Be here on time," she said and hurried out of the room.

"Start the dance?" His face grew flush.

"Do not tell me you have forgotten your hosting duties?"

"Uh … no. I haven't." He bowed, then pulled me close. "Ruth, will you do me the honor of dancing the first dance with me? And every dance after?"

Every dance after? My heart fluttered at the idea, but to dance every dance would mean he had claimed my heart. Had he? "I would love to," I answered, then stepped away from him. "I should prepare myself as well." I squinted at the tree again, then at Josh. "It does not make your face glow like the tree. It only makes you blurry."

He laughed and kissed me. I pulled away quickly and looked around the room at the few people doing last-minute touches. "People will see," I whispered.

He chuckled. "Now go get ready. I'm dying to see you in your ball gown." He winked and swatted me lightly on my hind end.

My eyes nearly bugged out of my head. "I cannot believe you just did that." I held my head up and tried to hold back my smile. "Apologize this instant."

He laughed and bowed low. "My apologies, Princess Ruth. I had a bit of a memory lapse and forgot that you are a lady."

"You flatter me, good sir, for I am not addressed as Princess Ruth. I am only known as the Honorable Miss Els—Roberts."

"Well, Honorable Miss Elsroberts, I've got to figure out how to tie a ruddy cravat. It may take me hours. I might miss the entire ball before I've figured it out."

"You had better not." I scowled at him and went up to my room to dress.

Once I had my gown on, I checked myself in the mirror. It felt good and right to be wearing my old clothes again, along with the many layers of undergarments. I was me again—apart from missing my hair.

I pulled the long gloves up my arms, glad they covered the bruises from my treatments.

A knock sounded at the door. I hoped it was not Josh. Perhaps he did not know he should meet me down the hall. I called through the closed door. "Who is it?"

"It's Sandy. I just—"

I opened the door. "Good day, Sandy."

"Wow! Where did you get that dress?" She stepped into my room and kicked the door closed behind her, then set a round box at her feet. "Spin around. I've got to see it."

I turned slowly. "It is one of my old gowns. My brother brought it to me."

"It's perfect. It looks authentic … it's much better than mine." She peered down at her gown. It, too, was pretty. The print was not what I would call in fashion for the early eighteen hundreds, but it would do.

"You look beautiful, and your wig looks perfect." I touched her curls. "It looks real."

"I've brought your wig." She bent to open the box, pulling out a wig of strawberry blond. It was pulled up in curls, and a white strip of fabric wrapped around the hair with a few curls hanging down to frame where the face would be. Sandy grinned when she saw the tears in my eyes. "Let's get it on you."

I lowered myself in front of the vanity mirror. Sandy stretched a cap over my head, then placed the wig. *Perfect.* The curls tickled my neck, just as they once had. Tears flooded my eyes. "It looks so real. It is perfect."

"Oh no! You can't cry. We've got to get your makeup on. There is no crying allowed." She handed me some tissues, and I wiped my eyes. Once my emotions were under control, she pulled out a bag from the box and began brushing makeup on my face.

It smelled strange. "I have not used makeup before."

"You haven't?" She laughed. "Then I will go light with the color. I wouldn't want it to be overwhelming."

Once she finished, I stared at myself in the mirror. "Wow! My eyes are brighter."

"It's amazing what a little color will do," she said, then clapped her hands together. "Well. I believe a special someone is waiting for you downstairs." She winked.

We walked together to the lift. "Do you think we should walk down the stairs?"

"And make a grand entrance?" she asked, then nodded. We made our way to the staircase and descended it with our heads high.

Near the bottom, I spotted Josh walking out of the ballroom. His breeches, perfectly cut jacket, and cravat made him appear as though he had just stepped out of the past. Well, almost. His cravat looked as if a toddler had tied it. With him being so dashing, it was easy to think I could take him into 1812. Our life together could be all I'd ever dreamed of if only I could share the truth.

He stopped mid-stride and stared up at me. His mouth hung open until he smiled, crossed the room, took my hand, and bowed slightly.

"Good evening, Honorable Miss Roberts." He kissed my hand and winked.

I suppressed a laugh. "You only use the honorable part when addressing a letter or the like, not when talking to me directly." I reached out and brushed his shoulder. "You look nice. Other than that, your cravat is a bit flat."

"Really? I worked so hard on it." He frowned playfully, pulled me into his arms, and whispered in my ear. "You look tantalizing."

The reaction my body had to that one word was unexpected and threw me off kilter. "Tantalizing?"

"Stunning, gorgeous, seductive, enchanting, alluring, beautiful ... take your pick." He kissed my cheek and stepped back to look me over once again.

My cheeks burned hot at his words. I nearly melted in his arms—but no. That would not do. I had a ball to attend. I cleared my throat, lifted my chin, and reached for his cravat. "Let me help you with that."

"You know how to tie a cravat?" His lips pulled into a smile.

"I was taught and helped by my father when I was young. I only learned one way of tying it. There are many." My fingers brushed against his freshly shaven neck. The scent of his cologne made me want to kiss it.

He cleared his throat. "Did your father wear cravats often?"

Every day. "At times, when we dressed up." I finished and smiled up at him. "Much better."

"What would I ever do without you?" He lifted my chin slightly with his fingertips, then kissed my lips.

Oh, I think I may never wish to wake from this wonderful dream.

With a sigh, I leaned away and lowered my head, knowing people were walking around us. *Was it common to kiss so publicly?*

We moved together into the ballroom while I tried to recover from his lips on mine. Friends were dressed in costumes from different decades of the 1800s. Most of their family and friends wore elegant clothing of more modern times. It was strange to see the mixture in the setting of a ball, but not disagreeable. I greeted my friends with hugs and kisses on the cheeks. Some looked so completely different with their wigs on, which made it difficult to recognize them.

I giggled when Steve arrived wearing a bright red, spiky wig. He smiled and pointed at his head. "I wore it in honor of Don. Go Essex!"

Josh and I laughed. "Bless you, Steve." I kissed the air beside his cheek and fought the tears that would ruin my makeup.

Steve scratched his head and wrinkled his nose. "I'm not entirely sure Essex colors look good on me."

The ballroom filled quickly. I was just describing how to address

224

a countess for Steve's American wife when violins, cellos, and other stringed instruments sounded across the room. Musicians struck strings with their bows, preparing for the first dance.

Those in the room moved back and made a space. Josh took my hand and led me into the middle of the crowd. My friends and their spouses took their places, and the dance began. Josh moved the wrong way. I whispered and gestured, miming the correct steps.

He was pale with fright. He would never survive the 1800's with his dancing. The thought saddened me. I doubt he would give up his life in this time for the boring, stuffy life he would lead in the past. If I were to have a future with him, I would have to give up my family and all I knew of my childhood, and my title, being the daughter of a Viscount would be erased. My place in society would be only a recollection of those who knew me.

My title and name in society could easily be given up. I would do it gladly if I could be in his arms for the rest of eternity. But … could I give up my family if it came to that? Could I live with the fact that we would have to travel through time to see each other? After all, it was infinitely better to travel a short distance through time than over many miles in a carriage. Occasionally, I *could* take him back to visit my family. Of course, I would have to teach him that kissing me in public and swatting me on the hind end was not commonly accepted, among other things.

"What are you thinking about so intently, my sweet Ruth?" Josh asked as we moved together in the familiar steps.

"Nothing of consequence." I dared not voice my thoughts of marriage when he had not yet mentioned it himself.

"When is this dance going to end?" he asked when we came together again, "It's taking forever."

I tsked and rolled my eyes. He most definitely could not survive the past.

The moment the song ended, Josh's attention was captured by someone behind me. He smiled, waved, and took my hand to guide me across the room. A couple, perhaps in their fifties, stood at one side, dressed elegantly, their smiles bright. The man's smile closely matched Josh's.

"Mum, Papa, I'd like you to meet Ruth Roberts. Ruth, these are my parents, David and Cynthia."

"Oh! It is a pleasure to make your acquaintance, Mr. and Mrs. Harrison," I curtsied.

"Oh my, you are playing the part! Please, call me Cynthia." She had the same eyes as her son, warm and inviting. "Josh has told us so much about you."

"Oh?"

"He wasn't exaggerating when he said how beautiful you are," David winked. *Like father like son, it seems.*

Heat rushed to my ears, and I glanced at Josh. He smiled and pulled me close. It was odd to be wrapped in his arms while standing directly before his parents. They chatted on as if it were the most natural thing in the world, smiling upon us with genuine happiness. My heart warmed at their welcome reception of me.

The rest of the evening went splendidly. We danced only a few of the old country dances. The rest were love songs and upbeat dances, which I found somewhat appalling. Josh wanted me in his arms as much as he could have me. He showed me how to dance the waltz and one called the quickstep. He moved me so fast around the room that I felt I was merely running along with him. Each time a song ended, I struggled to catch my breath.

When the next song began to play, I saw a grin spread across Josh's face. "The cha-cha."

"The what?"

"You've never heard of the cha-cha?"

I hesitated and soon found his arms around me once more. He moved his legs and hips to the music, showing me how to place my footing. I stood peering down at his feet, feeling helpless.

He counted along with his movements and pulled me into his arms to join him. I mimicked him the best I could. "A little quicker now. Move to the music."

"Where did you learn to dance like this?" I asked breathlessly.

"My mother."

"Your mother?" *Gracious! How could a mother condone such dancing?*

"She feels that all young men need to know the popular dances if they're to woo a girl," he winked.

Popular dances? Relax, Ruth. You are not in the past. I continued to watch his feet until comfort reached me. When I lifted my eyes, he moved a bit closer.

"You're doing well. Now, you need to move your hips." His hands slid down my body and stopped on my hips. He moved them side to side to the music.

"Joshua!" I gasped.

He laughed. "I'm merely showing you how to move those sexy hips of yours."

Sexy? "Yes, but the look on your face tells me you are enjoying it far too much." I forced his hands to my upper back and held his left hand.

"Move your hips, Ruth. You're too stiff."

I sighed and swung them side to side to the music, finding it easier to make the steps smoother.

"There you go. Nice." His brows moved up and down while he watched me.

"You are audacious." I tried to frown but found it difficult.

When the song ended, we went to the adjoining room for some

light refreshments and much-needed rest. After dancing until well into the night and after saying goodbye to friends and Josh's parents, we found ourselves alone in the ballroom once more. His hands rested at my waist, and my hands locked around his neck. We slowly danced to the music.

"What are you thinking about?" Josh asked, touching my brow and smoothing out the scowl I had not known I wore.

"Your parents."

"My parents make you unhappy?"

I smiled and tilted my head. "No. I was thinking how lucky you are to have your parents alive."

"How long ago did your parents die?"

Hundreds of years ago. "My father passed away when I was thirteen. My mother passed away two years later. In fact, my mother passed away on December twenty-first."

"You should go visit their gravesite. I'll go with you and take some flowers."

I stiffened. "No. We cannot do that."

"Why not?"

"It would not be a good idea … that is …"

"Where are they buried?"

"Uh … not far from here." I sighed. "Please, Josh. I do not want to talk about this right now." I leaned my head on his shoulder, and he held me tight. *What am I to do?*

Chapter Twenty-Seven

1812 England, Abbie

I walked the corridors of Shariton Park all morning, hoping for an opportunity to speak with Albert alone. When I had seen him this morning in the breakfast room, I had tried to convey my desire to talk with him, but I wasn't sure my winks and nods had worked. I was about to give up when I saw him carrying a folded stack of clothing down the corridor outside Lord Elsegood's room.

"Albert," I whispered and waved him over to a corner, out of sight. He looked around and walked to me hesitantly. "What is it, Abbie?"

"Since it's Christmas Eve, and tomorrow I won't be here to see you—" I frowned at the thought that I would have to spend the holiday with the neighbors, even if it was the Fosters. I sighed, "I've decided to give you your gift early."

"My gift?"

I nodded. "It isn't much." I held out the gift, unwrapped, for I didn't know how to wrap something without tape.

He took the photograph that I had carried with me over the last six months. I went out on a limb and retrieved it from my pack yesterday, along with another item I kept secret. His eyes widened in surprise when he saw the lifelike color of the photograph. "What is this? Did you paint this? How can you paint something so real?"

"I didn't paint it. And don't ask where it came from, for my lips are sealed."

"It looks exactly like you." He stared at the picture briefly while I studied his face. He had nicked himself, shaving on the spot along his jaw, and I found myself wishing I could kiss it better. He glanced down at me. "I did not get you anything."

I smiled. "Yes, you did."

"I did?"

I nodded. "And you're going to give it to me right now."

"Abbie, I do not know of what you speak." He appeared utterly confused, his brow furrowed.

"I'll give you a hint." I leaned closer, placing his warm hand against my cheek and standing on my tippy toes until I was only an inch away from his lips.

"Abbie." There was both frustration and longing in his voice.

I whispered, "Please."

A sound much like a moan came from deep inside him a moment before he pressed his lips to mine. He held my cheek with his left hand, and the other pulled me closer around my waist. He kissed my lips, cheek, forehead, nose, eyes, and along my jaw for quite some time. I even had the opportunity to kiss that spot on his neck ... several times.

He stopped and gazed into my eyes. "You do not know how long I have wanted to kiss you again."

"Perhaps just as long as I have wanted to kiss you."

"Happy Christmas, Abbie."

"Thank you for the best gift I could ever receive."

* * *

Present Day England, Ruth

"Happy Christmas, Ruth," Josh said when I opened my chamber door. Bashful warmth washed over me as I stood in his presence in my nightgown, with a shawl wrapped around my shoulders.

"Happy Christmas."

"Are you ready to go see what Father Christmas brought?" He took my hand to pull me out of the room.

This tradition of Father Christmas was not practiced when I was a child, but Celeste's stories inspired us to celebrate with gifts on Christmas morning. I wondered if Josh had gotten me anything special. I pulled against him. "I need to dress first."

"No, you don't. It's tradition to open presents in your pajamas." He waved at his T-shirt and flannel trousers, then tugged at my arm again.

"Highly unsuitable."

We walked down the stairs and into the drawing room, where another tree stood decorated. The night before, Josh and I, along with his parents, had sat in this room after dinner singing Christmas songs—most of which I did not know the words to. I had the opportunity to play some songs on the piano. I even taught them how to play the game of whist. We laughed and played well into the night until his parents retired to bed. They joined us now for Christmas morning, but would travel to spend time with other family members shortly afterward. It seemed odd to have guests for such a short time, and odder still that they could move from place to place so quickly.

"Are your parents coming downstairs?" I asked.

"When they wake." He smiled and sat me down on the sofa.

"Are there any other guests here?"

"Everyone is away visiting family for Christmas." He smiled and sat on the floor beneath the tree. Giddiness rose when I saw the presents I had wrapped and placed under the tree the night before. *I hope he likes them!* He picked up a large package and placed it on my lap.

I looked at the tag. "You got me something?"

"Well, of course." He rolled his eyes. "Why wouldn't I give the woman I love a gift?"

I pressed my lips together to hide my eagerness and opened the box to find a beautiful hat.

"I thought you'd like another one. This one might match more of your clothes. I've heard women like things to match."

"Thank you." I kissed his cheek and slipped on the hat. "It is very soft."

I moved to retrieve one from under the tree for him, but he stopped me. "Here's another." He held out a smaller box this time, and I began to open it gingerly until I saw him roll his eyes. I tore it open quickly to satisfy his impatience. Printed on the box was the image of a mobile phone much like his own. He laughed at the look of confusion on my face. "Don't worry. I'll teach you how to use it. I'm tired of not being able to find you. This is a big house, you know."

I laughed and waved my hand around me. "You mean this old cottage?" I kissed his cheek. "Thank you again, dear Joshua." I knelt by the tree, grabbed the wrapped painting out for him, and sat beside him on the sofa.

His eyes widened when he opened it.

I could not contain my excitement. "It is Shariton Park! It was painted back in 1810, I believe … perhaps 1811.""

"Where did you get this?"

"It has been in the family for years." *Almost years.*

232

"Is your family connected to the Elsegoods somehow?"

"Yes, in a roundabout way." I stared at him, and my smile faded. He seemed almost upset. "You do not like it?"

"Oh, I love it." He looked at me. "I don't know how you could have such a painting. There were so few paintings saved from before the wars. So many were stolen or destroyed, and not one that survived is of Shariton."

"Well, now it is home safe once again."

He put the painting carefully aside, pulled me into his arms, and kissed me passionately. The familiar tingles ran through my body.

"Dear me! I cannot wait to give you my next gift if this is how you reward me," I said breathlessly, kissing him again. *Oh, am I to be struck down for my indulgence?*

"Mm-hmm," he murmured against my lips.

I jumped at the sound of someone at the drawing-room door and reluctantly pulled away.

"Happy Christmas, Mum and Papa." Josh shot them a look of both annoyance and amusement. "Perfect timing."

"I'm guessing one of you likes the gift you received." David chuckled, entered the room, and sat in a high-backed chair. He pulled his wife down to sit on his knee. I blushed and reminded myself that it was normal for people to embrace in the company of others.

"Look what Ruth has given me, Mum." He held up the painting. "It was painted in the early 1800s by the same painter of the portraits upstairs in the study."

It warmed my heart that he recognized that fact.

"Amazing. Beautiful," they said together.

"I have another gift for you, Josh, but I want to allow your mother to open it. I suppose it would benefit her more."

"You didn't need to get me anything, dear," Cynthia said with a slight smile.

"I wanted to." I said, hoping I would not overstep my bounds. I pulled a small package from under the tree and gave it to her. She opened it and gasped.

"I have a rather large collection of old jewelry, dating back to the late eighteenth century and early nineteenth century, and I wanted to share it with you."

"This is too much, Ruth. This must be worth a fortune." She held up the necklace I had purchased myself during my first season in London.

I shook my head. "No. It has been in the family for years."

"Then you should keep it in your family." She moved to hand it back.

"Please, keep it. I want you to have it." Before she could protest further, I turned away and handed Josh the other portion of the present. "I know it is not customary to give men jewelry, but I thought this might be more for your late wife than for you."

He looked at me quizzically as he unwrapped the box. Inside were the earrings that matched the necklace that had once belonged to me and my mother.

He looked confused.

"They match the necklace you keep in the study," I explained.

His eyes widened. He grabbed my hand and pulled me from the room. The wrapping fell from the box, and we made our way upstairs. He stopped at his room and started to lead me inside, but I pulled my hand free at the door.

He went in without me, and returned holding a bundle of keys. Wordlessly, he took hold of my hand once more and led me to the study. He hurried to the glass cabinet and fumbled with the lock and key. Opening the door carefully, he lifted the necklace out and held the box of earrings up next to it. He turned them over, examining each piece with interest.

"They do match," he whispered. "How did your family come to

own these?"

"We have always had them," I whispered in return.

He glanced back at the paintings on the wall, then pressed his palms to his eyes and shook his head. "This is impossible. I don't understand how you could simply own these priceless historical artifacts. It's absurd to think …" He straightened, shook his head as if dislodging a difficult thought, then smiled crookedly at me. "Thank you for these." He laid the earrings beside the necklace in the case, a perfectly matched set. "Amelia would be so pleased." He paused and studied the painting Celeste had created of me. "It makes me wonder, now more than ever, who this young woman is that wears the necklace and earrings."

The person in the painting looked different from the person I saw in the mirror daily. My body had thinned, and my eyes had hollowed a bit. *Should I tell him? Would he believe me?*

Chapter Twenty-Eight

Present Day England, Ruth

"Come. I have a few more gifts to give you." He took my hand and kissed me before heading back downstairs.

"Well?" Cynthia looked at us with a smile. "What was in the box? We didn't get to see before you whisked out of here so fast."

"You remember the necklace in the study?" Josh asked.

"The one in the glass case?" David asked.

He nodded. "Ruth gave me the earrings that match."

Cynthia's head jerked back, and her eyes widened.

After the shock wore off and the questions were answered, we proceeded to give gifts. I received a pair of slippers and diamond earrings. The earrings won Josh a quick kiss despite his parents in the room. After we talked a bit and sipped hot cocoa, David and Cynthia stood. "We should be getting ready. We've got to be there to help with the meal soon."

After giving Josh's parents a fond farewell, I remained with him on the overstuffed sofa. Silently, he lifted my bare feet onto his lap. I stared at his hands on my feet, appalled. He pulled the slippers snugly up over my toes.

"They are so soft." I wiggled my toes and sighed.

"Like you." His fingers moved slowly across my ankle as he leaned over and kissed my lips. I gasped at the tingles that traveled up my body again, with more intensity. I shimmied out of his reach and pushed the bottom of my nightdress down around my feet. I held my hand to my chest to control the racing of my heart and stared at him in shock.

"Did I cross the line?" he asked with a slight frown, though his eyes were smiling.

I nodded. "I …" No words came to my mind, for it was a jumbled mess. I stood quickly and fanned my face, taking deep, steadying breaths.

He laughed as he stood and made his way to the mantle. "I guess this is a good time to give you another gift." He picked up two wreaths made of evergreen. They had pine cones and red ribbons wrapped around the green pine leaves.

"What is this?"

"They are for your parents' graves. When I found out you hadn't been to see them, I ordered them for you. I figured we could go together today to decorate their graves."

Tears moistened my lashes. *What ought I do? What ought I tell him?*

"I guess that's a yes?"

I did not answer for fear of what I might say.

"Go get dressed. I'll get you in twenty. Is that long enough?"

I nodded, then hurried from the room. Tears mixed with the water raining down upon me while I showered.

Before I knew it, we were headed down the drive and out the gates of Shariton Park, Josh at the wheel. "Where to?" he asked.

I pointed down the road toward the cemetery where they had buried Don. He drove slowly on the road and through town. When we reached the graveyard, he parked, and we walked through row after row of headstones. Finally, Josh stopped me. "Ruth. Are your parents buried here?"

I shook my head slowly.

"Where are they buried?"

I sighed. *I am cornered. I have to tell him.* "I will show you."

We made our way into the car again and I directed him back to Shariton. It was going to happen any moment. He would hear my explanation and believe I had gone mad. *I am going to lose him. But I am going to leave him someday soon, when my treatments are concluded. At least this way he will know my secret and know* me, *even if he decides I have gone mad.* I pointed at the road that led to the churchyard and he looked at me with his forehead creased before stopping the car.

"These graves are centuries old, Ruth. Are we going to wander around these headstones for a while before you tell me what's going on?"

With a heavy heart and a great sigh, I exited the car and walked through the gate. I could hear Josh close behind me while I made my way through the maze. I felt a little disoriented at first because there were so many new grave markers. I tried not to read the names for fear of seeing someone I knew. I spotted the two graves that belonged to my parents and noticed several more around them that were unfamiliar. I kept my eyes locked on my parents' graves and stopped before them. Josh stepped up beside me and read the markers out loud.

"William Charles Elsegood and Elizebeth Ruth White Elsegood. Ruth, they were born and died more than two hundred years ago."

"I know." I looked at him with tears in my eyes. "I was born in 1790, well over two hundred years ago."

He frowned. "If it weren't for the tears, I would believe you were joking … unless you're a terribly good actress."

"I am afraid I cannot act."

"Did you find the fountain of youth, and I'm dating a two-hundred-year-old woman?" He chuckled nervously.

"I have not lived all those years. I have only lived twenty-four of them. I traveled through time by way of a tree root."

His chin doubled as he laughed deep in his throat, then stopped as if he had been socked in the gut. He dropped the wreaths he carried into the snow at his feet. He appeared pale, and his hands shook. "A tree root?"

"Josh. Are you all right?" I stepped to his side and held his arm.

He shook his head. "It's funny, but I might actually believe you."

"Do you need to sit?" I glanced behind him and found the stone bench that had stood there for centuries. I moved him to it and brushed the snow away for us to sit. He sat down hard and placed his head between his legs.

"Is that better?" I patted his back.

He was silent for a moment, then lifted his head to look at me. "It all makes sense now. That odd tree near the horse you left … the light was never quite right around it. It nearly drove me mad trying to figure out why. All the things you didn't know or have never seen, and the way you talked about Shariton Park as if you knew it differently. The way you act—like a lady. The earrings and the painting. You brought them back with you when you went to visited your brother?"

I breathed fast with anticipation at him believing me. Joy seeped into my soul. *Does he truly believe me?*

He peered around at the gravestones. "Then your brother is the man in the painting—and you!" His voice squeaked. "That painting! That is you with the necklace!" He gestured at his neck as though he wore it.

I nodded. "My real name is Ruth Ann Elsegood."

"Then who are the Roberts? You've taken the name of Roberts, so…"

"Celeste Elsegood's maiden name is Roberts. Her father was Damian Roberts. Celeste was born in this time. She was the one who donated the money to Shariton before going back in time to marry my brother, Charles."

He leaned forward and covered his nose and mouth with his hands. "Celeste was a painter then? It's her signature on the paintings. Amelia spoke of her at times."

"Yes, she's a very talented artist," I said.

"So your brother … the man in the old-fashioned clothing, he was Amelia's ancestor." He looked at me. "And you're her … what? Great great great great great something or other …"

"Aunt." I laughed. "You make me sound so old."

"So that time when you came to me, telling me someone needed help on the telly?"

I blushed. "That was my first experience with the telly."

"So you weren't hallucinating?"

I smiled and shook my head.

Josh ran both hands through his hair and breathed out, causing his cheeks to bulge. He stood, pulled me to my feet, then walked me to my parents' graves. From the ground, he retrieved the wreaths and handed them to me. I placed them against my parents' tombstones, letting the peace relax my shoulders.

He smiled at me and took my hand in his. "This is so impossible … I can't believe it … but everything fits. Everything makes more sense now." He chuckled. "Am I going bonkers?"

"Bonkers? What does that mean?"

"See! It all fits. Bonkers has to be a modern word, and you wouldn't know it, would you?" He kissed me, then laughed. "I *am* going bonkers—or mad, as you might call it."

"Oh." I laughed. "I hope you are not going mad. There needs to be someone sane between the two of us."

"I may need some time to make sense of this." He paced back and forth for a time, then paused with his fingers over his lips. He pointed at my father's grave marker. "So, from what I understand, your family had the title of Viscount. Is that correct?"

I nodded. "My father passed that title on to my brother, Charles."

"So, are you Lady Elsegood then?"

I laughed. "No. I am known as the Honor—"

"Honorable Miss Elsegood." He nodded and touched my cheek.

"Was Amelia known as that also?" I asked.

"No. Amelia's father was a twin. The title of Viscount went to her uncle, Adam. The estate remained with her father because Adam didn't want to take responsibility for a crumbling estate that was losing money."

"I see. Well, I am happy it was left to Amelia then. She deserved to see it repaired."

"So, how does it work? Can you walk back in time any time you want?" He must have noticed my shiver because he rubbed up and down my arms to warm me.

"So far, it does work that way."

"Unbelievable," he whispered, then frowned. "So you came back for medical reasons?"

My smile faded. "Yes."

"And when you're through?"

I turned my head and regretted it the instant I did, for my eyes landed on the grave marker beside my mother's, and I could not miss the familiar name, my name, Ruth Ann Elsegood, engraved upon it. Before I could look away I had seen the date of my birth ... and my death.

Some unforgiving force pressed against my chest, and my eyesight darkened. "Take me back. I ... I am not ... well."

Chapter Twenty-Nine

1812 England, Abbie

"Had I known the Fosters invited other neighbors to Christmas dinner, I would never have agreed to come," I whispered to Celeste right before entering the dining room.

"I will help you bear it," Celeste whispered before she was escorted away. I followed along behind the group into the dining room. I sat beside the Russels and was left completely ignored, but at least I didn't have to act as though I enjoyed their company. The footmen brought out the main course in their stuffy costumes. Seeing them made me think of Albert's precious wig, and I felt a sudden pang. I noticed Mrs. Russel looking down her nose at me from across the table, and she glanced away as she took a rather large bite of meat. She must not have noticed how large she had cut it, being too busy scowling at me. Her cheek bulged as she tried to chew, swallowing before she could possibly have chewed enough. The instant Mrs. Russel swallowed, I knew she would choke.

Her eyes grew wide, and her mouth hung open. I waited long enough to see if she would cough. No sound came out. She pounded the table with her fist and caught the attention of those around her.

I stood and hurried around the table, knowing time was of the essence.

"What is happening?" someone asked.

"She's choking!" I called. Would anyone know the Heimlich maneuver? Had it been discovered yet? Given that no one else rushed to her rescue, I guessed not.

Instantly, I took charge and wrapped my arms around the woman's middle. She tried to push against my arms, and I fought back. "Knock it off! I'm trying to help you!" I yelled in her ear.

"What is she doing?" I heard someone ask at the same time that Celeste said, "She's only trying to help!"

I found the spot right under her ribs and locked my hands together. I jabbed her abdomen once, then twice. On the third attempt, I heard her lungs pushing air out of her mouth. She gasped a moment later. I dropped my hands to my sides and looked around her. There, across the table, on top of her oldest daughter's head, sat a chewed piece of meat tangled in her curls.

Silence settled over the room for what seemed like an eternity before Mr. Russel took hold of his wife's hand. "Are you well, my dear?"

"I think so," she responded with a hand over her heart.

I slowly stepped back amid the relieved exclamations of the guests.

"I'm well enough now. I was lucky I was able to get it out in time." She waved at her face.

Lucky she *got it out?* I frowned at Celeste. She frowned back. We knew what happened, and it had nothing to do with Mrs. Russel's abilities. I returned to my seat, receiving only glances from a few people.

Mrs. Russel didn't so much as acknowledge me.

The meal went on as if nothing had happened, and I was ignored once again. The only ones who continued to look at me were Celeste, Charles, and Miss Caroline Russel, the younger of the Russel girls. Once the meal was over, the women made their way into the drawing room. I walked to the window to sit alone and brood over the evening's events.

"How are you?" Celeste sat beside me in the settee.

I scowled. "Fine."

"You save a woman's life, which they all pass off as something incredibly mundane, then they ignore you, and you say 'fine'?" She shook her head and smiled. "Bravo, Abbie. I would have blown up and called them out long before now."

I laughed. "Do women actually call people out?"

She laughed. "Well … no, but sometimes I wish I could see the look on their faces if we did."

* * *

Present Day England, Ruth

I did not hear him enter my room. I had no idea I had an audience until his hand touched my shoulders. I gasped and turned around so quickly that my head protested in pain. After leaving the churchyard, I made excuses and hurried to my room. There, I stayed the rest of the day and into the night, crying until I caused myself a headache.

"I'm sorry I startled you," Josh whispered.

I checked the clock on my nightstand. It was one in the morning. "It is late, and you are in my chambers."

"I had to check on you." He touched my forehead. "All the nurses have the day off and won't return for a few days."

I sat up quickly and pulled the blanket up to my neck. "We are

244

alone?" My voice squeaked.

I could barely see him smile. "I'll be a gentleman. I promise."

I did not relax.

"I promise, Ruth," he whispered. "Why were you crying?"

"I was not crying." *What a fib that is.*

"Ruth, you were sobbing when I entered, and every time I walked by your door, I could hear you crying." He took my hand in his. "Tell me, please."

I shook my head, covered my face with the blanket, and cried … again.

"Please."

"I cannot. Not now. I still need some time … to think it through." I started to hiccup. *Why did this have to happen now? Now, when I have such a man in my life?*

Josh pulled on my hand, and I moved into his arms as he leaned over the bed. He kissed the top of my head, and I buried my face in his chest. He rubbed affectionately up and down my back while I cried. Knowing how little time I had left made it so much more difficult to be held by him. I wanted to be his more than anything, but I could not put him through losing a loved one again. I would have to leave … and soon.

I sat up. "I am fine now. You can go back to bed."

"Do you want to talk about it?"

"No. Not yet." I moved away from him to relieve the temptation of kissing him.

He watched me for a moment, then stood. "I'll see you for breakfast then?"

I nodded.

He walked to the door and paused. "I love you, my sweet lady."

My heart broke. *I cannot stay and hurt him.* "I love you," I whispered.

245

He shut the door, and I listened to his footsteps move away. With a wave, I flung the blankets back and hurried to my closet. My hands shook while I dressed in my old Regency clothes. I laced up my boots, put on my wig, tied my bonnet over it, and slipped my traveling coat on before checking myself in the mirror. *Me again.* I gathered the rest of my old clothes and folded them into my trunk. All my modern garments were left behind as I quietly walked out of the room with the trunk banging against my leg.

With everyone on holiday, it was easy to leave the house. I glanced over my shoulder at the large stone walls and shivered. It was terribly cold out, and I wished I'd had the foresight to bring my warmer coat. I hurried through the gate and did not slow down until well into the coverage of the forest. It seemed as though the walk took longer than I remembered. Perhaps the reason was that I had ridden a horse last time. Once I reached the tree, I paused and looked around, breathing hard. "Goodbye, my love. I truly am sorry." My voice cracked, and I sobbed once again.

* * *

1812 England, Celeste

Tap, tap, tap. I turned in my bed and moaned.

"Do they not know not to disturb us this morning?" Charles growled beside me. I opened one eye and could see faint light peeking its way through the curtains. The night before was Christmas, and we did not make it home until late. We planned to sleep well into the morning.

Tap, tap, tap. "Yes, yes. I hear you." Charles threw the blankets off and moved to the door, opening it.

"Sorry to disturb you, my lord." It was Herbert's voice. "I thought you should know. Miss Ruth has returned and retired to her room."

All sleepiness vanished, and I sat upright.

"Thank you, Herbert." Charles shut the door and looked at me with eyebrows furrowed. "Why would she come back now? Are her treatments done so soon?"

I shook my head. "No. The doctor said it would be sometime at the end of January."

"You do not suppose … something has happened?"

I shrugged. "Should I go to her?"

"Let her rest. If she made that journey through the forest during the night, then she needs her rest." He approached, kissed me quickly, and then walked to the door that joined our rooms. "Get some more rest. I am going to go check on the fields." He smiled and closed the door behind him.

I laid wide awake, knowing I wouldn't rest anymore tonight. Instead, I studied the curtains and thought about Ruth. Why had she returned? Did she simply come because she missed us? Had another friend passed away?

Those questions rattled through my mind as I went about my morning routine. It was well into the afternoon before Ruth left her room. I sat with Abbie in the east sitting room when Ruth entered, appearing fragile, her eyes red and swollen.

"Ruth!" I stood and guided her into my arms. She clung to me as if I were her lifeline. I pulled away to inspect her closer. "Why have you come? Has someone else passed on?"

She shook her head. "I finished my treatments early."

She did not look me in the eye. Something was not right. "Are you sure? The doctor said it would be January."

"I finished early," she repeated, smiling reassuringly. The smile did not touch her eyes.

"What is it, Ruth?"

She turned away. "It is nothing." She nodded to Abbie. "Greetings

247

again."

"Hi, Ruth. I'm glad you've come," Abby said in return.

Ruth sat on the sofa and breathed out in a gush. "What a long journey it was."

"Are you feeling well?" I sat beside her, keeping my eyes glued to hers, hoping I might catch a glimpse of the truth.

"I am well."

"Ruth. You've been crying."

She sighed. "It was difficult to leave my friends." Her voice caught.

"Why would you leave in the middle of the night?" I pressed.

"I could not sleep, and I was anxious to be back." She offered the same small smile and turned her attention to Abbie. "I have been anxious to get to know you, Abbie. When we first met, I was a little out of sorts, but I felt then, as I do now, that we shall be good friends."

"Good. I need more friends. Everyone around here thinks I'm a witch." Abbie smiled, but I could hear the bitterness in her voice.

"A witch?" Ruth tilted her head in question.

"The neighbors, particularly the Cromwells and Russels, are spreading rumors of the worst sort all around the county."

"Oh. I am sorry, Abbie."

Abbie shrugged. "It doesn't matter anymore."

My attention darted to Abby, and panic shot through me. Did Abbie plan to leave once the baby was born? Was I to lose her friendship so quickly? My heart ached at the thought.

Ruth scratched her head.

I reached out to touch a curl. "This wig is perfect for you."

"I got it for the ball." Her smile fell.

"Tell me about the ball." I leaned back in my chair. She told me of the music, the decorations, the food, the smells, the people, and most of all the dancing that was so unfamiliar to her. I laughed to think of what she had experienced. She shared about her friends and about Amelia

Elsegood, the late wife of Mr. Harrison—what she learned about this distant member of our family and how much she wished she could have known her. She told me of a horse called Norman and the time she rode on the golf course.

It was late afternoon when Ruth grew quiet. I sighed and stood. "Well, we have little time to prepare ourselves for dinner. We should go."

"Do we get to dine alone this evening? No neighbors?" Abbie asked with hope in her eyes.

"No neighbors."

Just then, the door opened and Albert entered. He nodded briskly and held out the silver tray containing a single calling card. I took it with some reluctance. We were not expecting visitors.

Mr. Joshua Harrison
Owner and founder of Shariton Park Cancer Treatment Centre

Printed below his name were his email address and phone number. My mouth dropped open, and I stared at Ruth in surprise.

"Shall I show him in, my lady?"

I studied the card again. "Yes, Albert. Please do." He nodded and left the room.

"Who is it?" Ruth asked anxiously.

"Why did you leave, Ruth?"

Her eyes darted to the door, then back at me. She didn't have a chance to answer before a man entered the room.

Ruth gasped and covered her mouth.

"Holy hotness," I heard Abbie whisper behind me.

"Ruth." His breath rushed out in obvious relief.

"Josh. What are you doing here?" Ruth's voice shook with emotion.

Josh's eyes darted around the room, landing on me. "You must be

Celeste," he said, eagerness alighting his eyes.

"I am."

He took my hand in both of his, holding it in a gentle embrace, and his eyes grew misty. "There are no words ... thank you for your generous—more than generous—donation to Shariton Park. You don't know what it meant to my late wife—your great, great, great, great ..." he smiled impishly, "granddaughter. We are indebted to you, as are all who receive cancer treatments there. Without you, it wouldn't have happened."

"Wow." I laughed nervously. "I was glad to do it. It was my father's money, you know, and when I came here, I didn't need it anymore, but I love this place, and so does my husband. You must meet him! He will be thrilled to learn how his descendants have maintained the estate ..." My smile faded. "Please accept my deepest sympathy for your wife's passing."

Ruth made a small noise in the back of her throat. I glanced at her, then back at Josh. His gaze was fixed on Ruth. "You must have a lot to catch up on. We'll leave you two alone," I said brightly. Giving Abbie a meaningful look, I led the way purposefully to the door. "We'll just be across the hall if you need us," I sang, setting off swiftly in the direction of Charles' study.

Chapter Thirty

1812 England, Ruth

"How did you find me?" I asked in amazement. He wore the same costume he had worn at the ball. If not for his poorly tied cravat, he would have fit perfectly in my brother's sitting room.

"It didn't take long for me to realize where you'd gone, and that odd tree root where I found you before—I knew that had to be it." He crossed the room and took my hand in his. He looked as though he wished to pull me into his arms, but after a glance at the open door, he held back. "Ruth, I've been worried sick about you. Why did you leave?"

"You should not have come here. I should not have told you." I tried desperately to hold back the flood of emotion, but my voice cracked, and the tears began to fall. Every fiber of my being wanted to drown in his arms, never to surface for breath.

"I had to. You left with no goodbye or note of any kind." He gently brushed my cheek with his fingers.

His touch caused my mind to cloud, but I somehow managed to speak. "I came back to stay."

Josh's eyes narrowed in confusion. "But your treatments are not finished."

I closed my eyes and tried to clear the fog from my mind. "I cannot finish treatments."

His hand froze against my cheek. "You are giving up?" Anger and hurt broke his voice.

I opened my eyes to see those same emotions in his eyes. I covered my face to hide the tears. "It is no use."

"You can't give up, Ruth." His chin trembled and his voice cracked.

"I am going to die soon anyway."

"What do you mean? You can't know that." He removed my hands from my face and studied me.

"That day in the churchyard, I saw my grave marker. I only have a week left, and it is not fair of me to make you watch me ..." The word would not pass my lips.

"That's not true. It can't be true."

"Josh ... I ..."

He pulled me into his arms. "No." His shoulders shook as he held me close. "No."

We cried for some time before either of us spoke. At last, he broke the silence.

"There must be some mistake. I just talked to the doctor, and he said your numbers look great. Your cancer is nearly gone now. He had high hopes for your full recovery." He stepped back and ran his fingers through his hair, shaking his head helplessly. "Come back with me, and he can test you again so we can be sure."

I shook my head. "I cannot. It is not fair to make you go through it all again."

He scowled. "Like it or not, Ruth, I lost my heart to you long ago. It doesn't matter where you go. I will lose you all the same. Quite frankly, I'm a little selfish, and I'd prefer to keep you close for whatever time is left."

I could not answer as the sobs tumbled out of me in great, heaving gasps. *Why is this happening to me? Why must I die instead of living a long, happy life with this wonderful man? It isn't fair!*

"Marry me, Ruth. Marry me right now. Let's not waste any more time." He pulled me closer and cupped my face in his hands, smiling through the tears sliding down his face. "Please say you'll be my wife."

Despite my misery, I smiled. I knew I needed Josh, yet it hurt to make him love and lose again. Maybe we were both selfish. I touched his handsome face and answered, "Yes."

He pressed his lips to mine. I could taste the salt of our tears as our lips moved together. When we parted, I dabbed at my eyes, laughing at the state of us. This man wanted me no matter how long we had left together. All thoughts of death and gloom fled. Determination pulsed through me. *I am going to enjoy the last week of my life. I am going to live it to the fullest.*

"Will you take me paragliding with you?"

"Yes!" He laughed, picked me up, and spun me around. When he set me down again, I remembered that Celeste still waited for an explanation of this unexpected visit.

"You cannot mention my death to my family," I said in a low voice, holding his gaze sternly with my own. "I do not want them to know."

His eyes narrowed in thought, hesitating, and then he nodded.

"I need them to believe I am living a full life when I return with you."

"If that is what you want."

"It is."

253

He smiled and gazed around the room. "So this is what this room used to look like."

"Let me take you on a tour of the house. You can stay the night and dine with us. In the morning, we will go for a ride, and I will show you what the grounds used to look like, then we can return."

"Sounds perfect," he said, stealing one last kiss before we left in search of my family.

* * *

1812 England, Abbie

"Mrs. Foster! What a pleasant surprise," Celeste greeted her guest in the entry hall.

"Lady Elsegood, I had to come and tell you myself how appalling I find the gossip regarding Mrs. Lambert!" Mrs. Foster looked fit to be tied. She turned to me, took my hand, and held it tight. "I hope *you* know, dear Mrs. Lambert, that I have not taken part in any of the slander. I *know* you are a modest and upright lady!"

"Thank you." Her emphatic kindness took me aback. Mrs. Foster had always been rather standoffish, yet I knew her to be a fair and decent woman.

"Would you care for some tea?" Celeste gestured toward a door leading to the west sitting room. We had yet to find out what was happening between Ruth and her mystery man in the east room.

"Oh, no, thank you. I do not wish to impose upon you a moment longer. I only hoped to pass on this information so you might set them straight," Mrs. Foster replied. She glanced around, leaned in close, and continued in hushed tones, "Mrs. Russel has been telling the whole neighborhood that you, Mrs. Lambert, *tried to murder her*!"

"What?" Celeste and I cried out at once.

What the crap?

Mrs. Foster nodded urgently. "She tells everyone that you used some kind of witchcraft to make her choke, and just when it seemed the offensive bite of food was becoming dislodged from her throat, you tried to force it back down!" Before we could react to this, she continued. "I was there, and I know for a fact that it is *not* true. I saw what you did to save her life, and I will not stand idly by and let that woman ruin you!"

I looked at Celeste and moaned. "This is only getting worse."

"Do not worry, Abbie. I will pay her a visit tomorrow and set things proper." Celeste took my hands in both of hers and held them.

The three of us turned at the sound of a man's voice. Ruth and the man from the future came around the corner. Her hand rested on his arm, and she smiled up at him.

"Ruth! You are back!" Mrs. Foster hurried to her and greeted her with a curtsy.

Ruth seemed momentarily surprised to see her. "Greetings, Mrs. Foster. It is good to see you again."

"You have been gone for far too long. I heard that you have been ill. I hope you being home is a sign that you have fully recovered," she declared.

"Yes—" Ruth's voice caught, and she cleared her throat before answering. "Yes. I am well now."

"And who is this?" Mrs. Foster looked pointedly at the man, who stood back with a polite smile.

"Forgive me, this is Mr. Harrison." Ruth gestured toward him. "Mr. Harrison, this is Mrs. Foster, one of our best neighbors."

"Good afternoon," he nodded.

"Are you here for long, Mr. Harrison?" she asked.

"No. In fact, I'll leave tomorrow. I'm here to escort Miss Elsegood back for one last medical treatment."

"Oh. Well, I hope to see you again. The country can be so refreshing after spending too much time in London," Mrs. Foster said. "Well, I must be on my way." She came to me and kissed my check. "It will get better once she is silenced."

"Thank you, Mrs. Foster," I said. Celeste and I walked with her outside and watched her carriage drive away.

I sighed. "At least we have someone on our side."

We rushed to dress for dinner, then met in the drawing room. I watched Ruth's sadness melt away throughout the evening. The man she introduced had come from my own time, and was the owner of the future Shariton Park. They appeared completely happy together.

It made me jealous.

After the kiss I shared with Albert on Christmas Eve, he went back to avoiding me. I tried to act as if it didn't bother me. I might have fooled him, but I couldn't fool myself. I was in love, and I couldn't seem to stop.

Seeing Ruth so blissfully happy with someone she was obviously smitten with caused my heart to ache for the same thing. The next day, after breakfast, they announced their engagement and said they planned to return to the future and marry right away.

Celeste was a little put out, for she wanted to be there for the wedding, but in her condition, she couldn't travel. Ruth reassured her that it would be a small wedding. Josh's parents were most likely the only ones that would be present. Charles, too, was upset, for he was to be called away on business the next day and couldn't be present either. Ruth said that once she finished treatments, she would return and have a big celebration to make up for it. That seemed to satisfy them both—at least a little.

Not long after breakfast, I watched a teary goodbye among the Elsegoods, especially on Ruth's part. She seemed the most emotional of them all. After they left, I walked the corridors well into the late afternoon.

The news of their engagement only caused me pain. Pain that was too much to bear.

Chapter Thirty-One

Present Day England, Ruth

My knuckles were white as I gripped the armrest of Josh's car. I disliked going so fast. *This is insane.* I could not even ride in a car without holding my breath in fright, and I was now heading out to the cliffs by the sea to go paragliding. *This is insane!*

"We're here," Josh announced. "Are you ready to get married?"

I nodded. We had decided to be married on the cliffs just before we took flight. His parents pulled up behind us and waved when we stepped out of the car. Two other men stood beside a car, dressed like a clergymen. They introduced themselves and asked me questions about my faith while Josh prepared the 'wing' we would be strapped to. I smoothed my elegant white pantsuit, taking steadying breaths. Naturally, I had wanted to wear a dress, but paragliding in a gown was not only impractical but hazardous, too, and I did not wish to give up our madcap plan for matrimony.

"Are you more nervous about the ride or the marriage?" David chuckled beside me. He had the same deep laugh as his son.

"Without a doubt, the ride," I smiled back at him. "I have no anxiety about the marriage," I spoke the complete and honest truth. I loved Josh and knew I wanted to share my life with him—as short as it would be.

"That's good to hear."

Josh stood, already strapped in, and waved me over. "Time to buckle you up."

I pulled my hat down on my head and joined him. David helped snap me in with several straps wrapped around my body, while Josh gave me instructions.

The ceremony was short and to the point, as Josh requested. When the time came to exchange rings, my heart dropped. I had no time to get him one. Heat rose in my cheeks as Josh dug in his pocket. Just as I was about to voice my folly and forgetfulness, David placed a ring in my hand. Traditions of marriage had changed over the years, which made it difficult to remember it all.

He winked at me. "I've got you covered."

I smiled in gratitude, then my face heated remembering another changed tradition that I had to look forward to. The kiss. "Thank you."

Josh took my hand in his and slid a ring upon my finger. I gasped when I saw the familiar stones and intricate workmanship of the gold. I looked up into his smiling eyes, tears clouding my vision. I happily said, 'I do,' with a shy giggle. We kissed with difficulty, as he was strapped behind me and people were watching.

"Smile," Cynthia said, snapping a photo. I smiled and waved at her, then kissed Josh again for the camera. This whole kissing in front of people had grown on me. I no longer felt shyness creep up on me each time. Perhaps I was too eager.

"Ready?" Josh asked in my ear after our helmets were snug on our heads.

"Ready." My voice caught.

"Remember to run until your feet don't touch the ground. You'll feel it pulling us back, so you must lean forward and run. Once we're securely in the air, sit back into the harness."

I nodded.

"Let's go." We started running forward, and I felt the pull against my body. My heart beat so fast I thought I would die right there, but of course I knew that it was too soon. I was not due to die for five more days—*what a strange thought.*

"The wind is perfect!" Josh called once we were in the air. "We lucked out!"

I did not respond for fear that if I opened my mouth, I would scream.

"How are you doing?"

I nodded.

"Are you breathing?" he laughed. "You're allowed to enjoy it, you know."

I let out my breath with a bursting laugh. Once I realized we would not plummet back to earth, I relaxed, but only a little. "I never, in all my life, thought such a thing was possible." I swung my arms out. "I am flying!"

Josh laughed with me, then pulled on the handle that connected to the wing. The sudden swing to the side had me squealing in delight. The cliffs below took my breath away. I watched the waves crash against the white cliffs and create white foam that floated on the water's edge.

"This is truly amazing. Now I can see why you love it so much." My voice was a continuous giggle. "This is amazing." I paused. "Celeste used to tell me stories of this century. She told me of all the awful things—the heartache, pain … suffering … wars and crime. I think she shared all that to frighten me away because she was afraid I would run off to see the mysteries of the twenty-first century for myself." I chuckled. "You know … it is not all bad. There is still joy, peaceful moments, and love."

"I suppose every century and time will experience the battle between good and evil," Josh mused.

"Yes," I agreed. "I am happy you are part of the good. Thank you for opening your home to the good—even though it brings heartache along with it."

"I wouldn't want it any other way." His voice grew soft, almost carried away with the wind.

After a few quiet moments, I held my hand out to look at the ring again. "This was my grandmother's."

"Really? Amelia and I never knew where it came from, only that it belonged to the family. I'm happy we can keep it in the family."

"We are married now." The realization hit stronger once my fear of flight was overcome.

"Now, I may call you my wife."

"Now that I am yours, what will you do with me?"

"I have a few ideas," he whispered.

I bit my lip and giggled. "This is incredible!"

"I'm happy this is your first experience flying. This is much better than flying in a plane."

"Celeste told me about planes long ago. I was amazed when I first heard of them. I never thought it possible. They must be the fastest things on earth."

"I would say the space shuttle is."

"Space shuttle?"

He laughed. "Did you not know? We've been to the moon!"

"What? You are jesting!" I laughed.

"That's it. I'm taking you to the planetarium. It will blow your mind." He pulled a cord, and we began spinning to the right.

I screamed and laughed. "Stop! Too much too soon!" I stuck my tongue out. "Ugh, I think I am going to be ill."

"All right, I won't do that again," he said with a laugh. "Have I told you how happy I am that you agreed to have our wedding out here?"

"Are you truly happy?" My smile faded for the first time since taking flight.

"I am."

"Even knowing we only have a short time together?"

"Let's not talk about that. Let's be in this moment," he said quietly.

"You are right. Forgive me."

"Will you do me a favor when we get back?" I could hear the laughter in his voice.

"Anything."

"I'm curious to see you in your old undergarments. Will you wear them for me?"

"Oh," I said with a squeak. If not for the cool wind blowing on my face, I might have overheated. I believed that was a sufficient enough answer for him.

When we neared the ground, I noticed his parents were the only ones who remained. His mom still took pictures, so I waved while we descended.

"Remember to run as soon as we touch the ground," he instructed, then pulled hard on the ropes. My heart thumped nearly as much landing as when we rose into the sky.

Once we hit the ground, I laughed, and I watched his parents hurrying to us. "That was amazing!" I couldn't stop giggling and smiling while being freed from the harness. I threw my arms around Josh and kissed him. He moaned and held me tight while we kissed. When I remembered we had an audience, I stepped away and blushed.

He took me around my waist, dipped me backward over his knee, and kissed me again. I could hear his mom taking pictures to the side of us. I laughed and waved my hand at my face when he set me back up.

"Well, my dear. It's time we left the newlyweds alone," David said, then gave us both a big hug. "Welcome to the family, sweet Ruth," he whispered, then smiled at me.

"Thank you." Tears flooded my eyes when I thought that I wouldn't get the chance to be part of his family for long.

* * *

1812 England, Abbie

"Please do not tell me nothing is wrong when I know something is." Celeste narrowed her eyes, letting them bore into me. "You have been moping about for days, and I have not heard you touch your guitar."

"I don't know what's wrong with me," I moaned and threw my needlework across the sofa in frustration. It was a stringy mess, anyhow. Time to give it up.

"Does this have anything to do with Albert?"

My head snapped up at the mention of his name. Warmth touched my cheeks, and I sunk into the sofa, knowing I'd given myself away.

"I know something is going on between you two. I saw the kiss you shared on Christmas Eve." One side of her mouth pulled into a half smile when she looked at me.

"You saw that?"

"I did. I even blocked the hall so no one could disturb you."

"You what?"

"Why do you think you were able to be alone for so long without someone finding you?" she chuckled. "This house is large, Abbie, but not that large."

I bit my lip and tried not to think too much about that kiss.

"So?" she prompted.

"Hum?" I asked, trying to hide my heated face.

263

"Is there something going on?"

"Not anymore," I grumbled.

"And why not?"

"He's a footman and I'm a lady—well, sort of a lady … and I'm a black widow." I wiggled my fingers and scrunched my nose.

"You have not poisoned him yet, have you?" she winked.

"It seems he was poisoned already." My smile fell. "He thinks that nothing can happen between us so long as I'm a lady and he's in the working class."

Celeste put down her needlework and looked at me like she was a mother about to give her daughter the most important advice she could give. It surprised me when she asked me a question instead. "Abbie, what would make you most happy?"

I shrugged.

"I think you do. Think about it."

Tears came to my eyes and emotion clogged my throat. "I don't dare voice it."

"Would you be happy continuing to live here?" she asked.

I shook my head. "I know I wouldn't. I want to become something more than someone who sits around picking fabric with needles—no offense."

"None taken," she smiled. "Do you love him?"

I nodded. "I've tried not to, but I can't help myself. I want a life with him more than anything."

"Then tell him. Tell him everything and take him with you. If it's meant to be and he loves you truly, then it will all work out." She smiled. "But you should wait until the baby's born. Traveling is dangerous so far along."

My heart fell. I couldn't tell her the other reason I was feeling down. I had begun to feel more and more strongly that I couldn't let my child be raised in this day and age. I wanted more for my child, just as I wanted more for myself.

I stood. "Thank you for the talk. I need some time to think." I paused when I reached the door. "Would it be all right if I dined alone in my room tonight?"

"I will have a tray sent up for you," she said. "In fact, I believe it a splendid idea, and I will follow your example." She stood and stretched, then held her growing belly.

I walked the gardens for a time and then the corridors. When I found myself at my favorite window, I sat and put my feet up. The sun hung low, close to setting, and I was determined to watch it from this window. I heard footsteps right outside the curtain, so I carefully peeked out.

I inhaled. "Albert."

He pulled the curtain aside and smiled. "I see you are enjoying a moment of solitude."

"Please, sit with me." I moved my feet, and he sat down beside me. A drop of sweat slowly trickled down his brow. His cheeks were red and he appeared tired.

"Are you getting sick?" I asked, laying my hand on his forehead.

"I am perfectly well," he said.

"Liar. You're burning up."

"I just finished a long run around the grounds on an errand. I am well."

"Okay. If you say so." *Men can be so stubborn,* "Can I ask you a question?"

"You already did," he teased.

I normally would have laughed if not for the seriousness of my question. "Do you love me?" I said the words slowly—this shy feeling was new to me.

His eyes widened. "Abbie ... I ..."

"It's a simple question, answered with a yes or no." My heart stopped as I waited for his answer.

"I do," he whispered.

My heart beat again, a little quicker. I smiled a little. "Then I need to tell you something." I cleared my throat and kept my eyes down on our joined hands. "You remember all those things I told you about my made-up world?"

He nodded and peered at me questioningly.

"Most of what I told you is true. Those things exist, but only in the time I came from."

His eyes narrowed in confusion.

"I was born almost two hundred years from now. I traveled through time and came here. I'm from America, but a future America. A place called California."

His thumb stopped moving and his grip tightened.

"I know you might think this is all absurd, but it's true." I felt panic rise in me at the look on his face. His lips pressed together, and his brows pulled together.

"Why did you come here?" he whispered.

"I came because Celeste and Charles were willing to help. I had found out I was with child, and I needed a place to hide away."

"You knew before you came that you were with child?" His voice grew shaky.

"I did."

"So you lied. Where is your husband?" He narrowed his eyes.

This wasn't going well. I needed him to believe me, and the truth had to be told. "I was never married."

He stood abruptly.

I took hold of his arm and held him. "Please, Albert. Listen to me." My throat tightened as if his alarm had caused it to seize up. "I love you more than anything, and that is why I told you this—in hopes that you will come back with me, to my own time."

He jerked his arm free. "You have wounded me, Abbie. You have

266

toyed with my heart long enough." He walked quickly away. I tried to keep up with him, but his legs were too long.

"Albert, please!" I cried as I watched him turn the corner and run. "Albert," I whispered and slid against the wall to the floor, my heart shredded in two.

Chapter Thirty-Two

1812 England, Celeste

I started to doze when a knock sounded at the door. I reached across the blankets, then remembered I was alone for the third night in a row, for Charles had traveled into town on business.

I opened the door to find Molly frazzled and frightened. "Molly, what's happened. Is Abbie unwell?"

"I do not know where she is, my lady. She was not in her room and I found this." She held out a letter to me.

"I don't understand." I took the letter and opened it.

My dearest friend in all of time,

~~I'm sorry~~ I apologize for leaving this letter and not speaking to you directly. But I'm a great big chicken when it comes to goodbyes.

Please forgive me, Celeste. I've been debating with myself for months over this, and I now know I can't let my child live in the past. I have seen nothing but heartache here, and I can't let my child live somewhere they can't live a better dream. I want my baby to become something more. I hope you can understand that. I pray you do. I thank you from the bottom of my heart for taking me in and treating me as your own sister. You'll always reside in my heart, and I'll remember all you taught me. Give Charles my love, and give yourself a great big bear hug from me. Again, I'm truly sorry for hurting you by leaving this way.

    Love always, your forever friend,
        Abbie Lambert

    P. S. I guess it wasn't meant to be.

The words were smudged, the letter tearstained. My hands shook as I reread the letter, trying to force my mind to make sense of it all.

"What should I do, my lady?" Molly broke through my muddled thoughts.

I looked at her and scowled. "Where's Albert?"

"I suppose he is retiring for the night."

"Take me to him." I pulled a robe around my shoulders and retrieved a hidden purse of coins from my wardrobe, then pushed her out the door. We hurried down the corridors and up a flight of stairs to the servants' quarters. When we reached Albert's door, Molly knocked. A groan came from inside. She knocked again just as the door opened.

Albert leaned heavily upon it, sweat glistening on his forehead, skin flushed with fever. "What is it?" he moaned, straightening right away when he realized who stood at his door. "My lady! I did not—"

"No time for that, Albert," I said, letting the anger touch my words. *How dare he get sick at a time like this!* "Abbie has run away." Molly edged away. My hand reached out to stop her. "Stay."

Albert's face turned ghostly white. "She what?"

269

"She's gone—and you, big buffoon, you let her get away," I loudly whispered so as not to wake the others. I threw the letter at his sweaty head. "She told you where she came from, didn't she?"

"Yes." His eyes narrowed.

"Well, she was telling the truth. Charles and I found her in the year 2012, alone and with child."

"Yes. She told me about the child."

"Did she also tell you that she had been taken advantage of and that none of it was her fault?" His eyes widened, and a look of pain crossed his face. "You did not let her get far enough to explain, did you?"

He swallowed hard and shook his head.

"Every bit of what she told you was the truth. I know it, and Lord Elsegood knows it. Even Sir and Lady Garrison know about it."

"It is true?"

"Of course, it's true. Now get your boots and coat on, and go find her. She's out there in the freezing cold, stumbling through the forest with a child in her womb, so you best make haste!"

He shut his door, and I heard him fumbling around his room. I turned to Molly. "You need to go with him. He does not look well."

"Go where? I do not understand." The poor girl appeared so confused.

"You will—Wait a moment, and I'll explain."

Once Albert was ready, we headed back down to the second floor. I pulled them into the study and sketched as I gave them instructions. "You two are going to travel through time, to the year 2012. Once you get out on the road, follow it until you come to the dead tree on the left. Go directly north from that tree. Keep that northern heading and search for the markings on a tree that look like this." I drew a mark that resembled the family crest. "You'll need to find this tree." I held up the drawing I had made of the large tree with the root arch. "It's the only one of its kind for miles, so you should know it. Go this way through

270

this arch. Doing so will take you forward in time. If you continue north, you'll come to a black road. Do not walk on the road or try to cross it. Stay on the side, wave your arms, and attempt to get someone to stop and help you."

Molly was faint, and Albert looked plain ill.

"If you can't find Abbie, make your way to the nearest hospital. After the long walk through the cold, she may end up there anyway, and you may need to visit a doctor also." I glanced at Albert, hating that he looked so weak. "Stay strong. You need to find her."

"We'll bring her back." Molly gave a small smile.

"I'll not expect you back—at least not to stay," I said sadly. "You'll both have a better life there." I gave them the coins. "Here's what is owed you, with an added bonus. Use it only when needed. The coins will be old and worth more than they are now. Remember all that Abbie has told you about the future. And watch out for the motorcars. They travel faster than a horse can. Charles is due back tomorrow. I'll send him to help as soon as he arrives." I hugged Molly and hurried with them to the door.

"Goodbye, my lady," they said together, still with a dazed look of disbelief.

"Take care of each other, and please find her." My voice cracked with worry.

* * *

Present Day England, Abbie

I leaned against a tree and groaned, blinking in the rain that fell on my face. The moment I passed through the arch of the tree root, the downpour soaked through my clothes. I had retrieved my pack and guitar before leaving Shariton but had left most of my clothes behind.

271

Exhaustion filled every pore of my being, and persistent, sharp pains dominated in my abdomen. It couldn't be a good sign.

Counting to ten repeatedly, I breathed in and out, desperately trying to calm my stupid heart. My tears of frustration mixed with the downpour as I peered through the trees. "I hate you for doing this to me!" I yelled at the jerk I once thought of as a nice guy. I hadn't thought of the father of my child in months. It wasn't until I was out in the forest again, feeling alone and helpless, that his face invaded my mind. I trusted him, and he left me like this. I hated him for it.

I hated Albert, too. I opened my heart to him, and he crushed it without a backward glance. "Never again," I said to the rain. I hated the rain, too.

I stood and pulled my pack tighter against my shoulders, gripping my guitar case under my arm, and walked toward Shariton. I had decided early on that being taken away to a hospital somewhere wasn't the answer I sought. I knew nothing of the healthcare system here, and I had no money to return home, so I headed toward the only person I knew I could trust—Ruth.

* * *

Present Day England, Ruth

"So, what did you think of the planetarium?" Josh asked as he finished whipping cream for the topping of a chocolate cake. He had insisted on teaching me how to cook, and making cake was first on his list of the best foods ever. I perched on a bar stool at the counter and watched him in awe. It had never occurred to me that a gentleman might learn to cook. As hard as it was for me to imagine myself, a lady, cooking, it was still more difficult to entertain the idea of a man of his standing in the kitchen.

It was quite late, and he said that having late-night snacks—especially chocolate ones—was essential in learning to cook. We baked in his personal kitchen, which sat far away from the guests that had remained during the season. It was meant for Amelia and him to have quiet dinners together to raise a family. It saddened me to think he would be alone in it once again.

"There are no words to explain," I said. "It makes one feel small and insignificant, does it not?"

"In a way, yes," he said. I sighed at his smile. Two days ago, we had leapt from the cliffs after saying, 'I do,' and I thought then that nothing could astound me more than that flight. Upon learning more about this vast world, the skies, stars and galaxies discovered in seemingly limitless space, I could not fathom the mysteries it concealed. Not the least was our ability to somehow travel through time and find one another. With all my heart, I wished I had more time to learn about these incomprehensible secrets.

"There is so much to learn," I whispered. *And so little time.*

The rumble of thunder followed a flash of lightning. "That's unusual at this time of year," Josh said, peering outside with a creased brow. He spread a small amount of whipped cream over the cake and handed me the spoon. "Is your mouth watering yet?"

"It has been since the smell permeated the air." I scooped a spoonful and watched the steam swirl and rise against the dark goodness within. I blew on it and noticed Josh watching me eagerly. My senses came alive, and the smooth, warm chocolate moved against my tongue. "Mmmmm." I closed my eyes as I chewed.

"It's good, then?" Josh asked with a burning fire in his eyes. He pulled me into his arms and kissed my neck.

"Very good," I squeaked.

Josh's lips found mine for a moment, then he chuckled. "Chocolate cake tastes good on you."

I laughed and pulled him back down to kiss me again, but before our lips touched, I jumped at the sound of a chime.

Josh looked confused. "It's well after midnight. Who would be visiting so late?" He walked to the door and I followed behind. Josh opened the door and gasped, his body blocking my view.

"What on earth?" He lifted someone from the ground, slowly backing up into the house.

"Who is it?" I asked with alarm.

He turned and I saw the round belly and pale face. "Abbie!" I shrieked. "You are soaked to the bone!" Thousands of questions flooded my mind as he carried her to the lift and down the hall to my room. "You undress her while I call for Kaitlyn. I think she's the only one back from holiday." He left the room, and I went to work undressing Abbie and redressing her in one of my own comfortable nightgowns.

Her teeth chattered uncontrollably, and she pulled the blankets to her neck.

"What happened? Why did you come alone and in your condition?" I asked, drying her hair with a towel.

"I was afraid." Her words were difficult to understand, slow, and slurred.

"Was someone unkind? Did someone try to hurt you?"

"I couldn't let … my child be born into that time."

"Whyever not?" I said a little defensively.

"Tell me the truth, Ruth … if you had no dowry, title, or family name … would you have any hope of … making a life? Would you have any hope of a future at all?" She coughed and struggled to speak.

Before I could answer, Josh and Kaitlyn hurried into the room, the latter with a cart full of medical items.

"What's your name, love?" Kaitlyn asked.

"Abbie Lambert."

Kaitlyn's eyes widened. "You sound American."

Abbie nodded.

"I suppose you don't have citizenship here?"

"No."

Kaitlyn frowned. "How far along are you?"

"I'm due sometime at the beginning of March," Abbie answered.

Kaitlyn checked her vitals, then put a stethoscope against her abdomen. Kaitlyn asked Abbie several more questions about how she felt and if she had family here. She was shocked that the girl had not been to see a physician at all during her pregnancy.

"Will she be well?" I asked once Kaitlyn finished.

"I think so."

"And the baby?" Josh asked.

"The heartbeat is strong. I see no reason why she shouldn't deliver a healthy baby, but she should be seen by a doctor. She's having pain, possibly Braxton Hicks." She frowned. "She's had too much exercise and has been too long out in the cold for her own good. She has a fever."

My heart quickened. Fevers were bad news in my experience.

"I'll give her something to bring it down." Kaitlyn's eyes spoke of worry and spiked discontent in my heart.

Five minutes later, the three of us left Abbie to rest. Josh shut the door behind us, and we shuffled out into the corridor. Kaitlyn motioned to follow her down the hall. Once our voices were from her door, Kaitlyn stopped the cart and looked at us.

"If she doesn't lose that fever soon, she'll need medical help. I don't have any clue what to do with pregnancy." She sighed. "I also don't know what laws are in place to prevent her from delivering the baby here. They may send her back to America."

This was all new, and confusing to me. I did not understand why they could not help her regardless. I lifted my hand to rub my temple but was startled when Kaitlyn snapped my hand away and held it, gazing at my ring in surprise.

"What do I see on this hand?" She smiled and looked at us with wide eyes. "Are you engaged?"

Josh pulled me closer to him, his hand wrapped around my waist. "Married, actually,"

"What?" She giggled and hugged us both. "That was sudden! The staff and some of our guests were betting on how long it would take for things to get serious, but none of us guessed it would be so quick." She giggled and hugged us again, "Why aren't you two gone on your honeymoon?"

Now I knew I blushed.

"Ruth doesn't have her NI number yet, nor her passport. Without her passport, we couldn't fly anywhere," Josh explained. "We're going to spend a few days in London, but now we should stay with Abbie until she's well."

"Speaking of Abbie," I stood a little taller, "I will pay for any care she needs."

Josh stared at me with disapproval. "You're not spending a dime on her. Your family has given enough. Let me take care of it."

"Celeste has grown very close to Abbie. You barely know her," I protested.

"If she's important to your family, then she's important to me," he said and gave a short nod. "Your family's my family."

I smiled and cupped his cheek with my hand. "I love you, Joshua David Harrison."

Josh leaned in, but before he could kiss me, Kaitlyn interrupted. "And that's my cue to leave. Good night! I'll keep an eye on Abbie and let you know if things get worse."

"Thanks, Kaitlyn," we said in unison.

"Alone at last." Josh kissed me, then scooped me in his arms and carried me to bed.

Chapter Thirty-Three

Present Day England, Abbie

"I feel like crap," I said aloud to the empty room. The digital clock repeatedly flashed 12 a.m. Beside it, several candles burned low, their light barely registering in the bright daylight streaming through the window. For a moment, I wondered if I hadn't traveled through time and was still stuck in 1812. But vaguely, I remembered someone entering my room sometime during the night and lighting the candles. The only explanation for it was that the power had gone out. Last night hazed together in my mind, and nothing around me looked familiar.

My large belly moved, and I realized what had woken me. I placed my hand on the spot where my baby pushed. "Are you as hungry as I am?" My voice sounded nasal, and my sinuses felt stuffed up. I sat and coughed for what seemed the hundredth time, and my achy body protested. I glanced around the room and found, to my joy, a TV. Where there was a TV and a radio, there must be a flushing toilet. And a hot shower!

I took the longest shower on record, sitting down and letting the water pelt my back. When I could bring myself to leave the warm, heavenly luxury of running water, I brushed through my hair (finally really clean!), donned the nightgown Ruth had dressed me in, and hurried down the hall. It was familiar, but the colors were all wrong. I walked in the direction of the stairs. There I also found an elevator. Flashes of memory returned to me, and I thought about my trip through the woods during the night. "I made it."

I took the elevator down to the main floor and wandered to the drawing room, then to the sitting room. No one seemed to be around. I heard a door shut and moved toward the sound. I paused and leaned against the wall when pain shot through my abdomen, and everything tightened. "Owww," I groaned. It lasted only a minute, and I continued my trek toward someone, anyone. The sound of a sports commentator echoed toward me. I followed the noise and found myself in a fairly modern room with couches, a TV, a pool table, several tables and chairs, and a few people occupying them. One bald, middle-aged man sat watching a sports show. He was the first to notice me, and he rose to his feet with questioning eyes. I gripped the door frame with one hand and my belly with the other.

"Who are you?" He hurried to my side and placed a steadying hand on my arm.

"Abbie. I'm a friend of Ruth's." I breathed deeply to push through the pain that had come again. "Do you know where she is?"

The man studied me. "Are you sick?" He felt my head. "You're burning up!" He turned to someone standing nearby. "Go get Kaitlyn."

He helped me to the couch to lie down. Wait. Everyone in the room had no hair. "Oh yeah, this is a cancer treatment center now, right?"

"Yes, and not a birthing center, so don't get any ideas, young lady.

I'm not catching any babies today," he winked. He propped my head up with a pillow and sat at my feet, watching me with brows creased.

"Thank you," I coughed, and he turned away.

The nurse who had helped me last night rushed in. "What are you doing out of bed?" she scowled.

"I dunno. I guess I wanted to see where I was."

She lifted her stethoscope to her ears and listened to the baby's heartbeat, then mine. It must have been fine because she didn't indicate otherwise. I scrunched myself into a fetal position when the pain and tightness shot through my abdomen once more.

"Are you having contractions?" Kaitlyn asked.

"Maybe."

She pressed her lips together and took my temperature. "One hundred and three!" She stood and took my hand. "Steve, go get Josh and Ruth. Tell them we need to get Abbie to the hospital. Hurry!" She pulled me to my feet and wrapped her arm around me. Steve was out of the room before I was steady on my feet. I put my arm around Kaitlyn's shoulders and let her walk me into the hall. We had gone only a few steps when Ruth and Josh joined us.

"I'll get the car." Josh hurried away, and Ruth took her place on my other side.

"What's going on?" Ruth asked.

"She's having contractions. If she births this baby now, it won't survive," Kaitlyn said.

My heart beat a little faster. Could I have put myself in greater danger by coming here than if I had stayed? I closed my eyes and prayed all the way to the hospital, hoping my baby would survive.

* * *

I passed the same four pictures hanging on the wall for the hundredth time as we waited for the doctor to check Abbie. Would she and the baby survive? A door clicked open, and I clutched Josh's hand when the doctor stepped out. He smiled and nodded. He had given her medication to stop the labor from continuing. She was doing well now, but she needed to be watched for the remainder of the day, and possibly through the night, to know for sure that it was doing its job. If it proved successful, she could return home, but she would be on bed rest for the remainder of her pregnancy. I sighed in relief. There would be no major travel for Abbie in the near future.

"I'm going to get something to eat in the cafeteria. Are you hungry?" Josh asked me.

I nodded. "I will join you. Let me tell Abbie first." I hurried into the room and informed her of where we were going.

"Bring me back some chocolate," Abbie smiled.

"I will," I promised, glad to see her in good spirits. She seemed much happier here than she had been in the past, despite her current situation. I walked with Josh to the cafeteria, where we ordered sandwiches and picked up many chocolate bars. While Josh collected our beverages, I searched for a quiet table. I wandered to a corner of the large room, and my eyes passed over a young woman sitting alone, her shoulders slumped and her head in her hands. As I studied her, I stopped short in shock. Her clothing, which at first seemed familiar, was, I now realized, out of place. I gazed in confusion at the white apron and the servant's cap. She leaned back and stroked someone's head. I stepped closer, spotting a man lying beside her on the bench seat, his head in her lap.

"Molly?" I asked.

She jumped and turned her head in surprise. Her eyes widened when she recognized me. "Oh, Miss Elsegood! You're a sight for sore eyes, you are!"

The man groaned and sat up.

"Albert!" I lowered myself into a chair at the table before I could faint dead away. "What are you doing here?"

"Looking for Abbie," Molly responded. "She has run away, and we cannot find her." Tears filled the girl's eyes, and she started to sob. "Albert got real sick, and I brought him here. They told him he has the flu, and then they told us to go home—but we cannot go anywhere with him feeling so ill."

Albert's head rested on the table in front of him. "Forgive me for not standing, Miss Elsegood."

"Do not think of it." I exclaimed. I noticed Molly's attention riveted on the sandwich in front of me. I pushed it toward her. "Eat, Molly, and I will take you both home." I did not know if I should reveal Abbie's whereabouts until I knew all of her story and why she had run away.

"We cannot go home until we find her," Albert mumbled.

"You are sick. I will take you home, then we will find Abbie." I helped the two up out of their seats and steadied Albert on his feet.

"Thank you, Miss Elsegood." He leaned heavily on me.

"It is Mrs. Harrison now."

"You are married, miss?" Molly's eyebrows rose.

"What's all this?" Josh asked, joining us.

"More friends from my *old home*," I replied.

"Ah," he said, looking sideways at me. I shrugged my shoulders helplessly. The thing was getting altogether out of hand. Josh turned to Albert. "You don't look so good, mate."

"He has the flu. We must take them back to Shariton Park right away."

"I'll take them, and you stay with—"

I cut him off. "With your friend … yes. You take them."

He gave me another odd glance but said nothing, escorting the two out of the building to his car. I followed them, thinking hard.

"This one is much nicer than the one we rode to the hospital," Molly said, settling herself into the car and studying the clean interior with approval. I helped Josh get Albert into the passenger seat and closed the door.

I turned to Josh and murmured in his ear as we embraced, "Keep Abbie's whereabouts secret for now. I do not know what has happened, and I do not want anything to upset her or cause her to deliver the baby too soon."

"All right." He kissed my neck and hugged me tight. "I'm sorry our last days together will be filled with hospital visits and stress."

I sighed. "At least I will be serving the needy and doing the Lord's will during my last days." I smiled at him. "I suppose it is a good way to go."

He kissed me goodbye and promised to be back within the hour. It was difficult to say goodbye, even for the short time we would be apart. Every minute counted.

* * *

Present Day England, Abbie

What kind of a future did I have? If I kept my baby, would I turn out like my mother? I knew she regretted keeping me. She had turned to drugs and alcohol as a coping mechanism for the stress and turmoil in her young life. My grandmother took me in, but she begged my mother repeatedly to take me back. I grew up unwanted. Was that the life I was destined to give my child? How could I be sure I would be any better than my mother when faced with the stress of raising a child alone. I wanted to be there for my children. Dependable. I'd told myself many times over that I would be, but fear and doubt berated my mind incessantly.

My baby moved inside me, and I gently pushed back. "I can be better. I have to be." A tear trickled down my cheek as I gazed up at the ceiling and counted the tiles until they disappeared beyond the curtain that divided the room. I had given up watching TV hours ago. The woman next to me had hers turned up quite loudly, and each time I turned on my TV, she turned the volume up even louder on hers. If I weren't already so beaten down emotionally, I would've fought back valiantly. My old self would've turned my TV up all the way, and then at the top of my lungs I would've sung a song or repeated—as loudly as I could—every word that was said on TV. I used to be an annoying brat who only laughed at what people threw at me.

Something had changed me. I felt broken.

Could a broken young woman raise a happy child?

"May I come in?"

I turned at Ruth's voice and wiped at my wet cheeks. "That depends on if you want to be accosted by a very loud television." I waved at the curtain next to me. The TV instantly grew louder. I rolled my eyes.

"As soon as the doctor releases you, you will get to stay with us at Shariton Park, in your own room with people waiting on you night and day," Ruth smiled, sitting on the bed.

"And be a leech," I grumbled.

She looked momentarily confused, and then understanding caused her to smile. "Forced to be a leech, as you might say. You will not be permitted to travel, and you may even be put on bed rest. So there is no way around it ... you are becoming a leech." She nudged my leg and smiled again. From the first moment I met her, I felt like she was a long-lost sister. The kind to be jealous of and get into heated debates with. The kind who would steal my clothes without permission, and then deny it when confronted. The kind who would thoroughly enjoy a

283

good prank.

Right now, I didn't want to smile. I wanted to argue. I had no reason to smile, but seeing Ruth's irritating smile caused me to return the favor with gusto. I gave her the cheesiest of grins. She had the nerve to laugh. After my smile faded, I frowned. "If you've come to get me to smile, you've succeeded. Bravo. Here's a pat on the back. Maybe one of the nurses will have a star sticker for you." I pulled the blanket over my head. "Now let me be sick and wither away in peace," I said, coughing.

"Now, what would make you say such things?" She pulled the blanket off my head. My hair snapped with the sound of static electricity and then went every which way. Ruth laughed, smoothed my hair, and sighed.

"Do you miss your hair?" I asked, my heart aching for her.

She waited for me to finish coughing before answering, "Yes."

"It will grow back in no time," I said. Focusing on Ruth's sorrows instead of my own felt better.

Her demeanor suddenly looked forlorn and weak. It was a physical change in her countenance that I found unnerving. She sighed and studied at her hands. "What truly caused you to come back?"

I frowned and tried to pull the blankets over my head again, but she held them down.

A crease appeared between her brows. "It was not because of the nobility looking down their noses at you, was it?"

I knew my facial expressions were too telling. I always gave myself away. I covered my face and mumbled, "Yes, it was."

She chuckled and pulled my hands away. "You cannot fool me. Tell me about it."

"Please. I don't want to talk about it now. I'm too tired."

"Very well. But you owe me a story when you are feeling better," Ruth said and stood.

"Wait. Did you bring me any chocolate?" I asked, hopeful.

She produced a candy bar with a wink. "We ran into some friends in the cafeteria, and Josh gave them a ride home. When he gets back, we will see what the doctor says, then decide if we will be making you a cake tonight at home."

I crossed my fingers, pressed my eyelids together, and whispered, "Chocolate cake ... chocolate cake ... chocolate cake ..."

Chapter Thirty-Four

Present Day England, Ruth

Abbie received her chocolate cake late that night. The doctor released her with orders for no traveling and partial bed rest. She could be wheeled about the estate, but she needed to keep off her feet. Her illness had improved so that all that remained was a small, irritating cough and a runny nose.

I kept her oblivious to the knowledge of Albert and Molly residing in the same building. Albert had recovered as much as Abbie had. However, Molly fell ill. We kept the lot of them separated from all other guests for fear of disrupting their recovery and treatments. I had to wear gloves and a mask when around them so that I, too, would stay safe.

When I woke on the morning of my death date, doom filled my soul, weighing me down. My time was nearly up. I needed to visit Abbie and force the truth from her. I knew there must be more to her departure than she had yet divulged.

When I entered her room, I found her in tears. I hurried to her. "What is wrong, Abbie?"

She waved me off. "Oh … it's nothing."

"Obviously, that is not true." I tucked her hair behind her ear.

She wiped her tears and tried to smile. "I'm all better now."

I stood. "Perhaps you need a change of scenery." I helped her out of the bed and into a wheelchair.

We rode the lift to the main floor, and then I pushed her along the corridors. We talked about the differences between the old and new Shariton. Some changes were an improvement, some things we wished had stayed the same. As I pushed her past the library, she stopped me.

"Can we go in there?"

"Of course. Do you wish to read a book?" I asked, wheeling her in.

"Well, I was wondering … did your family keep a record of the comings and goings of those at Shariton?" She sat up and looked around the room.

My brows rose. "Yes, as a matter of fact, we did!" I moved around the room in search of the familiar book. I came upon its faded spine tucked among those on the highest shelf. "Here it is." I pulled it from its home and nearly dropped the heavy volume. I placed it on a small table and sat beside Abbie. "Was there something in particular you were searching for?"

She shrugged and flipped through the pages. Each turn of the page released smells of old parchment. My heart quickened, thinking of what information this book held. Would she see my date of death in these records? I felt the sudden urge to pull it from her grasp and keep my secret hidden, but the urgency in her eyes kept me from following through.

She paused when she found the years 1812 through 1813. Her finger moved down the page and stopped. She gasped, covered her mouth, and stared at me.

My heartbeat stopped, and I swallowed to dislodge the lump in my throat.

"How is it possible?" Tears filled her eyes. "That you ... Molly and ..." she swallowed hard, "Albert. All of you on the same day?"

"What? I only knew of myself!" I moved closer to see it for myself.

"You knew of your death?" Her eyes widened, her voice raised.

I nodded and looked at the dates listed beside all our names. My mouth hung open in confusion. "How is it possible?" I stood. "I need to talk to someone. Will you stay here for a moment?"

She covered her face and nodded.

"I am terribly sorry to leave you at a time like this, but I need answers, and I am running out of time." I hurried from the room, making my way up to a guest room on the third floor. I continuously knocked until someone answered.

"One moment," I heard a male voice say.

The door opened a moment later, and I reached out to Albert and Molly, desperately needing to feel they were real and whole. "Tell me. What happened the day you left?"

"Uh ..." Albert looked at me in confusion.

"Did you leave Celeste in anger? Was there a problem of some kind?" My hands shook.

"No, my lady. Celeste begged us to come looking for Abbie. She gave us instructions on how to travel here, and we tried our best to do her will," Albert responded. "As a matter of fact, I wish to leave today and continue our search, if that is agreeable to you."

"Do not bother. She is downstairs," I said irritably. "She is recovering from illness."

He staggered back in surprise, and Molly gasped.

"Is there anything you can tell me that would explain why Charles would record our deaths as today?" I wrung my hands together, my heart pounding and aching.

"Our …" Albert swallowed, "deaths."

"Perhaps I should go ask Celeste myself," I said and took a few steps away.

"Oh, you cannot do that, miss," Molly said weakly.

"Why not?" I asked.

"The tree root was damaged," she responded, her voice failing her. "It was storming the night we left. Just as Albert and I passed through the root, a roar of thunder sounded right upon us. We ran for cover, miss, and then lightning struck so close it hurt our ears. I heard a terrible crack." She stopped and lowered her eyes. "The archway was collapsed, completely destroyed."

I stared at her in shock. "It's gone?"

"I do not believe it possible for us to return."

I turned away, holding my hand to my stomach. *This can't be!*

"Wait! Please, my lady, where is Abbie?" Albert followed me down the corridor.

"Albert, there is no more 'my lady' here," I whispered. "I left Abbie in the library." I stopped and looked at him with sudden understanding, "You love her, don't you?"

He nodded. "With all my heart."

A smile pulled at my lips, then disappeared as soon as it came. "Then go to her. She is now mourning your death."

I hurried away, heading outside. When I reached the stables, I found the new groom Josh had hired mucking out the stall. "I need Norman saddled."

"Right-o." He called and pulled Norman from his stall. A few minutes later, I was mounted and riding across the yard past the front entry. I faintly heard my name being called but chose to ignore it. I had to see for myself if we were indeed separated from my family for life.

Throughout the forest, I had to dodge great big mud puddles. I was afraid Norman would throw a shoe, so I tried to stay clear of the deep mud as best I could without losing my way. I was getting close when Norman started acting up.

"What is it, boy?" I asked and patted his neck.

The tree came into view at the same moment Norman started to buck. I screeched and tried to get a better grip, but my hand slipped. My body jerked forward, and my head collided with the back of the horse's head. Stars flashed when I felt my body fly back and to the right. My body jolted and pain shot through my head. Then everything went dark.

* * *

Present Day England, Abbie

I sat in the wheelchair feeling shock, which moved into confusion, then gloom. I knew when I came back that I was giving up a life with Albert, but seeing his date of death caused heartache like nothing I'd ever experienced. He'd had such a short life. If only he had come with me, he could've been spared.

As I sat there, despair surged through me. This wasn't supposed to happen. He should've been here with me. I pushed the book away, stood, and kicked the wheelchair, hurting my toe in the process.

"Stupid chair!" I cried, then laughed at myself. I always thought it was funny when people got mad at objects, and here I was doing just that. I lifted my foot to a nearby chair to rub my toe while I cried. I heard the door open, and a man cleared his throat. My back was to the door, so I couldn't see who it was.

"I'll be gone in a minute, and you can have the library to yourself." I sniffed and wiped my nose and eyes with my sleeve, chuckling at myself. Less than a year ago, I wouldn't have cared to wipe my nose in such a way. Now, it bothered me to no end, but at the moment, it was all I had.

"Would the lady like a handkerchief?"

I froze. I knew that voice, but the voice didn't fit in this space or my understanding of current events. "It can't be," I whispered and shut my eyes. *My mind is playing tricks on me.* I heard soft footfalls getting closer. A hand touched my arm.

"I owe you an apology."

A sob wrenched its way through my lips. *It can't be!* I opened my eyes and gazed at the hand on my arm. A smile spread across my face, and I followed the hand to the glorious masculine face I had fallen in love with.

"Please forgive me for my folly. I should have believed you." His eyes were glossed over with tears.

"You came," I said between sobs, "I …"

He touched my cheek with one hand and pulled me closer by the small of my back. My large belly pressed against him. His fingers moved to my chin, and his thumb touched my lips. "Please say you will forgive me."

"Only if you will … stay with me. I don't want to lose you again."

"I am all yours." His lips softly pressed against mine. My tears turned from those of sorrow to pure happiness. His kisses were warm and tender, yet passionate. Everything in me exploded with joy. I could run a mile. I could do anything.

I pulled away to catch my breath and laughed. "If you keep kissing me like that, I'll end up going into labor early."

He smiled and kissed me again, but only briefly. He placed a hand over my belly and held my hand with the other. "I know I am ill-qualified, and I have no any idea how to go about living this life you are familiar with, but … Abbie, will you be my wife and allow me to be the father of this precious child you carry inside you?"

"Yes!" I swung my arms around his neck and kissed him once. "A million times, yes!"

* * *

Present Day England, Ruth

"Ruth! Ruth! Come on, baby, wake up!"

I could hear Josh calling me, and I tried to answer, but only a moan came out. My eyes seemed impossible to open.

"Ruth! Please wake up! Show me those big blue eyes!" There was panic and desperation in his voice.

I wanted nothing more than to please him, but my eyes refused to obey.

His lips pressed against mine. My own were slow to respond, but respond, they did.

"That's my Ruth," he said, then kissed me again.

I moaned, and I tried to speak when he pulled away. My eyes fluttered, and I scowled at the piercing light. It won the battle, so I closed them again.

"Come on, love, and open your eyes." His voice was softer when he touched my cheek.

"I am trying," I mumbled.

His relieved laughter gushed from him.

My eyes finally opened, and focused on him. We smiled at each other before he scowled. "What do you think you're doing coming out here alone? Are you trying to make the grave marker true?" His hand caressed my face and head.

Grave marker? I stared at him, confused. "Where am I?"

"In the forest, by the root. Or at least, what's left of it," he responded.

"What happened?"

"By the look of it, I'd say you were thrown." He looked me over.

292

"Are you hurt?"

I moved my toes and hands. "I do not think so." I closed my eyes again. "I feel sick."

"Help is coming." Worry shook his voice.

"Where am I?"

He frowned. "In the forest—"

"What happened?"

He sighed long and heavy. "I think you have a concussion."

I tried to sit up, but he held me down.

"Stay down, Ruth. Keep still."

My head thumped to the rhythm of horse hooves. I frowned and moaned. Off to the side, someone approached. The thumping of my head ceased its intensity when a horse stopped beside me. The man appeared vaguely familiar.

He spoke with Josh and asked questions about my condition.

"Where are we?" I asked, feeling disoriented.

"She's asked that several times now," Josh frowned.

"I have?" Time and darkness slipped by. Josh called out to me again and again, telling me to keep my eyes open. I reached for my head and found it was tied to something hard that lay underneath me. I glanced around and saw trees moving by above me, and Josh looked as though he carried me on some kind of board, but I was now in a strange motorcar. None of this made any sense to me.

"Where is Josh?"

"Where am I?"

"Who are you?"

"Where is Charles?"

I dreamt of having tea and cakes with Celeste and the neighbors. A nurse was there with beeping machines I did not understand. There was a ball in the room next to me, and I could hear the music. Dancers were there, too. The dancers flew into the air, strapped into paragliding wings and laughing, and Josh was there holding my hand and showing me how to dance in the sky. Then, the nurse was there again, making beeping noises.

"Turn that noise off," I groaned.

"Ruth?"

"Josh?"

"Can you open your eyes?" His warm hand rested on my cheek.

I slowly opened my eyes and smiled at him.

"Are you awake for good?" he asked.

"What happened?"

"I believe Norman threw you." His hand rubbed mine.

"He did. Why would he do such a thing?" I frowned. "I thought he was my friend."

"Do you remember it, then?"

"Did I make it to the root? I remember I was trying to make it there, but I do not remember why." I rubbed my head and found something attached to my skin.

"It's the IV."

"Oh. I remember these. I have seen a lot of these lately, haven't I?" He nodded.

"Did I make it to the root?"

"Almost."

"Do you know why I went there?"

"I had a look at the arch … it was damaged," he said softly.

"Oh." My heart dropped at the memory of why I went there.

"There's no possible way of traveling back." His voice cracked.

I started to cry. "I will not see them again, will I?"

"No." He kissed my cheek. "I'm afraid not."

I held him close while I cried. *Never to see them again.* It seemed impossible to think that I could not laugh with Celeste or kiss my dear brother's cheek in greeting again. I would not race my horse with

Charles and walk the gardens arm in arm with Celeste. Never would I get the chance to see them hold their baby or watch their child grow.

After a good cry, I took a deep breath and sighed. Josh smiled at me as though he could not be sad about the news.

"Why do you grin at me, sir?" I frowned.

"Do you know what day it is?" He pulled out his mobile.

My heart skipped a beat.

He held the mobile out and showed me the time and date it displayed.

"The fourth?" My eyes felt as though they would pop from my head.

"The fourth," he said with a laugh.

"I am not dead?"

"I could pinch you if you like?" he winked.

"I prefer kisses," I said. He leaned on the bed and kissed me. Between kisses, I repeated the words. "I am alive!"

He sat back and wiped a tear from his cheek. "You and I are going to grow old together, raise a pack of lords and ladies, and see many friends beat their cancer, just as you will."

"I cannot wait," I said, then let him kiss me over and over.

Chapter Thirty-Five

Present Day England, Ruth (nearly two years later)

"What do you want done with this?" Abbie asked, setting a large box down on the edge of the couch.

"Set it there," I pointed. "I'll get to it in a moment."

"You should take a break. I wouldn't want you to overdo it and go into labor yet. Josh would likely strangle me if he came back and found you in the hospital," Abbie said, pressing her lips together.

"I've not lifted a single box, and nothing I've pulled from them has been heavy," I argued as I rubbed my large belly.

"Well, I need a break to check on Celeste. She's been napping long enough." She stood and left the dusty attic we'd been working in for days. I smiled when I thought of little Celeste toddling about. I was thrilled when Abbie named her daughter after my favorite sister-in-law. What a blessing it was to have Abbie and Albert around. Abbie was attending nursing school and had future plans to continue her schooling to become a chemist so she could do her part in researching a cure for cancer. She became interested in it during her stay here while on bed rest. After the baby's birth, she did all she could to make it into a good school nearby so she could be with her husband while he worked for Josh and me. I was so proud of her.

While Albert worked as a household manager at Shariton Park, he attended school along with Abbie and tried to keep up with her. Molly worked in the kitchen and took quite a fancy to a young man working in the stables. I expected to hear wedding bells soon.

I ran my fingers through my short hair and took a deep breath. For three days, we'd worked in the dusty attic, going through every box and drawer in each piece of furniture. After renovations were finished years ago, all the things that didn't have a place were put up in the attic and forgotten. Most of it was junk, like a lot of old Christmas decorations that didn't work any longer. There were only two things of value, one being an old shoe horn, the other a large desk. It seemed to date back to the turn of the twentieth century.

It had taken hours to go through it all, but now the desk stood ready to be moved downstairs. I noticed another drawer that I hadn't seen before, set further back, mostly hidden from the front. I pulled it open and found an old box. Carved across the wood box were the words: Letters from Great, Great, Great, Grandmother Celeste.

My heart quickened as I grasped the box from the drawer. Could it be? I slipped the top off and found a bundle of letters tied with ribbon. I started to cry when I recognized the handwriting. I carefully took off the ribbon and lifted the first letter. Atop the stack, there was a note.

To Ruth.
May these letters find you well and whole.

My hands shook when I opened the first letter.

January 8th, 1813

My dearest Ruth,

I began these letters in hopes of explaining some things and giving you the gift of knowledge. As I hope you know by now, Abbie ran away. I pray she found you and that Albert and Molly found her. I will never know your fate. The day after Abbie left, I sent Charles to look for her. He returned a short time later, reporting that he could not travel to you any longer. We are puzzled as to why and have tried many times since.

My heart aches over losing you and never knowing how you are. We decided the best way to go about this confusion, so friends and neighbors won't wonder where you are for years to come, was to pretend you had passed on. I will not write more on that, for it pains me greatly.

I refuse to believe you will not live a long life. If you do get a chance to read these letters, then I am quite jealous. This letter will be the first of many, for I am determined to write to you and tell you of all that transpires through our life together. As of now, I do not have too much news, so I will save you boredom and write again soon.

With all my love,

Celeste

I refolded the letter and laughed and cried. "All that time I thought I was going to die." I shook my head and laughed again. I cleared my tears and opened the next letter. It was dated only a month later. She wrote about her progress and her confinement. She wrote of the visits from Lady Garrison and how happy she has been to have her friendship.

The next letter was dated in April of that same year.

My sweet Ruth! How you would jump for joy if you were here! I have given birth to a healthy baby boy! Of course, you might already know this (if you have read the records). Damian Charles was born a week earlier than expected but is doing quite well. I cannot tell you how relieved I am that he is healthy. You know how much I fear the way medicine is practiced here, but I will not write more on that. He is well, and we are truly happy.

Another letter was dated a few months later, describing the new discoveries of having an infant. I laughed at her descriptions of his first laugh, and his first time grabbing hold of someone's hair.

"What are you reading?" Abbie caused me to jump.

I grinned. "I've found letters from Celeste." I stood and went to her side, eager to share my delight.

"Get out! Really?"

I passed her the first letter and watched her read. I read out loud more letters, one of which dated in the spring of 1815 was difficult to read:

I wish this letter had a happy ending. In my previous letter, you will have read about my anticipation of the arrival of my second child. But I am sorry to report that our dearest boy never took a breath at birth. Despite our struggles to get him to cry out, he would not take a breath. My heart is especially heavy in knowing that at a different time, he might have survived.

Charles has been a great comfort to me, as has dear little Damian. I do not know what I would do without them.

I wish you were here as well, my sweet Ruth.

I wiped the tears and read through several more. It wasn't until the letter in the year 1817 that I was able to smile again.

What a glorious day it is! Two days ago, I gave birth to Ruth Ange-lina Elsegood. The name fits her well. I am certain she will have light hair and blue eyes, just as you do. She cried so loud when she was born it made us all laugh ...

My body ached from sitting so long on the hard chairs in the attic, so Abbie and I retired to the drawing room to finish reading the letters. We laughed and cried as we read the stories she told of her two children growing older. Damian was quite the little mischief maker, as I remembered Charles being. Ruth did grow up with fair hair and blue eyes. It sounded as though she had her papa wrapped around her finger—years of letters told of them growing up. Ruth ended up marrying well and for love. Damian, on the other hand, married for money. His wife was good to him, but Celeste was sad they did not love each other. She was always a romantic.

The next letter in the stack, dated 1840, caused my heart to ache the most.

My dearest Ruth,

I write with a heavy heart, for I have lost my companion. The love of my life left this earth earlier this week due to an unknown illness. He has been weak for months, but of course, doctors could not find anything wrong.

Oh Ruth! How heavy my heart is! How can I go on? I feel I must die! I do not want to live my life alone!...

My shoulders shook, and I cried for my brother's death, though it had happened over a century and a half ago. It seemed silly to do so. I'd already mourned their loss months ago, but reading the sorrow in her words pulled at my heart, bringing back all the remorse and anguish. I continued reading well into the night, needing more.

I have good news, Ruth. I am a grandmother! Damian is such a proud father. I wish Charles could be here to celebrate with us. It has only been eight months since Charles passed on, and I find I can live again now that I have something to occupy my mind. Oh, what a blessing it is to have babies around again.

I read of more grandchildren that blessed Celeste's life. Most of her time was spent with them. She seemed happy but lonely when not in her children's and grandchildren's company. She wrote of trips to London and endeavors to open schools for the less fortunate. It was her joy and passion to see young ones learning to read. She taught her grandchildren to play the piano and to draw and paint. Her last letter was dated only a month prior to her date of death. She never mentioned feeling ill or worn down and only spoke of the joy in her life and how happy she was to live amongst her children.

Do you believe me wrong, Ruth, in meddling with the future and helping those less fortunate? Some of the ton have looked down their noses at what I do for the poor. I have tried not to be the leader in new endeavors so I do not make a name for myself in the history books, but I cannot let an opportunity slip by without joining in to help. How could I turn my back on the naked, the cold, and the hungry? I must do my part in clothing, feeding, and educating our future. It all starts somewhere. I find joy and peace in doing so. I have enjoyed a long life, and I have so much to offer. I will continue as long as the Lord sees fit.

I hope you find joy in your life, Ruth. I hope you live long and do everything possible to build the future as well. With all my love, until I can write again,

   Your dearest friend and sister,
   Celeste

At the bottom of the stack, I found one last letter. It was addressed to Amelia Sue Harrison, and under her name was written the date when it should be opened. That date was over five years ago, when Celeste had begun her life with Charles. Amelia was Celeste's descendant and Josh's late wife. The seal had already been broken, so I opened the letter and read.

Dear Amelia,

You do not know me, and there is no reason you should believe this anything other than a hoax. However, I hope to persuade you that I am a friend interested in your future and your well-being. I hope you will consider my words and follow my counsel.

You should recently have received a sum of approximately five million pounds. Do not be alarmed, for I am the one who donated the money entrusted to you to rebuild Shariton Park. My wish is that you do so right away, but I have another request. Please, dear Amelia, please convert it into a Cancer Treatment Centre. As a comfortable home for treatment and recovery, it will benefit so many, including members of your own family, now and in the future.

I also wish to press upon you the importance of keeping the contents of this letter a secret. I realize you may yet be wondering who I am and why I involve myself, and I imagine you are wondering why you would give my words any weight. Dear Amelia, I have been fortunate enough to see a vision of the future in which Shariton Park is restored and transformed into a place of refuge. I am blessed with innumerable descendants as beautiful as you. I wish I could have known you. I hope

302

you fill your heart with love and live life to the fullest.

My best wishes and love,

Your many Great Grandmother,

Lady Celeste Elsegood

Author's note...

Thank you for reading! I am honored you'd take the time to read what I have to share! I've got loads more coming, so please give this book a review on Goodreads and Amazon. Doing so will help me publish more, and have I got a plethora of stories to share, and between you and me, more than a dozen are already completed—rough drafts still—but completed. AND I've started over two dozen more. So, hold onto your seat, because it's all coming as quick as they can get edited and time permits.

I plan to bust out a time travel series of six (possibly more) that involves many different tropes we all love (friends to lovers, enemies to lovers, forbidden love and all that jazz). Plus, you'll get to follow characters through war-ridden Spain during the Napoleonic War and aboard Naval ships.

Now don't go thinking I only write time travel, because I don't. I've got some Regency, suspense romances, romantic comedies, and a cozy mystery with a bit of ghosts and comedy thrown in—all of which are completed and waiting for editing. If you can't wait to read all of this crazy that's been going on in my head, then follow me on Instagram and Tictoc for updates on what's new.

@AuthorChristineMWalter (both Instagram and Tictoc)
Check out www.authorchristinemwalter.com to join my newsletter!

Acknowledgments

There ain't no way in h-e-double-hocky-sticks I could have published on my own. It takes a village. There are so many people to thank, my head is spinning. There is so much to do and so many people involved in publishing a book, whether the author is self-published or not. To thank everyone sufficiently would be a monumental task of its own, and quite frankly, I could never thank y'all enough. First, I'd like to thank my children and my hunk of sugar lovin' husband for giving me time and support to write. Thank you to my editors, Alexa, Lynne, Lauri, and Shelley, for the crap load of junk you had to shift through to polish my work to what it is now. If there are any mistakes, they're all on me. Sometimes I can't see what's right in front of my face, so they are lifesavers. A huge shout out and thanks to Katie Garland at Sapphire Midnight Design for the beautiful cover. Thanks to my family and friends who have encouraged me in getting my stories out there. A great big appreciation to Lynette Taylor, you were the first to push me to write, so thanks for giving me confidence to do so. Traci, thanks for the pat on the back, the kindness, and the inspiration to keep going. Thanks to my Sweet Tooth Critique group for all your feedback. Also my ANWA writer's group. You ladies rock! Thanks to all the Youtubers, book reviewers, and other authors on social media who have shared their publishing stories and advice with the world. It's a huge support to those starting off.

And thank you to my readers!

Here's to dreams and many more stories! Cheers!

About Christine M Walter

Christine adores her husband, her three adult*ish* children, and her attention-seeking dog, Chewbacca, so much that she'll pause writing and reading just for them. Well, most of the time. When she's not drawn to writing, she often spends time in Lego building, painting, drawing, hiking, rock collecting, and off-roading through saguaro cactuses near her home in Arizona. Christine's artwork has been featured in the novel *Blackmoore* by Julianne Donaldson, as well as in the movie *8 Stories*. Christine has been the recipient of multiple awards in the first chapter contests and most recently won honorable mention for a first page contest from Gutsy Great Novelist and she won two awards in the ANWA BOB contest. Seeing new places and experiencing new cultures are top on her list of desires. In fact, her sense of adventure inspired her and her family to sell their home, move into a 400-square-foot RV, and travel the country simply to see and enjoy life outside of the norm. Best year ever!

You can reach Christine by following her on Instagram.

Insta- @AutherChristineMWalter

Check out her website at www.authorchristinemwalter.com and sign up for her newsletter!

AUTHORCHRISTINEMWALTER